DARK TRESPASS
BOOK THREE
A NECROMANCER'S
FIGHT

BY
MISTY DAWN TACKETT

Copyright © 2022 Misty Dawn Tackett
All rights reserved.
ISBN: 978-1-7373249-5-9

i

DEDICATION

For the readers of all things
weird and complicated.
Thanks for your support!

CONTENTS

Chapter 1
DEAN

Basic Maneuvers

We set up the room inside The Hillbilly Roost like a military operation. Everyone watched the video files with Lyle's proof of the Hedrix's possession. So many reactions filled the room—the most emotional came from Lydia and Rudy.

Tara had her arm around her mother as Lydia cried at seeing Lyle's pain and torment. Rudy's fists clenched, and he ground his jaw. His eyes filled with rage. He cursed often, but then he'd calm himself to comfort his mother.

Richard stood up and addressed the room. "Here is what we know. The Hedrix attacked our family seven generations ago with the knowledge that we are necromancers with a bloodline of Airmed's blessed children. He captured Alma and Esaw's daughter Willa and forced them to serve as Sevifk, and in return, he'd one day grant Willa her freedom.

The Hedrix searched down the line for a potential candidate who might produce an heir with multiple gifts. He aimed to steal their powers and make them his own, but he wasn't immune to our light energy, as for most demons with evil intent.

When he captured me at first, he drained me repeatedly in hopes that he could use my energy to build a tolerance before attacking Tara, using Lyle as his puppet. With my blood, he tried to slowly micro dose himself with Tara's over time, building up his immunity. He may have aimed to drain her, but he failed due to the safety measures I'd put in place, and with Lyle's help, we'd deceived the enemy."

Lydia raised her hand to speak. "So, when I found Lyle that night cutting Tara's leg and I, I killed him; I wasn't imagining seeing a demon whose intent was to kill my child?"

"What you saw was true. Only the Hedrix couldn't draw enough of Tara's blood, and the tool he used would never have worked to gain her power. You did the right thing killing him because you freed Lyle from the demon's torment and cast the Hedrix back to Hell."

Lydia nodded. "I always knew my actions were justified even though no one on the jury believed me when I said I killed a demon. Still, I wouldn't have done anything differently, and I have no regrets."

Tara took Lydia's hands. "Mom. Lyle told me to tell you he doesn't blame you for what you had to do. He said he still loves you and Rudy. He is free now. He ascended after he helped us find Dad."

Tears fell from Lydia's eyes. "Thank you, Tara. That brings me peace."

Richard smiled. "Now we know the Hedrix is responsible for capturing and turning Airmed's children into Sevifk and has used them to inhabit the dead, but he can only raise the dead by a necromancer's blood. Gina and Asher had risen by contact with Tara's blood, and Sevifk had possessed their bodies."

"Tara freed Alma's and Esaw's souls using the necro claw. More demons have risen, which we believed were Hedrix demons at first. But now that we know they still have Willa, the Hedrix may have used her to raise and possess more corpses. So, we may have an army of undead Sevifk on our hands.

His goal is to capture Tara and finish what he started. Alma has told us that he aims to rule humankind with Tara's power, as no doubt they will see him as a savior. He seeks the ability to come to our realm as he pleases and destroy any of Airmed's children who stand against him."

I raised my hand. "Richard, I'm of demonic necromancer bloodline. Has there been no opposition between the Hedrix and the demonic necromancers in the demon realm?"

Gina stood. "Alma wishes to speak." Her eyes changed to violet, and her voice changed. "A war has taken place between the armies of Hedrix and Necros demons in Hell. Esaw and I were made to fight, kill and steal what we could from the Necros's power. I've heard the Necros say that they, too, seek Airmed's Blessed to bolster their power to defeat the Hedrix. He has been torn between this mission to find Tara, claim her power, and continue fighting this war."

"Is that why Lyle had times of freedom from the Hedrix because he had to check on the war's progress?" Tara asked.

"Yes," Alma said. "Your blood is the key to ending the war one way or the other. Now you have proved that your power can help save the Necros and free the necromancers from their Sevifk forms, the Hedrix is more desperate than ever to claim you as his bride."

"HIS WHAT?" Tara screeched. "OH NO! OH, HELL NO!"

"Tara, you have already created an alliance with the Necros by mating yourself to Dean. And by giving him a dose of your power, you became enemy number one to the Hedrix army, even though their master still wants you as his own."

"That is why the demon at the crematorium tried to kill me. It was trying to get me to Hell one way or another," Tara said.

"But he couldn't have killed you," Richard said.

"Tell that to the burns on my hands that hurt like hell."

"This is bigger than we thought. We need to call in backup asap," Cannon said.

"I'm on it." Woody left the room and headed to his office.

"Danny, we'll need enough Holy water to make bombs," Cannon said.

"Uncle Danny!" Tara yelled.

"I know! Ready to go for that ride?" Danny smiled.

"Hell yeah!"

"A ride where?" Rudy asked.

"Come along, kid. Dean, you up for it too?" Danny asked.

"Always," I replied.

"Danny! Bring back my gladiator gear," Cannon said.

"Anything else?" Danny asked.

"Not unless you can think of anything."

"Okay, everyone gather around and join hands," Danny instructed.

"Is there room for all of us?" Tara asked.

Danny and I laughed.

"Everybody hang on tight," Danny said.

I felt the wind in my hair and Tara's arms wrapped around my waist. The Firebird screeched, and its wings flapped. Tara and Rudy laughed.

"Woohoo!" Rudy yelled.

"This is amazing!" Tara said.

"Welcome aboard, the Firebird Express, where we take you as far as your imagination," Danny shouted.

"This is badass, Danny," Rudy said.

"Just like me," Danny replied.

"What's her name?" Tara asked.

"How do you know it's a girl?" Rudy asked.

"Because Uncle Danny wouldn't dare ride a dude," Tara responded.

Danny and I laughed.

"This here is my girl Neveah!" Danny stroked her shiny black feathers, and Neveah screeched like a majestic bird of prey.

"She's beautiful," Tara said. Neveah made sweet perking noises.

"Neveah said thank you," Danny said.

"Where are we going?" Rudy asked.

"To my treasure trove. It's where I keep my most valuable things hidden and safe."

"This is where you went with Danny before?" Tara asked.

I pointed at the mountainside cliff. "Yes, it looks like we're almost there."

Neveah broke through the barrier, followed by thunder and lightning scattering across the sky.

"Tara, look!" Rudy pointed to the colorful banner streaming behind Neveah's tail feathers.

"Whoa! How beautiful!"

We landed on the cliff and dismounted. Tara went around with Danny to pet Neveah's head and praised the Firebird. Danny handed Tara and Rudy treats of raw meat to feed Neveah.

"You'll have to take us again, Uncle Danny!" Tara pleaded.

"I will. Now let's line up and join hands. Don't freak out or let go, or you won't make it inside." Danny motioned for us to follow him, and Tara took his hand, followed by Rudy and me.

He pulled us through the rock wall, and we stood inside his fortress of treasured keepsakes. Rudy laughed and pointed at the get-well balloon still floating from its pedestal. "You kept it?"

"Of course, I did! Why wouldn't I?" Danny asked.

"I didn't know it meant so much to you."

"It was a gift from you. Anything you've given me over the years, I've kept."

"I think that's sweet." Tara picked up her picture as a child holding the Easter Bunny's hand. "I remember this! Wasn't that you in the bunny suit, Uncle Danny?"

"Yes. You remember complaining about the box of crap you got in your basket?" Danny smiled.

Tara laughed. "How could I forget? I still don't eat chocolate-covered raisins."

"Rudy, Dean, your assistance, please," Danny called.

Danny was standing before the ancient armor of a Roman gladiator. He put the leather breastplate on Rudy and handed him a short sword. Then put a helmet on his head.

"Wicked! All these weapons and armor belong to Uncle Cannon?" Rudy asked.

"It looks in good shape, and I don't see a scratch anywhere. Did Uncle Cannon fight in this armor?" Tara asked.

"He did. And the reason you don't see any damage is that no one could get a strike on him. Spartacus trained your Uncle Cannon," Danny said.

"The Spartacus?" Rudy asked.

"The one and only."

"How old are you?"

"In relation to the creation of man, I'm still very young." Danny winked.

He handed me a lance and sword, then picked up a shield. Danny slid on a pair of arm and wrist guards and picked up a harpoon and a net. Then he went to the pedestal containing the small square of fabric.

Danny picked up a pebble, set it on the pedestal, then reached inside and pulled out the bound glass. He untied the binding and carefully sat the top piece down, pulled out his handy tweezer and scissors, and snipped a slightly large thread than before. He placed it in a tube which he sealed and put everything back together.

"What was that?" Tara asked.

"A piece of the shroud of Turin. It contains main ingredient in the Holy water I make."

Tara's eyes bugged out, and she made the sign of the cross.

"Where did you get that?" Rudy asked.

"From my family," Danny replied.

"Someone in your family was in the tomb of Christ?" Tara asked.

"My ancestors were travelers, and one of them witnessed the crucifixion. After Jesus rose from the grave and the Romans finished their investigation, no one was there for some time. My great grandfather snuck inside and cut a piece away, thinking it might come in handy. It turns out he was right."

"Your great grandfather was a grave robber?" Rudy asked.

"Possibly! I'm not sure. But this is the greatest treasure my family possessed, and the dream travelers of our family have kept it hidden over the centuries."

Tara and Rudy were in awe of their uncle. We left Danny's treasure trove behind, and Neveah took us home. We reopened our eyes and found ourselves standing in the bar, loaded with Cannon's armor and weapons.

Rudy looked around. "How in the hell did we do that?"

"Traveler family secret. It's the only thing I must keep to myself. At least until another comes along." Danny grinned at Billie, who blushed.

"Stop looking at me that way. You're making my ovaries weep," Billie said.

"That's what I'm counting on, baby! Do you want to make some Holy water with me, then practice making little miracles? My little travelers would like to explore your dark recesses."

"Danny!" Billie slapped at him playfully, and he nibbled her neck. Billie squealed and started running for the kitchen. Danny growled and chased after her.

The clattering of pots and pans falling erupted from behind the swinging door. Bren shrieked and came running out, waving her hand in front of her face. "Don't go in the kitchen for a while. It's getting a bit too hot in there."

"My armor and weapons!" Cannon took the helmet and breastplate off Rudy and put them on, then took the swords and stepped back.

Cannon began swinging the weapons in the air with deadly precision, and everyone stopped what they were doing to watch the magnificent display. He began teaching Rudy some moves, and he took to the sword like a natural. Perhaps Rudy had some abilities after all. Tara told me Rudy had dreams and visions that were accurate premonitions. He was strong and athletic, and his moves were fast and efficient. Rudy's downfall was being human and breakable, but his leg had mended well. His brace seemed unnecessary as I watched him move with stealth and grace.

Cannon proudly watched as Rudy wielded each weapon with skill and accuracy. They moved outside to practice and worked up to sparring. Tara and I came to watch, and Richard came out with Lydia.

Richard fitted Tara with the necro claw, and he and Cannon started showing her stances and basic maneuvers. Tara already knew how to throw punches and kicks, and my heart was pounding with excitement as I moved into the face-off with my sexy little warrior.

Alma and Stella joined us and coached Tara through her movements. I held up Cannon's shield, and Tara charged at me. The claw clashed against my guard, and sparks flew. We began to spar. Stella, Alma, and I surrounded Tara.

Tara moved with agility and increased stamina. Stella and Alma came at her faster with more force, and I tucked in tighter. A once uncertain, frightened girl transformed into a warrior as she found her fighting voice and moved like a champion.

Tara's power charged beneath her skin like riptides painting her body with exquisite designs that moved from her arms down to her wrists. It shined so bright it emblazoned markings on her skin with golden tones of Celtic artistry.

Tara spun through the air like a majestic bird tucking its wings and striking with her lethal talon. She moved swiftly and sure as sparks flew in every direction. And before Stella and Alma knew it, they were backing off and deflecting Tara's assault, barely able to keep pace.

We were all smiling and cheering Tara as she knocked us down; she was the last one standing. Cannon roared and dove at her, and she raised her gauntlet and deflected his strike. Tara began matching Cannon blow for blow.

Though evenly matched, Cannon was huffing and sweating as he swung his blades, and Tara hooked his long sword with her claw. She kicked his short sword from his other hand and spun up with her foot toward his head. Cannon caught her, but Tara used the leverage to pivot her body over his shoulder, pulling his sword toward his neck. She tugged Cannon's sword sharply to his flesh, which nicked him, and blood ran down his chest. His eyes widened with shock. Tara released her hold, and Cannon lowered his sword and dropped to his knees.

"That's never happened before!" Stella sounded shocked.

Tara's chest was heaving, and her power pulsated beneath her skin. She raised her claw in the air and cried, "I am Tara Raybrook, Daughter of the Goddess Airmed. I fight for my family, justice for Airmed's children, and the Necros. No evil will take what Airmed has given!

Everyone cheered, and she looked around and smiled. Cannon lifted Tara on his hulking shoulders and paraded her around as everyone chanted her name. She lept down, jumped into my arms, and kissed me. I carried my little warrior queen to our cabin while her family whistled and cat-called behind us.

Tara took the claw to my shirt and ripped it down the middle as I kicked the door shut behind us. She slid the necro claw from her hand and held it behind her as I walked us toward the kitchen table. She set it aside, and I kicked a chair out of the way.

She unfastened my jeans and pushed them down, and I pushed down her leggings as she kicked off her shoes. Tara fisted my torn shirt and pulled me to her. She kissed me hungrily, and we became wild with reckless abandon. She began sliding backward on the table, and I shuffled my knees till I was on top of her. Tara lifted her hips and met my thrusts. Her mouth broke away and panted.

"Dean! I need, I need." Tara's body quaked as she threw her head back. She cried out and tightly fisted my shredded shirt.

"Baby, you are so hot!" I kissed her neck, and she chuckled in a smoldering sexy voice.

"Oh, Dean! It feels so good! My power ebbs and flows with yours when we make love. Can you feel it?" She placed her hands on my chest and looked into my eyes. I felt her power pulsing everywhere, making me jerk inside her. She smiled wickedly, and I chuckled. I always felt more powerful with her. Tara allowed me to dominate her. But then she overtook me with her love, heart, soul, gorgeous brown eyes, and sexy body.

"You are so amazing! So amazing that I want to kiss Martina and your father right now for leading me to you."

Tara laughed. "I think I want to kiss them too, but in a familial way."

"I don't know. I might lay it on them pretty good." I grinned.

Tara laughed. "I don't think my mom would care for that, and Martina might get the wrong idea."

"How about a hearty hug?"

"That would do." Tara smiled. She looked at the necro claw beside her and sighed. "Do you think Airmed planned this?"

"I think she knows what she's doing. She chose you to fulfill a mighty role."

"I feel stronger and surer than I've ever felt."

"I've seen you change so much since we first met, Tara. I'm so proud of you."

"I would have never guessed I had it in me."

"How about now?" I smiled and moved inside her.

"Mmm! I love you, Dean."

I kissed her lips. "I love you too."

Chapter 2
TARA

Good Grief

Getting ready for Asher's funeral was more than finding what to wear and fixing my hair and makeup. I read over my speech and tried to pour the proper emotion into it without sounding like a fraud.

Gina was determined to attend, as was Alma, and they went to get ready with Martina's help. Mom and Dad were less recognizable with makeup, wigs, and colored contacts. We had to make sure no one singled them out in the crowd, though it was years since Gina's parents saw either of them. They were the most likely to remember them, which might cause issues.

Half of us rode in my truck with Dean driving and the other half with Cannon in his Bronco. Once we got to the funeral home, Trey, dressed to the nine's, pulled on his hat and went with Danny to retrieve the keys to the hearse.

I walked hand in hand with Dean, and Gina wearing a different blond wig and wide-brimmed sunglasses, held onto Rudy's arm as we went inside. Everyone went to find a seat, and I went to say a few kind words to Asher's family. Seeing Asher lying in that dark mahogany coffin made my stomach twist. I took a deep breath and continued to where his family sat in the front row.

Martina had come to do his final make-up last night, and she did a phenomenal job. I mentally noted how Asher looked like an actual corpse. He was as still as death, and I prayed Uncle Danny's fairie juice would still do its job for as long as this took.

Asher's brother, Christopher, wife, and two daughters sat beside Theresa and Kyle. Chris held his composure while his wife corrected the twin girls as they tried to move away from their seats.

"Hello, Kyle, Theresa." I greeted them with a hug and kissed Theresa's cheek.

"Tara, you remember Chris, Melinda, and their girls, Lexi and Justina?" Theresa asked.

"Hello." I smiled and waved politely. It would most like be the last time I saw them. Chris nodded curtly at me, and Melinda looked flustered as she lifted one of the little girls and passed her to Chris. Melinda snatched up their second child, who cried and whined, and handed her to Theresa. She settled down with a lollypop, and Theresa rocked her grandchild.

"It's good to see you again, Tara." Melinda stood and gave me and hug. I felt guilty for not remembering her name, but it wasn't like we kept in touch over the years. I patted her back and felt sympathetic for her motherly struggle.

"It's good to see you too, Melinda. You have your hands full."

"Oh! It was easier carrying them in the womb than what I have to deal with now. They're all over the place."

"I can see that. I want to tell you I'm sorry for your loss. It's been hard for all of us." I sniffed and dabbed my hand at my eyes which began to water as I pulled on recent emotions from losing Gina.

"I'm sorry for you too, Tara. I know you and Asher went your separate ways, but I know you still love him."

"I always will." I cleared my throat. "Well, I'm going to go up there. I'll see you all after the service."

"Tara!" Theresa called. Her granddaughter was falling asleep in her arms.

"Yes?"

"Thank you again for picking Asher's suit with me. Whoever dressed him and made him ready did a great job. He looks like he's, uhm, well-rested."

I looked at Asher and back at Theresa and smiled gently. The little girl in her arms looked so sweet with her blond curls and cherub cheeks. The lollipop was barely hanging on from her tiny lips. I pointed to it, and Theresa chuckled. She lifted it away and passed it to Melinda.

I moved away and went to stand before Asher and whispered, "Hang in there. We're in the home stretch."

Gina and Rudy came to stand beside me, and it was strange to recall how only weeks ago, Asher was standing by my side, looking down at Gina. Gina sniffed as she reached to touch Asher's hand, but I took her hand to make it look like we were comforting each other.

"They're watching! You can't make yourself obvious," I whispered.

"It's not me. It's Alma," Gina whispered back.

"Didn't you explain to her the importance of anonymity?"

"She understands now."

Asher's body took that moment to betray himself as he released a long, loud fart. The rancid stench permeating the air had me cupping my hand over my nose and waving the air with the other.

Rudy saved the day when he turned around and addressed the audience. "Sorry folks, too many eggs for breakfast."

I bit my lips and held my hand over my face as I turned and hurried down the aisle. Gina was fast on my heels as we ran to the restroom, pushed through the door, and we burst into laughter.

"Oh, good grief!" I cried.

Gina was laughing hysterically into her hands. "I can't. I just can't take it!"

"Oh, I'm so sorry!" Melinda looked at us as she lifted her daughter from the changing table and held the toddler to her hip. I grabbed a paper towel from the counter and held it to my face as I continued to laugh so hard it became hard to distinguish if I was laughing or crying.

"Oh, Tara!" Melinda put her hand on my shoulder. "I'm so sorry. Asher's passing has to be so hard for you!"

I heard a stall door close, and I peeked to see Gina had left me to deal with Asher's sister-in-law. I listened to Gina's muffled laughter, and I nodded my head to answer Melinda.

"I understand what you're feeling. I lost my nana last year, and I loved her so much."

I nodded again, and Melinda put her arm around me and rubbed my back. I felt a little hand pat mine and heard a sweet little voice say, "Peekaboo, I see you!"

I lowered the paper towel and saw a little angelic face with bright green eyes. I smiled at Melinda's little girl. "I see you too!"

"Peekaboo!" She giggled and then covered her face.

"Which one is she?" I asked.

"This is Lexi," Melinda replied.

"She has the Ferris green eyes."

Lexi peeked between her chubby fingers and stuck out her tongue. I returned the gesture, and she laughed. Lexi turned and reached out, and Melinda passed her to me.

Lexi felt light in my arms. So soft and cuddly. My heart melted as she snuggled into me and patted my chest. It felt like she was comforting me.

"She does that. I think she has my nana's gift of empathy. She seems to know when people are sad or happy. She's good at picking up others' emotions," Melinda said.

I held Lexi and swayed with her. "Thank you, Lexi. You made my heart feel better. She certainly has a gift." I tried to pass Lexi back, but she wouldn't let me go. Gina peeked out from the bathroom stall with her hand on her chest. She had an 'aww' expression on her face.

"Uh, maybe we should head back. I think the service may be starting soon." I walked with little Lexi in my arms, and Melinda held the door for me. I followed her back to her seat, and Lexi finally let go and returned to her mother.

"Thank you for the hug, Lexi." I blew her a kiss, and Melinda smiled. I breathed a sigh of relief after I turned to walk back to sit by Dean, and he was grinning at me the whole time. Gina moved past us and sat next to Rudy, just in time as Woody stood to give the opening prayer.

We went through the motions, and seeing Asher's family in tears was overwhelming, especially when Kyle and Christopher finally broke down and cried. The most valid emotions grip the heart when seeing a strong-willed man break down his walls and shed sorrowful tears. It touched me so that I couldn't contain my sympathetic grief. I made my way up to the podium and looked at Asher. I cleared my throat as I straightened the paper in my hands. I focused on the words I had written, and it felt like I was alone in the room reading a love letter to my dearest friend.

"Asher and I met in high school, and I was shocked when he asked me out at the beginning of our Senior year. I couldn't believe how lucky I was to have caught the eye of the most popular boy in school, and it didn't take long to fall in love with the handsome young man with striking green eyes.

He was charming and full of life, bringing out the funny free-willed girl buried deep inside a sorrowful shell.

We talked about spending our lives together. But his heart was so big and he had so much love to give that I couldn't hold him back from the true happiness destined for him. I will always love Asher. I never imagined it would be so soon that he'd leave us this way."

I shed genuine tears and took a moment to compose myself before continuing. "Asher said something to me when we met again at our best friend Gina's funeral. He told me, 'Tara. You deserve to be happy, and I don't want to stand in your way. Please remember the good times we shared. You'll always be in my heart."

I looked at Asher once more. "Asher, I will always remember and cherish our time together. You'll always be in my heart, and I'll always love you. Till we meet again, may God bless you, and may your rest in peace and be filled with joy."

Theresa was wiping away her tears as she leaned into her husband. Kyle nodded at me as I stepped down from the podium. Woody closed the service in prayer and told everyone where the burial would occur. People lined up to pay their last respects to Asher and his family.

I looked at the clock on the wall nervously as I shook hands and hugged people on their way out. Asher's family stood over him, saying their final goodbyes. Theresa placed something in the casket beside him, and Kyle put something in Asher's breast pocket. I was beginning to think they'd never leave, but finally, they walked toward me, and I hugged each of them, letting them know I'd see them at the gravesite.

I watched them walk outside and stand by the hearse. Woody closed the casket, and Asher began sneezing repeatedly. I ran up to the coffin, reopened it, and Asher looked at me. "God! I held that in for so long that I thought my head would burst. Here! Take this damn rose! My mother knows I'm allergic to that shit!"

"Shh! Would you quiet down? They're right outside!" I whispered.

Woody threw a handkerchief at Asher. "Stuff it up your nose and breath through your mouth. Danny will knock on the lid after the hearse moves, and he'll help you out and hide you. Keep your damn mouth shut and stay hidden till after we leave the gravesite."

"Man, this blows," Asher complained.

Woody rolled his eyes and closed the casket, and he, Dean, Danny, Cannon, Trey, and Rudy lifted the coffin and carried it out to the hearse. Asher's family watched as the men pushed the casket inside, and Woody closed the back hatch. He shook the family's hands and told them he was sorry for their loss.

It was another hour till we made it through the final proceedings at the gravesite, and I watched as an empty casket descended into the dark earth. I hugged Asher's family again, then went to my truck, where Dean helped me into the passenger seat.

I slumped, sighed, and yawned. Dean kissed my hand while he drove, and Gina and Rudy sat in the back seat. We followed the hearse back to the funeral home, moving behind the building under the car park. Dean pulled up beside it, Gina opened her door and jumped out, and Asher sprung from the hearse and jumped in the middle seat.

Gina climbed back inside and closed the door. They started kissing, and Gina moaned and cried, "Oh, Esaw. I missed you so."

"I missed you too, my beautiful Alma."

Rudy tried shrugging away from the two, and Dean and I laughed. "Tara!" Rudy cried. I looked back at the couple in the throes of heated passion. Asher's hands were up Gina's top as her hand was massaging between Asher's legs.

"Alma, Esaw! Cool it! You can wait twenty minutes till we get home and then have at each other," I said.

"Sorry, Tara. I have missed my husband, and we have yet to be together after your freed us," Alma said.

"I understand. But I'm exhausted, and my brother is next to you."

Rudy waved, and Alma looked at him sheepishly. "My apologies, Rudy."

Esaw adjusted himself and cleared his throat, "Sorry, friend."

Alma and Esaw composed themselves, and the ride felt long, but when we finally made it back to The Roost, the couple fled off together into the woods. Rudy climbed out and shook like creepy, crawly things covered his body.

"I need a drink!" he grumbled as he opened the door and went inside the bar. Dean and I followed him. Rudy grabbed a beer and went over to the pool tables. I slumped in a chair, and Dean stood behind me, massaging my shoulders. I dropped my head in my arms and groaned in misery.

"I hope and pray I never have to go through anything like that again!"

"It's over now. You did a good thing. Don't make any more mortal friends, and you should be good," Dean said.

"But there's still Bren, Billie, and Martina to worry about, and my mother and Rudy."

"Bren will be around for a long time if Zane has anything to do or say about it, and Billie is Danny's responsibility. Your dad and uncles can cover everyone else. You are relieved of any further obligations."

"Why did I feel so energized yesterday after sparring but feel so drained today?"

"Today was emotionally taxing, which tends to wipe a person out, mortal or supernatural."

Everyone else came inside, and Stella brought me a drink. "Damn girl, you look tired!"

"I am!"

"I've been in your shoes a time or two, girlfriend. It's never easy."

"Boy, do I know it!"

"Perhaps you should take a nap, honey," Mom said.

"I think I will." I pushed the chair back, and Dean took me a hand. "I'll come with you," he offered.

"No. I'll be fine. I'm just going to get a few hours and come back."

"I'm making dinner tonight around six," Mom said.

I leaned in and kissed her on her forehead. "Thanks, Mom."

Dad hugged me. "See ya in a few hours."

"I'll walk with you," Dean insisted.

"Alright." I leaned into him, and we went to the cabin. Dean helped me out of my dress, and I changed into a cami top and pajama pants. He brought me a water bottle, and I drank half before lying down. Dean kissed me and tucked me in before turning off the light at my bedside table. He went to sit on the couch and picked up a book to read.

"Aren't you going to hang out with the guys at the bar or something?" I asked.

"Tara, I'm not leaving you alone. You had a trying morning, which may leave you vulnerable in your sleep."

"Fair point, but I won't be out that long. Will you wake me in a couple of hours?"

"If that's what you want."

"How long do you think Alma and Esaw will have Gina and Asher doing the hanky panky?"

Dean laughed. "Tara, you think of ridiculous things when you're sleepy."

I yawned. "Yeah, well, I'm concerned about Gina and Asher out there having unprotected sex. And they're exposed out in the wilderness if there was an attack."

"Alma and Esaw are fighters and well aware of the possibility. They wouldn't go so easily again."

"But you saw how wrapped up in each other they were in the vehicle, and they paid no mind to their surroundings."

"That's because they knew that they were safe with us. Tara, please rest. You have to be sharp in the days ahead. Who knows when something bad will happen? I'm staying here to make sure you're alright, and if you keep it up, I'll strip naked and climb beneath the covers with you."

"That's not much of a threat Mr. Perrish." I yawned loudly. I lay my head down. My eyes grew bleary as I struggled to hold them open, and the last thing I saw was a bird that eerily resembled Danny's firebird, Neveah, flying past the window.

Chapter 3
BREN

The Next Level

Gina and Asher laughed and held hands as they walked by the camper. They looked so in love, and I couldn't tell if it was them or Alma and Esaw as they passed my window. The way they gazed into each other's eyes, I leaned towards the latter, as Gina and Asher would probably be arguing with each other.

I sighed at the sight of a love so true it spanned the centuries. I thought of the hardships Alma and Esaw faced with losing their daughter and having to make a deal with the devil to try and save her. It must have been torture to go against everything they believed, but that's the sacrifice some are willing to make for love.

I knew that Zane loved me, and I felt it even when he had manipulated and compelled me. His approach was reproachful, but I have learned since then that he had been through so much that he didn't trust that anyone could love him. Because who could ever love a monster?

Well, it turns out this woman did. And I was willing to do what I could to show Zane what I felt for him was pure and true. It was beyond lust and flights of fancy. Our hearts beat for one another. And the more we got to know each other, the more it felt like I'd found my soul mate.

I had a strong urge lately to offer myself to him physically, but I was still uncertain about using his and Dean's body to be intimate. It was the same body that had been with Tara. And even though we'd discussed the possibilities, it still didn't sit right with me.

I could feel and touch Zane's ghostly form. It was cold, and I was alright with that, but something was missing, and it was only that warm tangible, tactile physicality that triggered this urgency whenever Zane's hands touched me while he resided in his and Dean's form.

Tara smiled at us the last time Zane held my hand and kissed my cheek, and it was like she'd finally let go of her hesitation and was happy for us. Still, I was unsure if it was time to take Zane's and my intimacy to the next level.

My mind kept revisiting the old blue mason jar that Abigail had given me. I decided to keep it with me, and I'd bubble-wrapped it and stored it in my bedside drawer. I felt like I needed to keep it close in case of an emergency, though I had no clue what constituted one.

"Hello, gorgeous!" Zane greeted me.

He appeared before me, and I smiled. "Hello, handsome."

"Quiet the festivities today, don't you think?"

"I can't agree that a funeral qualifies, but knowing it was a farce, made it more interesting."

Zane laughed. "I'd say. Especially when Asher ripped a long, loud one and Rudy covered for him."

"That was Asher?"

"Yeah. I think the fairie juice had worked through his system and backfired."

"No wonder Tara and Gina ran from the room looking like they were about to die from laughter." I chuckled. "How is she?"

"Tara?"

"Yeah."

Zane sat beside me, took my hand in his cold, vaporous one, and kissed it with his cold lips. "She's fine. She was pretty tired, and she's sleeping now. Dean is with her."

"As he should be. Tara was amazing yesterday. I couldn't believe how fast she moved. And when she took down Cannon. Wow!"

"Yeah, that was pretty impressive. Our friend may have picked up a thing or two watching me fight." Zane grinned.

I nudged Zane's shoulder with mine. "I'm sure she did, oh mighty, powerful vampire that you are."

"Hey, I've got some pretty badass moves. You haven't had the privilege of witnessing my might and strength." Zane teased.

He got to his knees and began tickling me, and I screeched and started laughing. "Ahh, Zane. No! Please! Stop!"

I wiggled and kicked and pressed my arms close to my sides. There was no way I could hurt Zane, and I could still move through him if he allowed. It was an unfair advantage.

"Stop it, Zane, and kiss me!" I cried. He relented at my words and laid atop me. His ghostly form was light, and I wished for that weighted pressure that would sink my body into the cushions below me.

I felt the brush of Zane's lips and the gentle caress of his fingers as he stroked my cheeks. He kissed me with a fervent need to join our opposing forms as one.

"I can't wait to be with you in my physical body. You are so beautiful. I can feel your warmth. It must be disconcerting always to feel my coldness."

"No, it's not. I love you, Zane. And I'll take you however I can, and I can wait a bit longer to be with you that way."

"A bit longer? Love! I can see the eagerness in your eyes. You can't fool me! You long for me that same as I do for you. Maybe, I can convince Dean to loan us some time while Tara is resting."

"But, what about Tara? Who will stay with her to make sure she's safe? And won't she be pissed to find out we didn't check with her first to make sure she's okay with this? No, Zane. I don't want to go behind her back like that."

Zane huffed. "I get it. Perhaps we'll talk to her about it tomorrow. In the meantime, will you allow this vapey vampy to make you all steamy and moist in your happy center?"

"Only if you treat me to frosty vampire popsicle first." I giggled.

"Ooh, I likey!" Zane stood up, and his clothing dissolved into thin air. His erection sprung forward, and I licked my lips as I rose from the couch. I was about to take hold of him when someone screamed outside.

"What was that?" I asked.

"Probably Gina getting upset with Asher again."

"But why would she scream like that?"

"I don't know. Maybe Asher royally pissed her off this time."

Someone screamed again, and I jumped. "No, Zane. Somethings wrong!"

"Stay here, lock the door and hide!" Zane kissed me, and his clothes rematerialized as I followed him. He went out the door, and I locked it behind him, went to the bedroom, and pulled the partition closed. More noises sounded outside, and I heard a demonic growl.

"Hey, asshole!" Zane shouted.

It sounded like someone was thrown into a heap of metal trash cans. Footsteps stomped quickly away from the camper, and I went to grab my phone to call Dean. It rang twice, and Dean picked up. "Are you alright, Bren?"

"I think there's a demon attacking, and Zane just ran out after him."

"Stay where you are. I'm waking Tara now."

The call ended, and I tried to call back, but there was no answer. I called Woody next, and it went to voicemail. I was getting worried, so I tried Billie next with no response. Then, I called Stella. Still no answer.

Why wasn't anyone answering the phones?

It was quiet outside, and the sun was fading as I peeked out between the window blinds. I began pacing before the bed, staying close if I needed to duck beneath and hide. I kept checking my phone to see if anyone had texted. I tried to call a few more times. If anyone answered at this point, I'd be relieved. But, still, no one.

I heard footsteps running up to the camper, and I was about to dive under the bed when I heard Billie yelling my name. She began pounding on the door. "Bren. Are you in there? You must come with me. Hurry! Danny will take us to a safe place."

I ran to the door and looked out the window. Billie looked up at me with desperate pleading eyes. I grabbed the spray bottle of Holy water from my counter.

I thought it odd that she came here alone with no trace of another soul. I knew Stella had performed the protection vigil on Billie, but I needed to make sure. After what happened with Bryan, I wasn't taking any chances.

Billie pounded on the door again. "I promise you; it's me, Bren. We need to hurry. We're under attack, and Danny wants to take you, Lydia, and Martina with us to safety."

"Okay, I'm coming." I cracked open the door and sprayed Billie's face with the Holy water, and when nothing happened, she gave me a look that said, 'are you satisfied?'

I nodded and came out the door, and she took my hand, and we began to run. My heart tugged, and it occurred to me that I had left something behind. I pulled my hand free of Billie's and turned around.

"Bren! What are you doing?" Billie yelled.

"I forgot something! I need to go back and get it," I yelled.

"No, leave it! It's not important!"

"It is!" I cried.

I ran back to the camper. I had to get the jar. I couldn't let it fall into the wrong hands. I was almost there when Billie screamed, "Bren, look out!"

It was too late. A pair of strong arms locked around me and lifted me off the ground. I screamed as who or whatever had me took off running fast.

"BREN!" Billie screamed in the distance. We whipped past the trees, and the wind whistled in my ears as whoever carried me moved nearly as fast as Zane.

"Let me go!" I yelled and struggled to break free from its grasp.

I punched and clawed its back as it carried me with its arms locked around my hips, and its chest rumbled with a demonic chuckle.

I didn't know how far it had taken me before it stopped and set me down. I tried to run, but it grabbed hold of my arm and pulled me back. It pushed me to the ground, and I fell on my ass, catching myself with my hands.

I cried out as my palms landed on rocks, and my tailbone was shocked by instant pain that shot up through my spine. The intense pain made it hard to move. It must have bruised or broken.

My abductor paced back and forth. He looked like an average man; only his eyes showed what he was as the crimson glow shifted with his pacing. He growled and mumbled to himself like a stark, raving lunatic.

"Excuse me," I said. He ignored me as he continued to rant and seethe. "Hello!"

He stopped and hissed at me. My body jerked, and I cried as the sudden movement sparked an unbearable pain in my lower back and buttocks. It hurt at the slightest movement. I was able to shimmy and lean against a tree behind me but even doing that hurt. I grimaced and groaned through the pain before I finally settled.

"What do you want with me? I am of no value to you or your master."

The demon stared at me with those nightmarish red eyes, and his forked tongue tasted the air. "Human souls always have value in Hell."

"Is that where you intend to take me?"

"The master said to take all prisoners. You were an easy catch, foolish mortal."

"What is your given name?"

"You think me a fool to answer this?"

"I don't. I know you are a prisoner too. You were one of Airmed's children, and now you serve the wrong master."

"How do you know of thisss?" He hissed.

"My friend set two of your kind free, Sevifk. They are now back to their necromancer roots."

"You speak lies."

"No, I'm telling you the truth."

"Then tell me, how is this so?"

"I cannot reveal that to you, but if you take me back to my friends and cooperate, we can free you too."

"This is a trick."

"I promise you it's not."

"I'm to believe the word of a mortal girl?"

"What have you got to lose? I'm right, and you're set free. I'm lying, they kill you, and you return to Hell. Nothing changes. It's up to you. Do you dare to take the chance at freedom? Tell me your name. What were you called before the Hedrix tricked and changed you?"

"Antony. Now tell me how you know these things?"

"Antony. My friends have the powers your master seeks. He lusts for something that is not rightfully his. He has deceived many of your brothers and sisters over the centuries to find this power. My friend has freed Alma and Esaw from their Sevifk bindings, and she can do the same for you if you come willingly."

"So, you say I will earn freedom if I bring you back?"

"I promise it." I stared into the Sevifk's eyes. He nodded and came to lift me, and I cried at the shock of pain in my backside. He carried me over his shoulder, and as uncomfortable as it was, I bared it to save one more soul and have another champion on our side. But then something plowed into the Sevifk, and I fell to the ground and screamed in agony. Growling and fighting ensued, and I looked to see Zane in his and Dean's body battling the Sevifk.

"Zane! Stop!" I cried. He did not hear me or chose not to as he threw punches and swiped his claws at the Sevifk, who fought back with near equal measure. They growled and snarled as they circled each other.

"That is my woman you've taken, demon!" Zane snarled.

"I was returning her."

"I don't believe you."

"Zane, it's true! He was bringing me back. I told him about how we could set him free! His name is Antony."

"He hurt you. I'll hurt him too."

"No, Zane! Let it go. It was an accident. I'll be fine."

Zane continued to stare the Sevifk down. "I don't trust him. He could be lying to you."

"I would never reveal my name. What your woman tells you is true. I wish to be set free, and I will return her."

Zane moved toward me, still watching the Sevifk. A horn sounded in the distance, Sevifk's head jerked up, and he hissed. He charged and lifted me from the ground.

"I knew it! Liar!" Zane yelled.

"I do not lie!" the demon yelled.

The horn sounded again, and I screamed as the Sevifk lifted me above his head and threw me with great force. My body went sailing through the air, and I slammed into Zane's chest as his arms came around me, and together we hit something hard at our backs.

I cried in pain as I felt something sharp puncture my side and screamed as Zane freed me. "Here! He held something wet and metallic smelling to my lips. Drink this, and you'll heal. Hurry, my love."

I licked the liquid from Zane's hand, tasting blood, and he slowly lowered me to the ground. The pain faded away, and I placed my hand on my side and lifted it to find it covered with blood.

You'll be alright, Bren." Zane's voice was strained and weak. I looked to see that the Sevifk had run away, and Zane and I were alone in the dark.

"Thank you." I moved to stand and found the pain in my tailbone was gone. Zane was still leaning against the tree we'd hit when he'd captured me. He saved my life. I turned to kiss Zane and saw something sticking out through his chest.

"Zane?" I cried.

He was looking at me, still breathing. "I love you, Bren," he said weakly.

What I saw shocked me to the core. I began to cry. "Zane? No, no, no!"

This couldn't be happening! My hands trembled as I reached up and felt his heart pierced through his chest and speared by a jagged branch. It should have been me. The branch had pierced my side, and I could have survived it. But then I recalled the force of impact. My back would have broken in two, and I may have become paralyzed. No Zane had saved me, but now his life was in peril.

Zane was gasping as he lifted his hand and stroked my cheek. I held it and pleaded, "Don't leave me, Zane!"

The weight of his hand dropped in mine. Blood ran from his mouth, and his head fell forward. Suddenly, Zane's heart burst into flame and disintegrated into ash.

"ZANE!" I screamed. I fell to my knees and cried. "NOOO! No, no, no!" Footsteps ran up behind me.

"DEAN!" Tara screamed. I fell to my side and sobbed, and Tara came up behind me.

"Bren!" She shook me, but anguish consumed me as my heart became hollow inside my chest.

"He's dead!" I sobbed.

"No, he's not. Help me get him down," Tara pleaded. But I couldn't move. Tara pulled on my arm, and I rolled away from her.

"He's gone! Zane's gone!"

"What?" Tara cried.

"His heart!" I cried.

Tara gasped. "Oh, God! No! Zane?" Tara began hacking at the branch.

"What are you doing?"

"We need to get him down. I can heal him and bring him back."

The branch cracked, and I moved as Zane, and Dean's body slid away from the tree, and Tara began using her power to heal the gaping wound in their chest. She didn't realize that Zane's heart had turned to ash, and I knew there was no coming back for him.

Still, I sat up and watched as the wound in Dean's chest closed, but a large scar remained. Tara looked at the marred flesh, puzzled. "Why is it still like that?"

"Zane's heart!" I cried. "It's gone! Turned to ash!"

Tara's eyes widened, and tears sprung from her eyes. "No! Not Zane?"

Dean began to groan, and his hands went immediately to his chest. "My brother! I can't feel him!" Tara was sobbing, and Dean looked at her. His brow knitted together.

"What happened to Zane?" Dean asked.

"Zane! He's, he's!" I couldn't say the word—the one word I wished I'd never have to leave my lips.

"He's dead!" Dean confirmed.

I nodded.

Dean broke down and screamed, "NO! My brother!" Tara fell over Dean and cried with him. My hands brushed the ground and came up covered in ashes. Then something occurred to me.

A voice whispered in my head, *Put the ashes in the jar.*

"The jar!" I cried.

"What?" Tara asked.

"The blue mason jar Abigail gave to me. She knew!" I cried.

Dean stopped crying. "She knew that this would happen!"

"We have to put Zane's ashes in the jar. We have to hurry! It's back in the camper!" I rose to my feet, and Tara and Dean stood. A noise rustled in the branches above, and I saw a hulking figure falling toward Tara.

"TARA! Watch out!" I screamed.

But it was too late.

Chapter 4
TARA
Cruel Mind Games

I woke beneath the stars and heard water lapping. My arms were stretched, and my wrists were shackled. I pulled at my restraints, and short metal chains rattled and clanked against the wood. I rocked from side to side as I strained and twisted my body, but it was no use. The cuffs were too tight, and my bones wouldn't budge no matter how hard I tried.

"DEAN!" I screamed out to the night sky.

The last thing I remembered was healing him and Zane. No, Zane was dead! We were going to get the blue mason jar from Bren's when she screamed, and something big fell on top of me.

I didn't see what hit me, and now I was drifting in the water in a boat going nowhere. I had to be on the lake and confirmed it when I floated past the three wooden crosses where my uncles had perished.

Something bumped the boat's hull, and waves began to crash as I rocked wildly. The water hit my face, and I squinted my eyes and shook my head.

"HELP!" I screamed.

My voice echoed, but all that returned to me was the cry of a coyote in the distance. Something hit the boat again, and my body thrashed violently back and forth. I gritted my teeth as the shackles bit into my flesh, and I felt blisters burst and rub raw beneath the harsh metal.

A bird cried as it flew overhead, and it was hard to make out against the dark cosmic backdrop. Clouds rolled in and covered what little light the stars provided. The chirping of locusts in the trees grew louder as the boat rocked again, so hard that large amounts of water splashed inside, soaking my clothes and running up my nose. I coughed and sputtered.

"HELP! AHH!" The boat flipped, and I fell forward beneath the water. I screamed, and bubbles came forth. My arms strained painfully behind me, but I bobbed upward and caught my breath in the air pocket created inside the boat's capsized hull. I took in enough air that my body floated, alleviating the pain in my shoulders.

All I could think was how I would get out of this predicament. I was able to grip the boat's sides and kicked my feet. I began to move, but I had no idea where I was going. Thankfully, the lake wasn't too big, and I would eventually find shallow footing. I could drag the boat on my back and make it to shore. But then what? I was resourceful enough, so I knew I could think of something.

I had to stop, float and catch my breath. I prayed that whatever tossed the boat over didn't come back for me. With that in mind, I continued moving my feet. But the boat had bumped into something and stopped my progress. I rocked back and forth, trying to free it from the object in my path, and it wedged away, scraping along the side as I moved forward again. Just as my knees hit the shallows, I cried in relief as I was able to hoist the boat up on my shoulders. It was too heavy to stand up fully, so I trudged along, grunting and groaning.

Fresh air hit my face, and I stopped and panted. I was now up to my waist with jagged rocks digging into my knees. I groaned as I slid one knee forward, then the next. The shore was mere yards away. Something grabbed my ankles, and I screamed as my body was rushed back to the depths and under the surface. I saw a figure coming at me. It was a man, and he was stunning. He circled me and came up to my face, planting his lips on my mouth and blowing air into my lungs.

He held my face in his hands and smiled at me like this was some game, and I was the object of his merriment. I scowled at him, and though I was pissed, I couldn't help but notice his exquisite beauty. He had a muscular physique, dark hair, and electric blue eyes. He winked at me, and I yelled at him as air bubbles traveled from my mouth. "ASSHOLE!"

He must have found my tirade endearing because he laughed at me. He came face to face with me again, and I struggled to back away, but he captured my face and pressed his lips to mine once more before pushing me upward, and the boat flipped back over. I screamed ferociously at the sky.

"DICKHEADED-SACK-OF-SHIT FOR BRAINS!"

He grabbed the side, hoisting himself to where he crossed his arms on the boat and lay his head sideways to observe me. I coughed and spat at him, and he laughed.

"I knew I chose wisely. Hello, my little queen!"

My eyes widened in shock. "You're HIM!"

"Him who?" he asked with a tone of innocent curiosity.

"The Hedrix!"

"Yes. I am." He smiled wickedly. "Nice to finally meet you in the flesh, my love."

"I'm not your love, you asshole."

"Once I show how great I am, you'll fall hard and fast for me, little Tara." He grinned.

"Conceited much?"

"No. Women tell me how much they love me all the time. But, I'm willing to put them all aside for you, little songbird."

"Don't call me that!"

"Why? Because that weak little Necros does?"

"His name is Dean, and I will never put him aside for anyone, let alone you, you fucking egomaniac!"

"You have such a vile tongue for such a small beautiful creature. I will enjoy taming it with my own."

I spat at him again. "Never!"

"Oh, really?" He pulled himself inside the boat, and I pulled at the shackles in a futile attempt to break free. He crawled up my body like a predator till his nose touched mine and stared into my eyes.

The Hedrix pressed his lips to mine, and I clenched my teeth as he tried to push his tongue inside my mouth. I shook my head back and forth, groaning. The asshole pinched my nose shut and cupped his other hand over my mouth, cutting off my oxygen, and my head thrashed back and forth. My feet kicked, and I tried to raise my knee to crack him in the balls, but he had my legs pinned.

He threw his head back and laughed merrily at my distress. He removed his hand from my mouth, and I opened it to breathe. His mouth crashed to mine, and he inserted his tongue inside. I bit down hard, and he groaned. He backed away and laughed as he pressed his finger to his tongue, which came out covered with blood. "Mmm! So feisty! I love a woman who fights me tooth and tongue! We'll have so much fun together in the bedroom!"

"You're a deluded moron if you think I'll do anything to please you. I'll be your worst nightmare, and I'll repay you tenfold for everything you put my family and me through. You'll weep for mercy, and my boyfriend and uncles will take turns repaying you in kind."

The Hedrix grinned. "I look forward to it."

"You're a fucking fruitcake!"

"Oh, yes. That's my favorite! I can't wait to savor yours. I'll spread you wide on a platter and feast on your sweet cherry till you scream and beg for me to stop."

"You're sick!"

A bird screeched in the air, and the Hedrix looked up. "Awe, hell! Time to move this party to a new local."

I saw the same bird from earlier circling above. "What do you mean?"

The Hedrix didn't answer; instead, my vision went black, and I lost all connection with my surroundings. I blinked and looked around at my childhood bedroom. The door opened, and I went to sit up, only to find myself tied to my bed.

"Shit!" I wiggled and strained. A tall, dark shadow entered and came to stand at the foot of my bed. Moonlight hit its face and revealed my captor. He smiled cruelly and moved to sit beside me.

"Hello again, my love!" The Hedrix's hand came up, and he wore the false necro claw on his finger. He traced his hand down the side of my face; this time, I was not afraid as I'd been in my nightmare.

He planned to take me on a tour of every horrid dream I'd already experienced, so I knew his next move. The claw traced down my face and cut my bottom lip. I tasted the blood on my tongue, which tingled with my power. The Hedrix watched the motion and moaned with pleasure.

"Mmm, such pleasant memories we share." He ran the blade down my chin, neck, and between my breasts. "You've become quite the beautiful woman, Tara. I couldn't see it back then, and if I'd only been more patient, we wouldn't have gone through all the ups, downs, and mind games. You would have been mine already, ruling by my side."

"Good grief! You sound like every bully romance novel I've ever read! Could you get any more cliché? It's pathetic!"

"Ahh! You hurt my feelings, love!"

"That's not all I plan on hurting! Go ahead, sweetheart! Show me what you're packing, then we'll see who's begging for mercy once I get my hands on you."

"You see, Tara? Only a month ago, you were still a frightened little girl. Now, look at you. I've helped you grow a backbone. It's what you'll need to rule by my side."

"That's where you're wrong! How can I rule by your side when you're squashed beneath my feet?"

"Hmm! It seems I've broken you irrevocably. You're past the point where I hold you captivated in fear, and you've grown too big for your scaredy pants. What should I do about that?"

The Hedrix tapped his chin with the blade tip as he pondered in thought. "I could do? No, I already did that one! Hmm! Maybe? No!"

"What's wrong? Run out of tricks to pull out of your ass?"

"Oh, Tara! I've only just begun! I could do such dirty things to you, but I pride myself on being a gentleman. How about I make a deal with you? And before you refuse, consider this! I don't usually make fair deals, so you'd better think wisely before turning me down altogether."

"I'm listening."

"If you come with me and lend me just a teeny-weeny bit of your power, become my queen, and allow me to bed you whenever I wish, I'll allow you to bring your little love toy along to pleasure you as you see fit."

"I'd like to propose a counteroffer."

The Hedrix smiled. "I'm listening."

"I want you to free all the Sevifk and Willa, end the war with the Necros, and strike a peace treaty. Then allow Dean and me to have time to travel the world together for a year. You'll leave my family and friends in peace. Then I'll follow you to Hell with Dean, lie in your bed, and let you take me. Then while you sleep, I'll cut your fucking heart out with a spoon and feed it to the Hellhounds!"

The Hedrix laughed with delight. "Awe, my precious jewel! You are rare indeed! I was nearly ready to strike a deal with you till you ended it with my death at your hands, and I'm afraid that will never do. But I will still uphold my first offer. And since you're so callous, I will not adhere to your offer's terms.

You may have your Necros boyfriend, but I will torture him if he looks at you in my presence. The war will continue with you at my side, watching as my Sevifk and fellow Hedrix tear down the Necros and steal their powers. I will torment your dear family with empty promises and nightmares, and together you and I will rule over the humanity of this world with our combined powers."

I rolled my eyes. "Blah, blah. Blah, blah, blah, blah. Blah! That's not going to work for me either, dearest! I'm afraid we've reached an impasse, so you might as well let me go because the way I see it, you are so desperate for my power; the thought of tasting it makes you cream your underoos. And I want to give my light to you so bad it makes me ache with need. The thought of destroying you makes me want to dump my cherry fruit cake in my panties and lick whipped cream from my talons as I purr."

"Holy shit! I've never heard a woman speak like you! Damn, Tara! I'm so hot for you right now. Just look at me!"

The Hedrix stood up, and there was a massive bulge in his pants. My eyes widened, and I was frightened at what I saw. Maybe I should have kept my big mouth shut. My threats contained too much innuendo, but I never intended to get this demon all hot and bothered.

Why me?

But then it occurred to me that perhaps I could use my feminine wiles as an advantage. It seems men, and even those of the demonic variety, tend to be led by their penis. And the Hedrix was so hot for me that maybe I could take him for a ride. Not like that! But perhaps? If I played this right, without letting him have me? The thought gave me the heebie-jeebies.

"My, you are a big boy! Aren't you?"

"Baby, I will gladly show you how big and powerful I am."

"Oooh!" More like *Ewe!*

If he weren't such a conceited, arrogant, power-hungry, dipshitted, douche-wadded, evil megalomaniac who'd tormented and tortured everyone I loved, he'd be every girl's fantasy. He looked like a fallen angel, which he probably was. Alas, he fell for the wrong team, and this girl enjoyed her humble pie in the sky, handsome, heart of gold, worthy Necros demon man. However, Dean was more angelic than this asshat.

I poured on some sugar like sweet Martina, batted my eyelashes, and giggled. Was this sly demon as single-mindedly dumb as Bryan the pencil-dick rapist? Sell it hard, Tara! He looks like an eager buyer.

"So, you want a taste of my power? You'll have to play things my way, big boy!"

"What do you want of me, my queen?"

Man, he was as stupid as I thought! How did he convince all the others before me to trade their souls? I understood Alma's and Esaw's predicament, but this went too smoothly. But maybe he wanted me to think I was gaining the upper hand.

"You can start by untying me from this bed. How can I touch my king if my hands are not free to roam his sexy body?" The bindings broke instantly, and I sat up. "Can we go someplace a little less tragic? Unlike you, I'm not so fond of the memories here."

"I understand. That man's hands touched what was mine. The pitiful doctor got what he deserved."

I wanted to rip out the Hedrix's tongue. He was the one who made Lyle do all those sordid things to me. The bird screeched outside my bedroom window.

"How does that damn bird keep finding me?"

"We'd better hurry away from here, my king." I ran my finger down the demon's bare chest and smiled.

"I know where to go next." He took my hand, and I became dizzy as my vision blurred and my head spun. I landed on the Hedrix's lap as he sat in a chair. We were in a room that didn't look familiar.

Gina entered, talking to herself. "Stop it, stop it! Get out of my head!"

"Gina!" I rose only to have the Hedrix pull me back down again. He locked an arm around me, and I sat cooperatively.

"Just watch," he whispered in my ear.

Gina cried as she picked up a gun and magazine from a dresser and sat on the bed. The Hedrix walked into the room, pushed her hair back, and whispered in her ear.

"Why are you still tormenting me? I shot you dead, asshole! Okay! I'll do it for her! Promise you'll leave her alone!" Her hand was shaking as she picked up her phone, and she held it to her ear as it rang and rang.

"You've reached Tara. I can't come to the phone right now. Please leave a message."

The beep sounded, and Gina spoke.

"Tara…. I'm scared. Something is making me do this terrible thing, and I have no choice. It wants me to kill myself, and if I don't, it's threatening to come for you. I'm willing to take a bullet for you, Tara, because I owe you this much. Forgive me for what I'm about to do." She pushed the magazine into the gun and pulled back the slide. Gina's hands trembled as she turned the gun to her chest.

"I'm so sorry, Tara." Gina sobbed.

I turned away as she squeezed the trigger and cried as the loud fire rang. The Hedrix grabbed my chin and turned my head to see Gina's body on the bed. The gun lay beside her, and blood pooled out beneath her. Gina's eyes stared blankly at the ceiling, and her phone was still on the call to me. The Hedrix doppelganger stood over the bed, looking down with a smirk on his face. He looked up at me, smiled, and then turned and walked out the door.

"Gina!" I ran to her with my hands outstretched and my power burning down my arms, ready to save her. But as soon as my hands landed on her, she disappeared. I fell onto the mattress, and the fresh blood seeped into my clothing and covered my hands and face.

I pushed myself up, and the Hedrix clapped and cheered. "Bravo! Gina was such a brave little soldier, and she sacrificed herself to save you. Loyalty is one thing I admire. Humans make good little pets when it comes to love. Will you be loyal to me, Tara? I can make all the pain go away."

The Hedrix pressed his chest to my back and ran his hand down my cheek. He pulled me flush to him, and I felt every ripple and bulge of his body. I shivered, and he chuckled. He was revolting, vile, and manipulative, and I knew he was on to me. His hand moved to my erratically beating heart. The Hedrix cooed and swayed with me.

"Oh, little Tara! Did you take me for the big bad wolf, and you were to be my avenging little red riding hood trying to pull the wool over my eyes? I've seen this scenario enough times to know better. You thought you could trick me by temptation? I am no fool like that imbecile you shoved over the cliff. Speaking of which."

The scene changed to another room. A young woman lay crying in bed as a man stood and pulled up his pants. I immediately recognized Bryan's face. He leaned down and yanked the woman's hair, and she cried in pain. Bren's tear-streaked face appeared as Bryan leaned down and spoke in her ear. "Mr. Andrews sends his regards. If you ever come after him for child support, I have my orders to come back and kill you."

Bren began to sob. Bryan kissed her cheek, then let go of her hair. "I'll see you in class tomorrow, baby!" He left the room, and Bren curled up in a ball and pulled a blanket over herself.

The Hedrix shook his head. "Sick bastard! That's something I would never do."

"Why are you showing me this?"

"You see? Your actions were justified! That's another thing I want from my queen. To make a swift judgment and make the guilty pay. Bryan deserved his death."

The nightmarish scene with Bren faded, and I stood with the Hedrix on the ridge to the cave where he'd hidden my father. The same cliff I had pushed nightmare Bryan to his death.

"All this time, I have tested you." The Hedrix pointed down, and I saw myself holding onto the cliff face with fear and desperation.

The Hedrix yelled at my duplicate. "I'll see you again soon, Tara!"

"FUCK YOU!" I screamed back.

The asshole chuckled and smiled at me standing before him now. "You have passed my tests. Yet, you continued to waste your time protecting those who can defend themselves. You're in love with a man who's only shown you the smallest fraction of your capabilities, and not once has he proved to you what he can do.

You love a god who condemns humanity to a life of pain and misery just to take it in the end, and for what? He sent his son, who could heal and raise life from the grave, yet Airmed has blessed many children with the same gifts. Think of the lives you could save. The many you could heal. There would be no more pain and suffering. Humans could thrive and make the world a better place where life is worth living without depending on unanswered prayers.

And they would worship us, Tara. We'd live a life of luxury, travel the world, and see all the realms. There are wonders beyond this world so beautiful you'd wonder why you ever hesitated to be with me."

He lifted my chin to look into my eyes. "Tell me, Tara. What do you say?"

I smiled sweetly and responded. "I must say, you make it sound so appealing. I would love to live in a world without pain, suffering, and death, but a place like that already exists."

I pushed myself away from the Hedrix's hold. "You tell me you have tested me, but the same holds for all humanity. All of God's children face trials in this world. This life is not perfect, and our bodies are only supposed to live for a short while, and when we die, we will receive our eternal bodies, free from pain, misery, and death.

I don't seek to be some false deity, using my power to deceive people into believing they can rely on me alone. My power is not greater and never will be as great as HIS. I might be one of Airmed's blessed, and it may be my calling to help others, but it is not for sale to the highest bidders to gain riches and glory.

And as far as seeing the world, I can do that with or without anyone by my side. And one day, in Heaven, I will see beauty beyond all measure that will make me question, WHY WOULD I HAVE EVER CONSIDERED BEING WITH YOU?

You are an evil, manipulative deceiver who finds joy in people's pain and misery. You are the cause of every trauma and hardship my people have faced. You are vain and selfish and an egotistical power monger! I could never love or be with you. You would have to take me by force, and I would vomit every time you make love to me. You are death incarnate and the putrid bile that gives me severe indigestion.

You are incapable of knowing true love because you would never consider laying down your life for another. Instead, you take, steal and destroy. You are the thief in the night. A cold-hearted coward and slithering snake! I could love a snake better than you. That poor creature you crushed with Lyle's hand didn't deserve that fate.

Lyle was innocent, and you tortured him for your selfish gains. But guess what? My father deceived YOU! You could take from my father and me, but you'd never get the power you so desired, and you never will as long as I live. So you might as well kill me if you can, Hedrix. Though I don't know how you could because you are NOT a necromancer!"

The Hedrix scowled, crossed his arms over his chest, and smoke wafted from his nostrils. His disgusting tongue forked and flickered at the cloud in the air. "Poor, Tara. You've bought into all that foolish rhetoric and spout such a pathetic diatribe at me. It seems I must do more to break you. But you can't say I didn't ask nicely."

The Hedrix seized my arms, and I yelped as he turned me toward the cliff's edge. "But like all little birds, it's time for you to spread your wings, as I must push you from the nest. I know you enjoy flying. Why don't you sing a sweet song for me on your way down?"

The Hedrix kissed me on my cheek and shoved me over the edge. I didn't do the asshole the courtesy of screaming in fright. If this was my fate, so be it. I spread my arms and let the wind take me. The tree canopy came closer, and I welcomed the pain. I would take it rather than spend one more moment in his presence.

A bird screeched, and I looked to see a giant black eagle approach!

"Neveah!" I called. She screeched again, dove, and sailed closer, and just before I collided with the trees, I landed safely on her back. I cried with joy as Neveah rose into the air, and I could hear the Hedrix roar in anger from above. I turned and flipped him off; it was the only birdsong I'd ever give him. I laughed and crowed into the sky like Uncle Danny would do. Neveah cried out in acknowledgment and soared with me over the mountains.

Chapter 5
TARA

Renewed Alliances

The lake glittered with the risen sun on Uncle Woody's property, and Neveah circled before landing on the shore. I breathed in the fresh morning air and cried out like a warrior in victory. I hadn't defeated the Hedrix yet, but I'd claim this as a battle won.

I slid down Neveah's side and went to pet her head. "Thank you, beautiful girl." Neveah chirped sweetly and nuzzled into my shoulder.

"TARA!" Uncle Danny called.

"DANNY!" I saw him, my father, mother, and Rudy beaming at me. I ran and jumped into Danny's arms crying in relief.

"We were so worried about you, baby girl."

"You sent Neveah to find me."

Danny smiled. "I did. Dean told me the Hedrix had taken you, and Neveah was the only one who could. I was watching over you. I'm so proud of you for how you handled that beast."

"I was in the lake last night. I called for help, but no one heard me."

"Tara, the Hedrix had you halfway in the dream realm," Danny said.

"But, I," I turned to look back at Neveah, but she was gone.

"We were praying, honey," Mom said.

"I know, Mom. Thank you." I hugged her. "Where are Dean and Bren? Are they okay?"

"They are okay. Dean has been searching for you. We had a huge battle on our hands. We captured thirty Sevifk," Dad said.

"Thirty? How is everyone?"

"Unfortunately, we lost Zane," Danny said.

"I know. I was there just after it happened." My heart ached with sorrow, and my eyes watered.

Dad put his hand on my shoulder. "I'm so sorry, Tara. The Hedrix kept us distracted so he could steal you away. But every Sevifk we captured is waiting for you to set them free. They want to help us defeat the Hedrix."

"Good! Any enemy of that bastard is a friend of mine."

We walked back to The Roost, and I saw Dean sitting with his head in his hands. Bren was across from him, holding the blue mason jar with dirt and the addition of Zane's ashes, the ashes of his heart.

"Dean," I said softly.

"Tara!" He stood and wrapped me in his arms. "Thank God! I was so worried! Are you okay?"

"I am. I'm so sorry."

"Why? You didn't do anything wrong."

"No. I'm sorry for Zane. I couldn't save him." Tears rolled down my cheeks.

"He died protecting Bren. It's the way he wanted to go, laying his life down for someone he loved. He would have done the same for you or anyone here. It's just that I feel so empty inside now. Half of me is missing, and his heart is no longer there. And I, I just don't know what I'm going to do without my brother." Dean broke down and cried, and I held him. Dean squeezed me tight, and his body racked with grief. I cried with him, and we stood together for the longest time.

Bren was mourning while clutching the jar to her chest. Dean let me go, and I went to Bren and wrapped my arms around her. Bren's tears splashed down on the jar's lid. "We never got the chance to be together physically. I wanted to feel the warmth that matched the love we shared. We talked about it just before he died, and I asked him to wait because we would speak to you today. Our love was unique and too short. I miss him. I'll never love another the way I loved, Zane. My sweet, corny vampire." Bren sniffed.

"I'm so sorry, Bren. I would have given my blessing, and I should have much sooner. I just never thought that this would happen. I feel terrible and selfish."

"Please don't. I'm not angry with you, and you are not selfish. You're the most giving person I know. I'm happy you are back and safe."

"Me too. Do you know what you're supposed to do with Zane's ashes?"

"No. I knew to put the ashes in the jar, but I didn't know it would be the ashes of Zane's heart. This jar will remain with me always."

I didn't see or sense Zane's spirit, and I wondered what had happened to him. Where did a vampire's soul go?

Dean went with me to see the Sevifk that waited inside the bar. We walked through the door, and the demons rose from their seats. Thirty pairs of crimson eyes glowed as they observed my approach.

The Sevifk dropped to one knee and bowed their heads. They pounded their chests and cried out in a warrior's salute. There were men and women dressed in different clothing styles from various periods. These bodies had recently risen from the grave, and the Sevifk possessed them with the blood of another necromancer. The Hedrix thought he could send an army and get away with me, but he was sadly mistaken. He already let me slip through his hands, thinking he was teaching me a lesson.

It all backfired on him, and now those he'd tormented and changed bowed to serve a better cause. Alma and Esaw stood to either side of the Sevifk and smiled. I didn't feel the necessity for this display of loyalty, but I knew this was their way.

My father presented me with the necro claw, which he helped slide onto my hand, and one by one, I touched the blade to each demon bowed before me. I saw a glimpse of their previous lives as Airmed's children, and I went with the positive emotions I felt with each memory as I lightly pierced their skin and wished for their freedom.

As each of them stood, their eyes changed to their natural hues. Their bodies expelled the rush of decayed insects, and they took their first breaths of freedom and cried out in relief.

We spent the rest of the morning celebrating, and I learned their names and gifts. Many told stories of how the Hedrix had deceived and tortured and changed them. The Hedrix forced them to serve and fight against the Necros or face cruel punishment that involved hurting someone they loved. Because some of their gifts remained, they could steal some of the Necros' power and weaken them.

It was a huge travesty. But where there was war, there were spies. A secret alliance had formed between some of the Sevifk and the Necros. They knew coming here was an opportunity because word had gotten around in Hell that the Hedrix had found Airmed's blessed. They staged a show that would satisfy their cruel master but planned to surrender.

Though not all knew this plan, it worked out because Airmed's children were now tasting their first victory in ages. Many had loved ones to find and protect from the threats the Hedrix made long ago. But, for now, they vowed to stay and fight until the monster's death.

The Necros needed my help, which involved gifting them with a small dose of my power. I was gladly willing to provide what they needed because it would be well worth it if it helped turn this fight around.

We had to accommodate thirty extra people. We gathered what we had available and turned the bar into a shelter, moving tables and setting up cots with bedding, but there wasn't enough.

I went with Dean, Woody, Cannon, and Stella to get supplies and clothing for our guests. We ended up at one of the big buy-in-bulk stores, where Stella and I went to find essential clothing, shoes, and undergarments with a list of sizes.

Cannon, Dean, and Woody took flatbed carts and picked up more cots, sleeping bags, pillows, and toiletries. We ended with twelve shopping carts filled with food, water, clothes, and other necessities. Several store staff members had to help check out and load my and Cannon's vehicles. And Woody swiped his black credit card to the total five thousand-three hundred and sixty-two dollars. We had enough supplies to last for a few months.

When we returned to The Roost, everyone helped unload and set up inside. We had an industrial kitchen and plenty of service wares. But the challenge was providing showers for everyone. Dad and my uncles had plenty of helpers as they built two tented outdoor shower systems with PVC piping and a few propane water heaters.

Our new friends felt tremendous relief after getting a hot shower, fresh clothes, and food in their stomachs. Rudy, Trey, and Billie had set up a projection screen and put on some movies, and everyone sat and watched as Bren and Mom passed out popcorn and drinks.

The different reactions of so many faces felt like watching children ooh and ahh at something new. Most of these people had died long before all this technology came along. Because all they remembered were the simple things from their pasts and their experience in Hell.

They laughed at the comedies and action movies, cried at the drama and romance, and scowled at the war movies. But they also learned modern language terms and how the world worked today. They would leave equipped with all the knowledge they needed when they left The Hillbilly Roost behind.

Woody put the word out for help locating their people, though many probably changed their names and moved around to avoid suspicion of their prolonged mortality. They wouldn't recognize their loved ones in these different bodies. Providing new identities would also cost Woody a hefty amount, but he was willing to help, and everyone vowed to pay him back in time.

I didn't have nightmares anymore; instead, I dreamed of battles and victories for my brothers and sisters. It was my turn to comfort and watch over Dean as he grieved for Zane in bed each night. The loss of his brother devastated him.

I couldn't imagine living an entire life with another person residing inside you, feeling a second heartbeat and all their emotions, but loving them so deeply that you could overcome any obstacle together. He carried a second soul, another essence, and a constant reminder that somebody was always there for him. Dean and Zane experienced everything together, and now all that remained was a scar as a painful reminder of the brother he lost.

All I could do was be there for Dean. I held him, made love, prayed with him, and let him go through all the emotions. I brought our pet rubber duckie, Charlie, and we took a bubble bath. I made Dean laugh and smile like he'd done for me after Gina died, and I told him everything that happened while the Hedrix held me captive.

"He offered the world, and you turned it down for me?" Dean asked.

"Should I have taken his offer? I could be a queen in Hell now, and you could be my number one in my harem."

"As long as we could take little Charlie along and make him your number two." Dean made the rubber duck squeak like it was excited.

I laughed. "Well, the deal was we'd travel the world for a year first. I think little Charlie would enjoy seeing the seven wonders on the back of your motorcycle. Then we still needed to have our dance and make love on the beach."

"We could have added a sidecar to bring Bren along, but now that won't be necessary." Dean hung his head and sniffed.

"Bren can still come along. Did you see her new fashion accessory? She carries Zane around in an over-the-shoulder bag and double-wrapped him in bubble packing to keep him safe."

"I think she's gone a little overboard. She's losing her marbles."

"Maybe so, but she's dealing with her loss the best way she knows."

"I know. Tara, would you have really consented to allow them to be together physically? I heard you tell her it should have happened sooner, but given the circumstance, perhaps your reply was made out of sympathy."

"Perhaps it was at first, but realizing this was her loss too, I put myself in her shoes, and I know I would be devasted if we hadn't had our chance to be together. Still, it might have made the grief even more consuming, having had such an experience and knowing it could never happen again."

"Better to have loved and lost than never have loved at all? Is that what you're going for?" Dean's eyes glistened and threatened to spill over.

I took his hand, kissed his fingertips, and then nibbled each one. He chuckled at my attempt, but his callouses didn't allow the same ticklish effect as when he did it to me.

He returned the favor, and I screeched and giggled uncontrollably. Dean kissed my hand and smiled, but tears still dropped into the soap bubbles below.

"Life will never be the same without him. Thank you for being here for me, Tara. I don't know what I'd do if you hadn't gotten away from that asshole. I might have gone on a madman's rage mission and ended up in a tragic predicament."

"I wouldn't have left you behind. You'd have come along with me and helped me escape. Then together, we'd make our way to the Necros and give them that power boost. But then you might have to fight off a legion of horny soldiers and get trampled. Then I'd have to send in Charlie to save your ass." I pressed Charlie's squeaker, and Dean laughed.

"It doesn't work that way, Tara. When you did that with me, we were already mated. We sealed the deal, and I stamped my claim on you so your power boost no longer has that same effect on others, and we'd be safe."

"That's an idea!"

"What?"

"I allow myself to be captured and bring you with me. We escape and make our way to the Necros."

"No! Absolutely not happening!"

"But I!"

"Nope!"

"How can you?"

"Not listening!"

"Will you even?"

"It's a big fat NO, Tara! That's a risk I'm not willing to let you take! Your father is already discussing ways to get your power to the Necros. Your life is too valuable to risk, and no one here will allow you to do that."

"UHG! FINE! You're right! But, what if I get captured again?"

"That's not going to happen either. We have a team of experienced fighters willing to make a stand to keep you safe."

"I'm not expecting to sit out from any fight. I'm capable of holding my own."

"I know that, Tara. That doesn't mean you must face this battle alone or step in and try to save everyone. They see you as their leader, so lead. But let someone have your back. It goes both ways in battle, and the soldier who tries to do it all loses all. Everyone here would be lost without you. Even heroes need sidekicks and a following." Dean took Charlie and pushed the squeaker, and it sounded like the rubber duck agreed.

"You make a valid point, but does Charlie have to always agree with everything you say?"

"He is a wise quacker. He understands more than either of us." Dean smiled and pressed the squeaker again.

I laughed. "Well, he needs to start paying some bills around here since his has a lot to say."

Dean dunked Charlie under the bubbles.

"Where does he think he's going?"

"You scared him! He went into hiding!" Dean teased in a grave tone.

"Why?" I chuckled.

"He told me you were going to take his mouth away. He doesn't want to lose his bill. How's he going to eat?" Dean's bottom lip quivered. I laughed, and my hand chased Charlie under the water as Dean moved him about, only I grabbed something else.

Dean smiled deviously. "That one doesn't have a squeaker, but it agrees with your hand now."

I laughed. "Oh, really? Does it make bubbles if I squeeze it?"

"You can try it and see!" Dean grinned.

"Okay!" I squeezed Dean's erection, and bubbles broke the surface. I laughed again when Dean lifted Charlie out of the water and squeezed rubber ducky pee at me out of its bottom hole.

"Ahh! Bad duckie!"

Dean began cracking up, and my heart filled with joy. I smiled at Dean as I stroked him. He tried to pull my hand free, but I smacked him away. "Let me do this for you. I want to. Just relax, baby."

Dean closed his eyes, and I first worked him with long, slow strokes. I built up speed, and his breathing became heavy. I reached down with my other hand and massaged his scrotum. "Does that feel good?"

Dean nodded, and I worked him harder. He was slippery and smooth, and it made me hot to have him this way.

"Mmmm, Dean! You are so hard, smooth and thick. Do you know what you do to me when you are inside my body? You make me so wet, and you feel so good. You strike my sweetest places, and I ache with intense pleasure. You build me up and make me want more. Your body is electric. You course through me, fill me, and I burst and quiver for you. I desire you. I hunger for you. I…"

Dean groaned and shook. "Ahh! Fuck woman!" Dean's muscles flexed as he pushed himself to stand and stepped out of the tub.

Dean lifted me and hooked my arms and legs around his body. He carried me, dripping wet, and lay me on the bed. His beautiful blue eyes held my soul captive. The heat of his gaze drew me to the deep-set flame of past that burned and melded our souls together. He slid between my thighs, and I gasped. He began to move and my nipples rubbed and tightened against his chest. His pace quickened as my hands roamed the tight muscular lines of his chest, arms, back, and ass. I held him tight and pulled him deeper with each thrust of his hips.

Dean kissed me, and the decadent gliding sensation of our wet naked bodies made me light up from head to toe. Power buzzed in my veins, my blood rushed, and I throbbed in an achingly beautiful way.

Dean kissed my neck and then worked down to my breast, where he sucked my nipple into his mouth. His tongue pressed and swirled around my areola, and then flickered my taut peak. My body zinged, and the orgasmic sensation shot through my core.

My slickened muscles clenched around Dean's thick, hard cock. His momentum increased, and I moaned and begged him not to stop. Dean's fingers circled my throbbing clit, and I rocked my hips, meeting Dean's powerful thrusts. I screamed his name as my body arched off the bed, my toes curled, and I quaked. My heart pounded like a riot in my chest. "Ooh! Ohh! Dean! Dean! I, I need. I can't." My body continued to shiver.

Dean kissed me and made a deep, sexy chuckle. "You shouldn't start things you can't finish." He slowed his movements but continued. "Mmm! Do you know what you do to me when I'm inside of you? You turn me into a beast, and I have to take you hard and fast. To hear you moan and scream my name and feel every ripple of your tight wet pussy. And when you squeeze my dick! Mmm! It's so hard for me to hold back, but you feel so delicious, and I want everything I can get out of your divine womanhood. I want to worship at your altar and taste your wine. I want to give you my best offerings again and again. I desire, crave, and hunger for you, Tara. I'll never get enough."

I was still riding the waves, but Dean's movements and words caused my heat to rise. I licked at his lips, and he opened for me. I bit my lip and felt my power tingling on the tip of my tongue. I swirled my tongue around Dean's, and his blue eyes widened in surprise. They flashed, and his pupils dilated.

Dean groaned and began bucking his hips. He drank down my offering and pulled more. It was the tiniest amount, but it was enough to send him over the edge. His biceps bulged as he lifted me, and my legs went around him. He seated me on his erection, and I cried out. I swear he'd grown in girth and length and I stretched to accommodate him.

Every ripple and nerve inside me quickened with hot energy as Dean took my hips and rocked me. We panted into each other's open mouths as our tongues danced around one another. Dean moved faster, and my aching nipples rubbed against his chest as my breasts bounced. Dean grunted and groaned as I moaned. My body was on fire, and what was soapy water before turned to sweat as Dean and I burned together.

We lost track of time and fell into delirium. Dean fell asleep, and I watched him. Every so often, he twitched and moaned. He was dreaming and had said his brother's name like he was directing him. Dean's brows furrowed, and his body jerked. He breathed heavily, eyes rolling back and forth beneath his lids.

I wanted to wake him because it seemed like he was having a nightmare. But, at the same time, I felt he needed to follow through on whatever he was experiencing. Something important was happening. I had a distinct gut feeling that Dean was somehow helping Zane.

"Where are you right now?" I questioned.

Dean's lips parted, and he said, "Go this way."

Chapter 6
ZANE

Awe Hell

A beautiful voice called, and I yearned to be with the woman who beckoned me. My body ached, and my muscles burned with fatigue. And why did I feel like I got separated from someone else? I felt this void like a large crater in my chest, and I couldn't make a reason for it. I was naked and walking alone in the wilderness. Every stone, thorn, and thistle I stepped on hurt my bare tender feet. The sky was a reddish hue and overcast with a hazy drift. Where had I gone? What happened to me? Why can't I remember anything? And where was I going now?

I felt thirsty, but I didn't know for what. My stomach felt like it had caved in on itself and my eyes grew heavy. I wanted to lie down and rest, but something pulled me to keep moving. I heard water trickling, and a voice said, "Go this way."

I quickened my pace to find the source, pushed through thorny brush, and my skin burned as the sharp needles scored and broke my skin. But I saw it. A small stream ran down rocks, and I cupped my hands to catch a drink. Even the water here was red, but I was so thirsty, I didn't care if I drank poison at this point. I slurped the red liquid, groaning when it hit my tongue. It didn't taste like water, but it was bittersweet and familiar to me.

I drank more and more till I had my fill. My upper gums ached, and I pressed my fingers to them. I was startled when two sharp points pierced me, and I held my hand up and saw I was bleeding. Then it hit me. I drank blood, and I had fangs.

I was a vampire!

How could I forget something so significant? I looked at my arms and legs, and they had healed. My feet no longer hurt, the fatigue left me, and my muscles strengthened. I began to run and whip through the trees. I felt in my element, like I belonged here, returning to my origins.

I made it to a wide rushing river. A high stone wall stretched for miles in both directions was on the other side. I could try to jump across. There were rocks I could land on, so I sprung forward and landed on the first. From there, I leaped again and made it to another, then once more, I made it to the other side. I looked back, satisfied at my accomplishment.

As I looked both ways down the wall, there was no telling where it ended. I began to climb, and I scaled it with ease. Once I reached the top, I couldn't believe my eyes. A majestic city awaited me, and a mammoth jeweled tower rose high in its center, disappearing into the hazy clouds.

"Someone has a huge ego and must be compensating for something." I jumped from the wall and landed deftly on my feet.

"Halt!" a female voice commanded. Something sharp poked my back, and I raised my hands.

"Can I speak?" I asked.

"State your name and the reason for your intrusion within my master's walls," the woman said.

"My name is." Wait! What was my name? The woman nudged me persistently, awaiting a response. Nothing came to mind except the letter Z.

"I am Z."

"And why are you climbing the wall instead of entering through the checkpoint?"

"I didn't know there was one. I came from the forest. That way." I pointed.

"State your business, vampire!"

"I don't know. I just got here. I am lost. I can't remember anything. I was hoping to find someone who could help me."

"Keep your hands up and turn around."

I turned slowly and was face to face with a striking redhead in a guard uniform. Her ruby eyes glowed, and she scowled fiercely at me.

"Where are your clothes?" she asked.

"I don't know. That's another thing with which I need help. I just woke up in the forest and made my way here. As I said, I don't remember anything. Could you tell me where I am?"

"You are in the City of Syadestese, the Kingdom of the Hedrix master, Izrazyk. You have broken our law by entering our border without going through the checkpoint, and I am placing you under arrest."

"As I said, I wasn't aware of a checkpoint, and I was looking." My words were cut short as a charge of power zapped through my body, and I fell to the ground and blacked out. When I woke again, I was hanging upside down from a wooden pole with my wrists and ankles tied. I saw a soldier's backside carrying one end as my body rocked.

Was I to be placed over flames and burned?

"Where are you taking me? I didn't do anything wrong!"

"Quiet, vampire!" a male voice commanded.

I still didn't have any clothes. People paused in their activities and watched as the soldiers carried me through the village. Sounds of everyday life filled my ears as people talked and conducted business. We were passing through a marketplace where some peddled, and others shopped.

A man said to one of the soldiers, "Take him to the slave market."

"Slave market?" I asked. I grimaced as a whip lashed my side.

"You do not speak, vampire! Not until your new master says so!"

I looked at this man. He was nothing, and I could have taken him down in a second. Yet by the fancy clothes, he held some matter of higher station. If I knew anything, it was not to challenge a person of stature. At least not out in the open, surrounded by guards.

I was to be sold off to the highest bidder. I'd better play this right. I didn't get a chance to look at myself in a mirror, but by the condition of my body, I must not be all that bad looking.

The soldiers carried me through a crowd of people shouting bids for whatever poor soul stood on display. We stopped, someone cut my bindings, and I dropped to the ground with a grunt. I was grabbed and lifted, then prodded forward up some steps. I stood on a stage before a large crowd in all my naked glory.

An announcer yelled, "The next auction item is a male vampire with a strong physique and a promising prospect for harem work. Do I have my first bid?"

"One thousand!" a man cried. More people began shouting as the bids came in and went higher and higher. I put on my come-hither smile and posed, showing off my muscular prowess. Many women were shouting and raising the stakes higher, trying to beat each other out of the bidding. I started to enjoy all the attention.

A harem boy didn't sound all that bad. I wasn't sure what all it entailed, but it must be something worthwhile if all these women wanted me. The bids reached forty thousand, then a voice shouted from the back of the crowd. "One hundred thousand!"

Everyone turned to see who had made the high bid, and a hooded person had their hand up in the air. They did not reveal their identity, but I could tell it was a woman by her voice and delicate hand.

The auctioneer called, "One hundred thousand going once, twice. Sold to the hooded mistress in the back! Come up and claim your winnings."

The hooded female moved through the crowd to the stage. She handed a man a leather purse as shackles went around my wrists and ankles and a collar locked around my neck. Chains connected them with a leash, and the woman took hold and tugged.

I leaped off the stage and followed her willingly because what else was I supposed to do? Where else could I go? If I were to be her harem boy, I had no choice.

We made our way out of the crowd, and I followed the mysterious woman. She stopped at a booth and purchased a shirt, pants, and boots. She unlocked my bindings and tossed the articles of clothing at me.

"Get dressed," she commanded.

I pulled on the clothes, slipped my feet into the boots, and looked at my body. I supposed I looked like everyone else here now. I saw a full-length mirror and stepped in front of it. I didn't know what beauty standards were for a man or vampire, but I got the feeling as I looked at myself that I had plenty to offer, considering how the women in the crowd reacted. I had messy, dark blond hair with lighter blond ends, shining silver eyes, and full lips. My facial structure was lean and masculine, and my nose was straight of nicely proportioned to my face. The clothes I wore looked common, so I didn't stand out, and I was appreciative of my new master for my digs.

"Thank you, miss?" I began.

"Not here!" the woman responded. "You must come with me. We have to hurry back before he returns."

"Where? Who?"

"I said, not here! I will explain when we get back. Come now!" The woman put my shackles back on, and I allowed it. I could have easily run away, but I had a feeling I should stick around to find out why she wanted me.

We took back streets with few to no people and arrived at another wall. Only this one went around the massive tower I'd seen from the first wall I'd climbed. The woman stopped and paid a guard, and we entered through a cellar door. Once inside, my eyes adapted to the pitch darkness. We ascended a spiraling staircase and stopped at another door, where the woman pressed her ear to it and listened.

"Where are," I began to ask.

"Shh!" she silenced me. She listened a moment longer, then lightly tapped on the wood. It was a secret knock, which someone on the other side returned. She responded with another signal, and the door cracked open. She slid through, tugged on the chain, and I followed quietly.

We hid behind a vast tapestry and walked along for a stretch before reaching another door, where she and another hooded figure repeated the process. Again, we entered still concealed and traveled forward till she halted her steps.

"I will remove your shackles now, but you must promise to stay with me and do as I say," she whispered.

"I will," I whispered in return.

She took off my bindings. "You will be safe in this part of the castle, and you must not make your presence known. Whatever you see or hear, you must not interfere. The consequences are dire. Thousands of lives depend upon maintaining order within these walls. If you decide to be someone else's hero, everything we've worked hard to achieve will be for nothing. Do you understand?"

"I stay hidden and don't interfere with anything? Even if someone is hurt, tortured, or killed? Even a beautiful woman?" I asked.

"Correct. It is unfortunate, but if you were to intercede, many lives would become forfeit, and all the progress we've made with the Necros alliance will collapse. Many more will die, and their deaths will be on your hands."

"Does this include you?"

"Even me. Especially me. Do not try to be a hero. Since I was a small child, I have lived here and have endured more than anyone could imagine. I have gained the trust of Izrazyk, the Hedrix master, and I can withstand anything he does to me, so if you get any ideas about becoming my savior, don't. Don't look, speak or act. Whatever he does to me might look bad, but I can handle it."

"You have my word." I bowed my head.

The woman removed her hood, revealing long lustrous raven hair and a face that could evoke any man's fantasies, with violet eyes, luscious ruby lips, and flawless porcelain skin. She removed her cloak, and her body had perfect curves in the flowing sheer blue dress. Her arms were bare and covered with small scars like someone had cut her repeatedly. It made me growl in anger, but she shushed me again.

"I have explained everything to you, vampire, and what's on the line. You must maintain your composure, or I will have to kill you myself."

"How would you?"

"My blood. I am a necromancer; enough of my blood will kill you, so don't try me. I will ensure you are well fed by others in the harem."

"What is your name, mistress?"

"I am Willa Flores, daughter of Esaw and Alma and one of Airmed's blessed."

"Why does this sound familiar to me?"

"Because you are Zane Perrish, brother of Dean and in alliance with Tara Raybrook, Airmed's blessed. Izrazyk covets your brother's mate for her powers. You died in battle against one of the Hedrix masters' Sevifk demons. But they are innocent pawns. More of Airmed's children who were captured, transformed, and forced to do his bidding under duress of torture and threats against their loved ones."

My memory came rushing back to me. I was fighting one of these demons who had my woman. "Bren! My love. He had her, and I fought the Sevifk. He threw her in the air, and I caught her. My heart!"

I ran my hands over my chest. My chest?

"My brother?" I asked.

"He still lives. Only you died, Zane."

"Oh my god! This isn't right! I'm a vampire! I can't be killed."

Unless?

"You were staked through the heart, Zane. No vampire survives that. You are in Hell. It is your fate. Someone had to die to come and help with my escape to the Necros. You were chosen for this task."

Tears fell from my eyes. "My brother? My Bren? Tara?"

"It will be all right, Zane. They are all okay. I need your help."

"You seem to have a system going. You can leave and return without notice, and people are already helping you. Why am I here?"

"Because you are a vampire, you can mediate between the Sevifk and the Necros. Vampires serve Hedrix and Necros and have a low standing, and they go unnoticed as servants."

"Well, isn't that a shot to the balls? We are a superior species in the land of the living."

"Superior to humans. But, your Necros brother controlled you, did he not?"

"Dean and I are equals, and we have each other's backs."

"Had. You're not with Dean anymore. Look. You have your own body now, and you are your own person. You have a say in your destiny. You can flee if you wish, but you will forever travel alone in this realm with no one to have your back. Or, you can stay and help in this fight "

"I was already helping Tara. Why would I flee now?"

"I'm giving you the option. It will not be as easy in Hell as when you were alive. And if you die here, that's it. You exist nowhere. And vampires are a silver a dozen, and no one cries for their loss here."

"No vampire holds any sway in Hell?"

"Only sexually. Your race makes entertaining bedfellows. That's why the women went crazy bidding for you, even some men. They crave your body and blood."

"The women here drink vampire blood?"

"They are demons. Of course, they do."

"What else am I good for?"

"The highest station you may rank is as a guardsman, which is why I acquired you. You will become one of my detail on our journey. Once Izrazyk returns, he will rest for a day and return to the battlefront, and I will be at his side. He wishes to flaunt Tara and me to the Necros and make them bend. Once they see he has both of us, they will kneel. Tara is our last hope."

"He didn't capture her, did he?"

"He did, but she got away."

"How do you know all of this?"

"My mother and father are still linked with me, keeping me updated. The Sevifk Izrazyk sent to distract your friends surrendered themselves, and Tara freed their souls. They are preparing for the next attack, but we must try to get to the Necros before that happens. We are to meet with a Sevifk, who is supposed to bring a gift to help the Necros."

"If I am supposed to remain hidden, how will you present me as part of your new detail? Doesn't Izrazyk know who I am?"

"That's the thing. He doesn't. My mother told me that Tara boosted Dean's power and shielded you before Izrazyk could learn of your existence."

"But I look exactly like my brother. Won't that give me away?"

"That is an easy fix. Come!"

Chapter 7
ZANE

Make Believe Over

Willa led me to a room with women and men dressed in scant clothing. Some danced while others lounged about, engaged in conversation or intimate acts. They must be the Hedrix's harem.

A young woman ran up to Willa. She had dark silky skin and long multicolored braids. She assessed me with emerald green eyes and had fangs like mine—another vampire. "This is the vampire of which you spoke?"

"Domonique, this is Zane. He has come aboard as the replacement for my former guard Leander. I wish to have his hair made dark, and I do not care for the looks of his eyes. Find something more suitable to my liking. Perhaps obsidian. I don't need fair eyes distracting me."

"Pity. His silver eyes are striking, and I'd love to run my fingers through those luscious blond locks. He is very handsome," Domonique purred.

I grinned at the ebony beauty, and she smiled seductively.

"You can run your fingers through his hair as much as you desire while dying it black. Make him as classically gothic as possible without looking like a dramatic angsty human. I need him to portray an experienced guardsman, not a potential harem boy," Willa instructed.

Domonique took my hand. "Come along, Zane. We're going to have some fun."

I smiled as I let Domonique guide me to another room that looked like a day spa. Women began giggling as they watched me walk inside. A voluptuous blond in a white Grecian-style dress approached. "Ooh, Domonique! Who do you have here?"

"This is Zane. He's the mistress's newest guard, and she wants me to give him a make-over."

The blond and another dark-haired beauty came to fawn all over me. Their hands were touching and grabbing me everywhere. I jumped and yelped when a hand squeezed my ass and another groped my package. I pushed their hands away, and they groaned in disappointment.

"Ladies. Please, control yourselves. I have a girlfriend."

"Awe, poor darling! She must be lost without you," the blond woman said.

"Of course, she is. I know I would miss such a fine tail. You are a masterpiece of masculinity," the other said.

These women kept cooing and coddling me, and the old me would have had them eating out of the palms of my hands. But I was in love with Bren, and even though I was dead and gone from her, it didn't mean I was ready to jump back in the water.

"Oh my! It is true love. How tragic," the blond said.

"Wait! How do you know she isn't here, back at our home waiting for my return?" I asked.

All three women laughed.

"Sweetheart! You have fresh soul written all over you. You are too genuine, and you wear your heart on your sleeve. You smell like you just arrived from the wilderness. That's where the new arrivals always end up. From there, destiny guides them. You are lucky Willa found you."

"Where did Willa find you?" Domonique asked.

"I was captured by a guard and taken to an auction where Willa bid on me and won."

"See? I told you she knew it was today," the blond said.

Dominque had me sit in a chair and wrapped a cape around my neck. She mixed a dark paste in a bowl and then applied it to my hair.

"What do you mean?" I asked the blond.

She rolled her eyes. "I mean destiny, sweet cheeks! Willa has the sight, and she can communicate with those beyond this realm. These are her other gifts aside from her necromancy."

"She knew she'd find me today?"

"Yes. I'm Adria, by the way. It's a pleasure to meet you, Zane." The blond kissed my lips, took my hand, and cleaned my fingernails.

The dark-haired woman with Asian Indian features began washing my feet. After finishing the dye application, Domonique applied a minty cucumber mask to my face. I relaxed in the chair and sighed as the women gossiped and giggled as they rubbed my chest, arms, and legs with fragrant oils. I couldn't believe this was Hell because I felt like I was in Heaven.

Think of Bren, think of Bren, I repeated in my head.

I pictured Bren in a sheer golden gown with open toes sandals. Her dark hair flowed down past her shoulders in voluminous curls, and her eyes smoldered in smokey makeup. She walked toward me and knelt before my wide-open legs. She looked at me with those gorgeous green eyes and smiled with ruby lips as she ran her hands up my thighs.

Zane, I want you! Her voice echoed.

I snapped out of my fantasy as a riot of giggles erupted, and I opened my eyes. The dark-haired woman smiled and giggled as she looked at the rigid tent beneath my pants. Her hands were dangerously close, and I sat up and gently pushed her hands back and smiled.

"Sorry, ladies! I was daydreaming about my lady."

"What is her name?" the dark-haired woman asked.

"Bren."

"Tell us about her?"

"Yes, Zane. Tell us," Adria and Domonique implored.

"My Bren is brave, intelligent, and stubborn as a mule. She is giving and caring but also strong and a survivor. I made the mistake of trying to make her mine through compulsion, and when she found out, she was angry with me. But then I saved her from an evil man possessed by a demon, and when she felt how my heart beat for her, she melted.

Bren's beauty steals my breath away every time I see her. And when she touches me, I remember no other woman before her, nor will I ever want another. Her dark brunette hair smells like a fresh spring bouquet touched by the evergreen rain, and her green eyes sparkle like water catching the morning sun. Her lips are lush, soft, and sweet like ripened berries. Her breasts are bountiful and supple, and her body drives me to my bassist primal instincts.

The way she loves me and lets me love her sends my heart racing like a thunderbolt across the sky. She is my soul mate and my best friend."

All of the women sighed dreamily.

"I would give up this life of luxury to have a love like that," Adria sighed, "Bren is a lucky girl."

"You are a catch, Zane," Domonique said.

"I could never love a man that way," the dark-haired woman said.

"Why would you say that, Saharah?" Adria asked.

"I don't want to go through such heartbreak. You know our life doesn't allow such a luxury as love. I would no longer wish to be if I did lose someone that way," Saharah replied.

"You do not know of which you speak, Saharah. To love that way is everything. It is a risk, but to have such an experience is worth it," Adria said.

"But, have you been in love?" Saharah asked.

"Almost," Adria replied.

"Almost doesn't count. Besides, look at poor Zane. He daydreams but can no longer hold his Bren. The longer he is in Hell, the more his pain will be as he grows tormented by memories of a woman he will never see or touch again. From what he describes, she is Heaven bound. I am sorry, Zane, but it is best to try to forget her as soon as possible. Hell will make your sorrow paramount."

"Why don't you ask Willa if you can come with us, Saharah?" I asked.

"Why would I do that?" Saharah looked confused.

"Maybe you need a change of scenery. A fresh perspective," I offered.

"Oh, no. Our Master would not allow it," Domonique said.

"Maybe if you offer some service to him along the way. Not sexual, but what you are doing for me now."

"He does get extra moody when he comes home from a battle," Adria said.

"Lean your head back," Domonique instructed. I did, and she rinsed the dye out and shampooed my hair. Her fingers massaged my scalp, and goosebumps rose on my arms and legs.

"You have magical fingers, Domonique." I groaned at how good her fingernails felt on my scalp.

Domonique leaned down and whispered. "That isn't the only magical part of me."

Adria and Saharah giggled.

I chuckled. "I'm sure you're right."

"I am here for you if you wish to try me, Zane." Domonique kissed my lips. I turned my head aside before she could kiss me more, and she grumbled in defeat.

"Your loss! My girls and I could make you feel so good, you would forget all about…."

I growled and sat up. "Don't you dare finish that statement! We were getting off to a good start, and I'd like to remain friends."

"My apologies. I didn't mean any harm. Please!" Domonique gestured for me to lay back.

"I'm sorry I snapped at you."

She laughed. "You call that snapping? That's nothing! You should hear when our Master…." An enormous roar cut off Domonique.

"He's home! Quick! He needs to hide!" Saharah cried.

Domonique wrapped a towel around my head and took my arm. "Quickly! Follow me!" Domonique raced through a door to a balcony and shoved me inside a crevice between two columns.

"Stay here!" she whispered forcefully. She headed back inside and closed the door.

Izrazyk's voice boomed through the closed door. "Where is Willa?"

From this spot, I could hear voices carrying like running through a pipeline.

"I am here, my lord," Willa said. "What ails thee, Master?"

The Hedrix roared in anger. "I had her, but she got away! Tara is headstrong and manipulative. I aimed to teach her a painful lesson, but a god-damned bird swooped in and saved her, and she got away."

"What can I do for you, Master?" Willa asked.

"You will accompany me to the battlefront tomorrow morning and ride with your guard to steal more power from the Necros!" Izrazyk boomed. "And you will bring it back to me along with the dead, and I will put their heads on pikes. You will sit with me on my steed for all to see, and they will know their time is soon ending!"

"As you wish, Master. Master?" Willa asked.

"What?"

"My former guard Leander perished while you were away. I took the liberty of selecting a new one. He is a vampire, a well-trained and seasoned fighter. He would do well to ride with me and aid in your quest."

"Very well. Where is this new guard?"

"He is being briefed by General Krelm."

"When he is finished, you will bring him to see me. Adria and Saharah! To my bed-chamber now!"

"Yes, Master," the two women replied.

"Domonique! Whatever this mess is, clean it up!"

"Yes, Master."

After several minutes, the balcony door opened, and Domonique appeared.

"You can come inside, but you must remain quiet while I finish with you. Willa said to tell you; you will now go by Sergeant Jeremiah Vansbrie from the Second Battalion out of Ardromezor."

I nodded and kept repeating my new name, rank, and station in my head while Domonique finished rinsing my hair. She gave me a sharp haircut and a clean shave. She put a pair of black contacts in my eyes. And when I saw my reflection in the mirror, I no longer recognized myself.

My eyes were the eeriest feature, as they looked like a dark endless void, but I was rocking the jet-black hair. My clothing was part Dracula, part Three Musketeers with my dark cloak and kickass boots. The sword and pistol were fun additions, which I couldn't wait to use.

Willa came for me, and when she saw me, she smirked. I held my hands out and did a spin. "What do you think?" I asked.

"You pass. What's your name, soldier?" Willa asked.

"My name is Sergeant Jeremiah Vansbrie of the Second Battalion out of Ardromezor."

"Thank you for joining my guard, Sergeant Vansbrie. You answer directly to me and your Master Izrazyk above all else, but you will always address him as Master."

"Who was my former commanding officer?"

"Lieutenant Rishclaw. Your battalion made headway in Ardromezor, and Rishclaw sent you into the city with a few others as requested, where I selected you as my new head guardsman."

"How did you gain the trust of the Hedrix Master?"

"I spent the first few years watching my parents tortured. Then Izrazyk sent me away for training. He would come to see me often and steal my power, but my development was slow at such a young age.

He promised to free my parents if I cooperated, but I knew this wasn't true. I never saw them again, but I recently connected with them when Tara set them free.

My sight and communication ability developed before my necromancy. I staged a coup where I saved Izrazyk's life from an assassination attempt and revealed my ability to foresee important events, which I have directed in his favor. He still doesn't know about my other gift. My spies have worked with the Sevifk and Necros to deceive the Hedrix into thinking Necros have lost many soldiers. Only 'the dead' have gone underground and continue building their resistance. Still, they need a power boost from Tara. They have fought for so long, taking a toll."

"What has Izrazyk done with your power?"

"He's collected it over the years, keeps it in a hidden vessel, and takes from it in small doses. He desperately wants to have the necromancer power, but it doesn't stay with him long, and if he tries to take more, it makes him ill."

"He's done the same to Tara and her father. Why is he so desperate to become the same thing he despises?"

"He is envious of the Necros because of their power. He wants to have the powers of life and death to decide who is of value and who is not. He wants to rule Hell and the living realms. He wants to be a god."

"Wow! Someone must have taken away his favorite toy when he was a child, and he never got over it. You said you were one of Airmed's blessed, yet he has not accomplished his goals. Not that I'd want him to, but why?"

"I don't have what Tara has."

"And what's that?"

"The ability to separate her light from her darkness, but he doesn't know this. Tara has the key to release whichever she chooses. But you should never speak of it here. If Izrazyk figured this out, the scales would tip drastically in his favor if he got hold of it."

"Noted. Is there anything else I need to know?"

"We ride tomorrow morning to the battlefront. You are to accompany me to capture as many Necros as we can. I am to steal their power and bring it and the dead back to our Master. I will send word ahead of this, and the arrangement will provide what Izrazyk desires. The Master is a vain demon. Feed his ego, and you'll pass his tests. Come, now we must go to meet him. You follow my lead on how to salute and greet our Master."

I followed Willa down a grand corridor lined with dramatic tapestries and paintings portraying a man with dark hair and startling blue eyes. He rode a gallant black steed, wore shining golden armor, and was victorious in every scene. Of course, this was the Hedrix master. I could see why Willa called him vain.

We approached a double door where two guards opened them for Willa, and I followed her inside. Izrazyk sat propped up in a massive bed with Adria and Saharah pleasuring him. They were half-naked, and Izrazyk was. Holy Moby Dick! The demon had an enormous!

"Master!" Willa saluted with a fist pound to her chest, a head bow, and an aggressive hoot. "This is my new first guard, Sergeant Jeremiah Vansbrie."

I stepped forward and saluted and hooted just as Willa had.

"Master!" I looked straight at Izrazyk's forehead. I knew to stare him directly in the eyes would evoke a challenge, which I was all for, but I didn't want to start something I couldn't finish with the other guards around.

The women in the room needn't get caught up in the crosshairs. So, I played my role like a good little soldier at stood at attention. All my years of military training made me believable in my current position. It was challenging to hold a serious face as the women moaned and cooed as they kissed and touched the Hedrix below his waist.

"Where have you come from, soldier? Who was your commanding officer?" Izrazyk asked.

"Second battalion stationed at Ardromezor, Master. Lieutenant Rishclaw sent me to your opulent city at the request of Mistress Flores, along with others who serve your magnanimous cause. It is an honor to stand in your presence, Master."

"It is indeed. Tell me about your experience?"

Willa and I had not discussed this, and Willa paused her breath for a split second, but I had this.

"I have served on the frontlines in thirty-eight battles over the last eighty years, engaging the enemy in hand-to-hand combat. I am ninety-eight percent in marksmanship and number two in swordsmanship. I can throw a blade and strike a man's eye or heart at one hundred sixty feet even more if he is not running. I can run faster than every vampire in my regiment, and I have worn down a powerful Necros as he challenged to control my bloodlust."

"You've accomplished all of this, and I am now just learning of your name? And who is number one in swordsmanship?" Izrazyk asked.

"You, of course, my master!" I bowed my head, laying it on thicker than blood and molasses.

"How noble of you to recognize this, Vansbrie. I believe Mistress Willa has chosen well. We ride at dawn. And Willa? See to it that fresh horses are ready for Adria and Saharah. I wish to bring them along."

"Yes, Master, I will see to it," Willa replied.

"One more thing, Willa."

"Yes, my lord." Izrazyk beckoned Willa to come to him. She climbed onto the bed and crawled on her hands and knees. Saharah and Adria cried out as he shoved them aside, and I clenched my fists behind my back but kept my face neutral.

When Willa was within reach, she yelped as the Hedrix grabbed her arm and yanked her forward. It took every ounce of restraint to keep my monster calm. I swallowed thickly to keep from growling as Izrazyk reached inside Willa's cape, wrapped his arm around her waist, and pulled her onto his lap.

I thought he was about to do the unthinkable, but instead, he pulled a knife from a holster at Willa's back and took hold of her arm. He pressed the tip into her flesh, making a small cut, then wrapped his lips around the wound. He took a single sip and groaned. Without warning, he released Willa's arm and threw the knife at me. It sailed past my head, missing the tip of my ear by mere centimeters, and embedded into the door behind me.

I hadn't even flinched, and the Hedrix laughed.

"Did you see that, Mistress?" He turned Willa around in his lap to face me. "He knew I could have struck his eye, but he didn't move, not a jerk or the tiniest flinch. You have indeed chosen well, my love." Izrazyk squeezed Willa in his hold and kissed her cheek. He released her and smacked her ass as she crawled away. When he looked at me again, I bowed my head.

"You are dismissed, Vansbrie. Willa, show him to his quarters."

"Yes, my lord." Willa and I saluted and turned to walk towards the doors. Adria and Saharah were moaning again, and the Hedrix chuckled. Before the guards opened the doors, Willa pulled her blade free and tucked it back into her holster.

We exited the Hedrix's chambers, and Willa turned in the opposite direction from where we first came and continued to another door. We moved in silence down the spiral staircase and stopped.

"You did well, Jeremiah Vansbrie. Do you require sustenance before you rest?"

"I drank from a fountain in the forest before making it to the city. I suppose it wouldn't hurt to top off before tomorrow."

"You found a blood fountain in the woods? Someone is looking out for you. Come, I will call Domonique to feed you."

Willa pushed through the door, and we entered another hallway, less extravagant than the last, but it still mirrored the arrogant display of the vain master. She opened another door and walked beneath a waterfall that parted as she passed. I followed and didn't feel a drop land on me.

We were in a large suite, and Willa opened another door. "This is where you will sleep."

"Do you not have a detail following you everywhere you go?"

"I used to, but I ended that long ago. I can fight for myself, but Izrazyk will take no chances outside the castle. That is why you will accompany me everywhere we go."

Willa picked up a device that resembled an old telephone and pressed some buttons. "Domonique. Sergeant Vansbrie requires a drink. Thank you." She ended the call and walked away.

"Where are you going?" I asked.

"I need to wash after being touched by him." She went through another door, and I heard the water running. The steam fogged the room, and I stood and waited.

A knock sounded at the main entrance, and I went to it. A feminine voice spoke. "It's Domonique. I bring you a drink."

I opened the door, and Domonique stepped inside and closed it behind her. She wore a sheer gown that left nothing to the imagination. Her colorful braids were to one side over her shoulder. Domonique smiled at me with her full lips and sparkling emerald eyes. She was a gorgeous woman, but she was not my Bren, and I would not fall for her allure.

"Where do you wish to have me?" Domonique asked. I swallowed thickly and pointed to a chair. Domonique's hips swayed as she walked to it, then sat. She tilted her head to the side, placed her hands on the chair's arms, and waited.

My fingers grazed along her dark silky skin, and Domonique closed her eyes and hummed. I got down on one knee, wrapped one hand around the back of her neck, and pulled her forward. Vampires fed from each other, but it was more an act of intimacy that served as a survival tactic when times were tough and humans were scarce.

There were humans in the harem Willa could have chosen, but Domonique was in her trusted inner circle. It would be my second time drinking from another like me. Dean and I had only come across a few vampires in our travels. One of which shared herself with us for one night. She tasted sweet, and I wondered as my fangs hovered over Domonique's neck if she'd taste the same.

I sank into her flesh, and she purred. I drank of her, and she tasted tantalizing and refreshing. Domonique's blood made my thirst increase, and I wanted more. It was not a good thing. Would my blood lust return now that I didn't have Dean to help me keep it under control? I was in Hell, so did it matter anymore?

Domonique's hands gripped my head, and she ran her fingers through my hair. She moaned lustfully and spread her legs so I was between them. My hands went to her hips, and I pulled her closer. She gasped and pleaded, "Take me, Jeremiah!"

I pictured another pair of green eyes and quickly broke away. I zipped across the room, putting distance between us, and Domonique looked distraught, then disappointed.

"My apologies, Domonique. I do not wish to be led astray. I thank you for your offering. I must rest so you may leave."

"Of course. I'm here and of service to you anytime, Jeremiah Vansbrie. Unless I am with our master, consider me at your call." Domonique's eyes roamed up and down my body, and she smiled. She turned to leave, making a show of her assets as she swayed in a seductive motion toward the door. She knew how to work her body to tempt a man, and it was difficult to let her go.

"Good night, Mistress." Domonique bowed before going out the door and closing it behind her.

Willa was standing in a long flowing gown. She walked past me, poured a glass of water, and carried it to her bedside. She opened a small metal container, took a pill, swallowed it with the water, and laid down.

"What is that?" I asked.

"Something to help me sleep."

"Oh! Rest well, Willa."

"Rest well, Jeremiah."

I went to my room and removed my cape, sword, pistol, and boots. I lay down, closed my eyes, and thoughts of Bren took over my consciousness. My heart began to ache at not having her here with me. Would I never truly see her again?

I thought of how Alma and Esaw escaped, and Tara freed their souls from the Hedrix's influence. Would it be possible for me to find a body to inhabit and return?

Oh, how I desperately wanted to go and do that, but I didn't know if it would work the same as when I shared a body with Dean. Could my soul merge into his body as Alma and Esaw did with Gina and Asher? Would I still be able to vampire vape away to visit Bren?

Somehow, I didn't think it would work the same anymore because, technically, I wasn't alive or undead, and my heart was no longer in Dean's chest.

My sweet, beautiful Bren! Do you miss me as much as I miss you? If I could hold you in my dreams, I'd do so every time I closed my eyes. Please remember me, my love. I must find a way back to you. If a demon can come back to the living world, then perhaps so can a vampire. Wait for me, my love.

Chapter 8
BREN

Hanging Up The Hang Up

I carried Zane everywhere I went, and he never left my side. I had the bubble-wrapped blue jar with his ashes in the bag I carried hanging from a hook while I showered.

I thought of him as I washed my body and touched myself, imagining it was his hands, but it wasn't the same. I felt so empty inside. How will I ever get past these emotions?

I dressed and sat with my coffee and unwrapped the jar, and set it on the table so Zane could enjoy the morning sunlight with me. "Good morning, Zane. It's going to be another beautiful day. I'm feeling a bit down in the dumps, though. I know I say it every morning, but I miss you. I'm learning how to fight, and I'm not half bad.

My training partner served in World War II just like you did. His name is Jeremiah Vansbrie, and he was a Sergeant Major in the 2nd Infantry Division in Normandy and France. He's a nice guy. I wonder if you ever crossed paths?"

I sipped my coffee and watched as Jeremiah walked past my window. He was a handsome man, though this was not his original body. Still, he was tall and lean with jet black hair and dark eyes. He reminded me of Zane, with a near identical facial structure. He was kind and had a peaceful temperament, and I enjoyed talking with him.

A knock sounded at my door, and I got up and let Jeremiah enter. He looked at the blue jar on the table and smiled. "Zane is getting some sun today?"

"He sits here with me every morning," I replied.

"How are you feeling today, Bren? Are you up for some exercise and fresh air?"

"Yeah, I guess."

Jeremiah looked sympathetic. "Did I ever tell you about the woman I met on leave during the war?"

"I suppose I'd recall if you had." I sat at the table. "I'm sorry, I'm feeling a little bit off this morning. Would you like some coffee?"

"I understand. And no, thanks on the coffee. I had some already."

I gestured for Jerimiah to have a seat. "So, what was her name?"

Jerimiah smiled and sat before me. "Her name was Adria, and she was a buxom blond beauty with a witty sense of humor. We met at a USO club in England, where we hit it off on the dancefloor and spent the next few days together. She was easy to talk to, and I wanted to kiss her from the moment I met her.

When we finally kissed, it was just before I had to leave again, and I'd asked her if I could write to her. She gave me her address, and we wrote back and forth for several months. I'd fallen in love with her and wanted to propose to her the next time I saw her. On my next leave, I returned to find her, but no one had seen her for days. I had received her letter three weeks prior, so I thought her feelings for me hadn't changed. Every word she wrote led me to believe she loved me too. A few days later, someone discovered her body behind an abandoned building, and witnesses said they'd seen her with a large man with dark hair. I knew the bastard had murdered her, and her death was highly publicized, so I couldn't use my necromancy to bring her back.

I learned the killer's identity when the Hedrix found me and offered me the opportunity to see her again. He had murdered my Adria and took her with him to Hell. He brought me there, too, and made me a deal. If I served in his army, I could have her back. Foolishly I agreed. I saw Adria with his harem one day and approached her. My Sevifk form disgusted her, and I told her it was me, but she just looked away. I didn't see her again after that. I spent the rest of my time in battle and eventually moved on."

I place my hand on Jeremiah's. "I'm so sorry."

Jeremiah shrugged. "That's love and war for you. Trying times will test a person's character. It's not the best life for two people in love. You think if you can make it through each battle, you'll make it through everything else. Some make it, and some don't."

"I feel like I'm in a battle now between moving on and hanging on because I keep believing Zane will return to me one day." I turned the jar so the sun could reach Zane's other side. It was ridiculous sunning a vampire's ashes. The sun didn't hurt him when he was alive, though, like all the stories led one to believe. But perhaps that was because he shared a body with his necromancer brother, and Dean acted as a shield of protection. I never got the chance to ask if that were true, and Zane was the only vampire I'd met.

"I believe Zane was an exception to the rule, and we'd have made it. I would have waited for him through any war. I guess that's what this feels like now. We're training for a battle and don't know when it will come, but we keep hanging on for that victory and the homecoming reunion."

"I can see that about you, Bren. You're a very dedicated woman, and I admire you. If Zane could return from Hell, I'd gladly share this body with his spirit so the two of you could be together."

I froze. What exactly did Jeremiah mean by that? He hadn't let on that he liked me in that way, but he was certainly attentive to me. When Jeremiah put his hands on me to show me fighting moves, it didn't seem like he was coming on to me either.

Perhaps, he was making this offer out of the kindness of his heart because he knew what it was like to have loved and lost. But then I knew the answer when Jeremiah gently took my hand in his.

"You remind me of Adria. You are a kind and beautiful woman. I know you are grieving Zane's loss, and I don't want to push you into anything. I want to let you know you enamor me, and I will wait for you as long as it takes to decide. Until then, I'd like to continue to be your friend and train together. I promise I won't make any moves on you. I am a man of honor. I'll always be here for you if you wish only to be friends."

I looked into Jeremiah's dark eyes, like looking into the depths of hope. Hope is an eternal emotion. It goes on and on, searching for the light at the end of a tunnel. I was in that tunnel with my heart still dedicated to Zane, but I saw Jeremiah's hope and didn't want to dismiss it so quickly.

It had been three weeks since Zane passed and a few days less when I'd met Jeremiah and started working with him. Sometimes Dean and Tara would pay attention to our training together. At first, I thought it was just them checking on my progress. But, now that I thought about it, maybe they saw what I couldn't see with Jeremiah's attentiveness.

He was fun to be around, and he made me laugh. My stomach clenched at the thought of moving on from my past with Zane. It still felt like I was betraying him even to consider the idea. No, if I thought this way, it was still too soon.

"I like you, Jeremiah. You are a good man."

"I hear a 'but' in there," he said.

"Yes. There is. But don't be dismayed by what I say. It's only been three weeks since Zane passed, and we met a few days after. You are charming, kind, and fun. I enjoy talking with you, and we work well together. You kind of remind me of Zane, as I remind you of Adria.

Maybe our similar backgrounds have tied us together in some cosmic way. We've both loved and lost wonderful people and see those same qualities in one another. I'd like to remain your friend, and I don't want to shoot down your hopes. But, as you already know, these things take time. And maybe if you stick around long enough, we'll see where this goes."

I lifted my hand away, and he moved his hand back to his lap. Jeremiah stood up and smiled. The hope was still there, but he took a breath and let it go. He held his hand to his chest over his heart, which reminded me of the first time I'd felt Zane's heartbeat. Did Jeremiah's heart feel as strongly about me?

He was more reserved than Zane and concealed his emotions, unlike Zane, who wore his heart on his sleeve. Jeremiah was dark and quiet, while Zane was a beaming light that refracted from everything around him. Zane called people out, while Jeremiah aimed to see the good in everyone. It was like Dean's tattoo on his chest that now had a scar beside it. One was the light in the darkness, and the other was the darkness in the light. Neither was bad, but you didn't have one without the other.

"Well, I'll see you outside whenever you're ready," Jeremiah said.

"Okay." I smiled encouragingly.

Jeremiah went out the door, and I looked at the blue jar. "I wish I knew what you were thinking right now. Would you approve of Jeremiah Vansbrie? He wouldn't have dared come near me if you were here. I will try something different today, and I hope you'll forgive me."

I kissed the jar. "I love you, Zane."

I wrapped it back in the plastic packing bubbles and put it back in the shoulder bag hanging from the hook on the wall. I reached to take the handle out of habit but stopped myself. My fists clenched, and tears threatened to crest my lower lids. I could do this. I vowed I'd always keep Zane with me wherever I went, and I didn't care if everyone looked at me and talked.

They felt sorry for me, but no one said a word of discouragement or called me insane. Everyone around me accepted it because they knew the pain I felt. The further I walked away from Zane, the tighter my stomach knotted. I wanted to step back and grab that damn bag. I bet Zane would call me crazy for doing this to myself.

Bren! What the hell do you think you're doing carrying around a jar of ashes? I'm in here! He'd point to my heart. *Not there!* He'd point to the jar.

I put my hand to my chest. "You're right, Zane! You'll always be in my heart!" I grabbed the door handle and stepped out into the sun. I felt naked without the bag across my body. I stretched my arms in the air and took a deep breath. "I'm doing this for us."

I stretched my body and prepared to run. I felt safer now that our camp was full of warriors ready to take up arms at a moment's notice. Once I was limbered up, I started at a light jog. I made my way around the camper and headed toward the lake where Airmed's fighters sparred. People paused and looked at me like I had grown another head as I passed.

"Good morning." I smiled and waved. Most of the men watched me with big smiles, and the women took the opportunity to knock them on their asses. I laughed but continued on my route.

"BREN?" Tara called out in surprise.

"Morning, bestie!" I waved and continued.

"Bren! Wait up!" Tara yelled. She caught up with me. "Are my eyes deceiving me, or are you flying solo this morning? Where's Zane?"

I smiled and patted my chest. "Right here!"

Tara smiled. "That's awesome! Did Jeremiah come to talk to you this morning?"

"He did. Why do you ask?"

"Well, he told me about something he'd gone through and asked if I thought it might help to share it with you."

"He did, and it did help. Zane's hanging out in the camper. I thought I'd give him a break today."

"You came to this decision on your own? Or did Jeremiah's story have any influence?"

"I suppose it was a little of both. Tara, have you noticed anything about Jeremiah?"

"In what way?"

"I don't know. Maybe it's just me, but he resembles Zane, only if Zane was more gothic and reserved."

"He does sort of look like Zane and Dean, like a yin-yang cousin."

"That's what I thought when I looked more closely at him just a little bit ago. Jeremiah's love story and how he lost Adria was tragic. He told me I remind him of her."

"I think Jeremiah is into you."

"He is."

"BREN!" Tara grabbed my arm and stopped me. "What did he say to you?"

"He confessed that he likes me and understands I'm still grieving. He doesn't want to push me into anything, and we're friends unless my feelings change."

"This is good, Bren! Dean and I have noticed how you get along so well. You're right about him being Zane's polar opposite, but I think the two of you complement each other like kindred spirits. Don't get me wrong. I'm not pushing you either, but I see how he makes you laugh, and you work so well together."

"I like Jeremiah too, but I'm not at that level yet. I think I could be someday. I told him to hang around. I still need time."

"I get it. No one, least of all myself, expects you to move on so soon. Zane is still a part of us. He always will be. It's been hard for Dean too. I can't help but think that wherever he is, he's not letting go either. I feel like he's going to return any day now."

"Do you think it's possible for him to come back, like Alma and Esaw and the rest did?"

"At this point, I believe anything is possible. I just wish I had some sense of where his spirit is. Dean keeps having these dreams like he is in a battle at Zane's side. Zane doesn't see or hear him, but Dean keeps guiding him. It's like he's watching over him."

"Perhaps he is. You'd know better than any of us, right?"

"I most certainly do! So do Danny and Rudy. Alma has told me that Willa has reached out to her and Esaw. They began hearing their daughter again a few days after being freed from their Sevifk possessions. Rudy has had dreams of Willa in dark places consorting with spies. There's a new player in the game, too, a tall, dark gothic-looking man who is there to help her."

"Do they know who the man is? I mean, tall, dark and gothic could be anyone, but that description fits Jeremiah."

"I don't know. I'll ask Alma later today. A liaison is supposed to rise tonight, a Sevifk spy who can take my power to the Necros. He will meet up with Willa at a graveyard and deliver the package. My dad and I created a concealment vigil, so my power will not be recognizable."

"That's great news, Tara. I can't help but think how easy it's become for the Sevifk to come here, grave rob a body, and rejoin the living world."

"And you're thinking or hoping that is what Zane might do?"

"Well, yeah! But Jeremiah made me an offer."

"What offer?" Tara crossed her arms over her chest and gave that appraising look her Uncle Woody does.

"He offered to do a Gina and Asher; only he'd allow Zane to bunk with him so we could be together."

"Oh my god, Bren! Jeremiah has got it bad for you, girl!"

"Yeah, I know. And it makes me wonder if I could love Zane and him both in the same body?"

"Well, around here, it's not unheard of." Tara laughed. "I mean, I love Zane, but not that way. And Gina and Asher have kind of blended cohesively with Alma and Esaw. Gina confessed their love life has become pretty crazy, but she still calls the shots if things get too bizarre."

"That gives me hope. Maybe it's possible. Zane is, was used to the whole body share thing with Dean, but this is another man who has feelings for me, and I couldn't imagine he'd be cool with it."

"Can I tell you something, and you won't get mad?"

"What?"

"The night we officially introduced you to Zane, we were joking about having a three-some slash four-some. I was mostly against it. But?"

"Tara? What aren't you telling me?"

"Okay. I may have fantasized about what it would be like to be with Zane a time or two. I immediately berated myself. Zane felt more like an annoying brother to me."

"I may have tossed the idea around in my head, too. I'd never done anything like that before, but if I were ever brave enough, I couldn't think of two people better than you and Dean. I was getting desperate to be with Zane before, you know." I swallowed my grief.

Tara hugged me. "Oh, Bren. I still feel like a total selfish bitch for holding back."

"Let it go, Tara. I might start bitching at you for beating yourself up over something neither of us could control."

"Awe, look at you putting me in my place! I wouldn't say it was old high school bitch Bren, but more like assertive, no ass-kissing, Bren. I like it."

"Well, this is ass-kissing me, letting you know I've learned from the best."

Tara and I laughed.

"Let's go kick some ass. I saw a couple of guys back there checking you out who need to be put in their place," Tara said.

I smiled. "That sounds good to me."

We began to run, and I pictured Zane cheering me on with a battle cry.

Go and get 'em, Beautiful!

Chapter 9
ZANE

The Other Man

The field below was a massacre of sweet perfume, and my fangs were itching to bite. Perseus whinnied as he rose on his haunches, not taking well to a new rider on his back. He must sense my blood lust rising. I patted his flank and talked him down. "Easy horse! I don't care for animal blood."

But it will do in a pinch.

Willa was at Izrazyk's side, awaiting his order to ride into the fray. We had already gone over the plan earlier this morning while Adria, Domonique, and Saharah distracted Izrazyk in his tent. When the Hedrix master gave the signal Willa and I rode full speed. We made a show of swordplay, knocking a few Necros down along the way. Some men wore a green band around their arms to signify their roles as players in the farce. They turned to run over the hill, screaming as they dropped out of sight.

Willa and I charged after them, and on the other side, where we made the exchange for four of Izrazyk's dead stripped and changed into Necros's uniforms along with the green bands displayed on their arms. A stipend of the Necros power was spilled into four wineskins containing mostly Hedrix blood.

The dead were tied by their ankles and tethered to our saddles. We rode back around the fight, dragging the fresh corpse whose faces were ripped away to ensure they were no longer identifiable.

One green-banded soldier jumped and grabbed at Willa's leg, and I threw my knife at his pre-confirmed false eye. He screamed and dropped to the ground, and we continued to ride, making it back to Izrazyk, who was laughing with great joy.

"Well done, my mistress!" Izrazyk lept down from his steed and went to the four corpses. He lopped off their heads and put them on spikes one by one. He mounted his black horse and beckoned Willa to come. She took Izrazyk's bloody hand, and he hoisted her onto his lap. He fisted her braid and crushed his lips to hers.

"I think I will finally bed you tonight, Willa. What say you, Sergeant Vansbrie? Care to join us? I will lend you my Adria and Saharah."

I lost my bloody appetite, but I kept my pretense and bowed my head. "If it pleases you, Master, it would be an honor."

Willa cupped Izrazyk's chin and traced her thumb across his mouth. "Master?"

"Yes, Mistress?" Izrazyk's blue eyes gleamed as he looked adoringly at Willa.

"I have received intel of a new weapon said to release a toxin into the air. I believe the Necros plan to move it tonight. They aim to launch it at your castle and can do so from a vast distance. I would be honored to head the detail with my first guardsman to intercede and confiscate this weapon. If you allow it so, Master, Vansbrie has experience with weapons of this sort, and he can devise a launch system superior to that of the Necros. We can strike them first."

"Is this so, Sergeant Vansbrie?" Izrazyk asked.

"Yes, Master. In Ardromezor, we launched an attack with a missile reaching a target of over thirty kilometers."

Willa whispered something in Izrazyk's ear, and he grinned. He raised his sword in the air, and a horn blew. The Necros soldiers were already on the retreat. A footman handed something like a megaphone to Izrazyk, who began yelling out to the valley below.

"See the heads of your men delivered by my mistress! And she has brought me your power! It will not be long until you bow to me and surrender everything!"

He held the wineskins, and the horn blew again as Izrazyk's soldiers chased the Necros over the hill. The Hedrix and Sevifk stood at the top and cheered in victory. Archers launched flaming arrows at the retreating men. Their lack of honor disgusted me, but I presented a wicked smile. Izrazyk looked at me, and I bowed my head.

"Well done today, Vansbrie. We shall ride back to the castle and celebrate our victory. And we will plan for our next campaign."

"Master?" Willa asked.

"Yes, Mistress?"

"Of which campaign do you speak?"

"We will attack in the Earth realm, and together you and I will capture our new queen."

Domonique, Adria, and Saharah sat in the laps of high-ranking Hedrix soldiers, pouring blood wine into the men's mouths.

Izrazyk raised a toast. "Tonight, we drink the blood of our enemy."

Izrazyk tipped his head back and downed the contents of his chalice. The Hedrix cheered and drank. The Hedrix blood they unknowingly consumed was diluted with red wine to not overdoes on the Necros's power, which was minimal but gave them enough of an energy buzz to keep them satisfied.

It wasn't long before the men were drunk, and they sat and feasted, tearing dripping bloody chunks of meat off of large bones with their teeth while music played and all of Izrazyk's harem danced and entertained his guests.

I walked the room's perimeter, watching the moronic display as the demons crushed scarab beetles with their fist and then brought them back to life, cheering every damn time. They behaved like imbeciles, laughing and slopping food and wine everywhere. All the while, Willa sat on Izrazyk's lap, and he played with her hair and kissed her neck. She strained to keep her face away from his with a look of disdain. I felt ill for her.

Domonique brought me a chalice on a silver tray and bowed. "A gift from our master and mistress. It is human blood." I could smell it, and my mouth watered. I took the cup, raised it toward Izrazyk and Willa, and bowed my head in gratitude. The Hedrix master motioned with a bored flipped gesture for me to drink.

I smiled in return and tipped the chalice to my lips. A divine burst of flavor exploded on my tastebuds, and it took all of my control not to down it all in one go. I could use more than this, and I thought back to the fountain in the forest. Perhaps I should have stayed there and lived out my existence in the wild.

"What human provided this?" I asked.

"Saharah, sir. Do you wish for more?"

I drank the blood and handed the chalice back to Domonique. I nodded and continued walking, watching, guarding a room of buffoons engaged in sinful debauchery.

Willa gazed my way, and I paused. Izrazyk was running his fingers along the waistband of her pants. She grabbed his hand and brought it to her mouth, where she took a finger and began kissing the tip. Izrazyk looked pleased, and he smiled at Willa as she swirled her tongue around it.

She leaned in and spoke in his ear as he grinned and nodded. Willa rose from the Hedrix master's lap, and he slapped her ass hard as she walked away from him. Three more women and a man replaced Willa and began fawning over their master.

Willa came my way, grabbing a carafe of red wine, placing it to her lips, and tilting it in the air. She swallowed greedily, then lowered the bottle and wiped her mouth on her sleeve, making a disgusted face only I could see. I smirked, and she scowled.

I walked behind a tapestry, and Willa joined me, grabbing my arm and walking us quickly to a door. We were inside a dark stairwell where Adria, Domonique, and Saharah waited.

"It is time. Everyone understands what is happening. Izrazyk will receive word that we were captured and held captive at a false location. He will suspect this and send troops to confirmed Necros hideouts where Sevifk will pose as prisoners and feed him information that will send him on a wild goose chase. Meanwhile, we will take the 'weapon' and deliver it to the Necros commander, Yuen Koh, in Ardromezor."

"But isn't that where the Hedrix battalion crushed the Necros?" I asked.

"The grapevine is an efficient way of relaying many half-truths. Ardromezor is where the largest alliance of Sevifk, Necros, and even some of the Hedrix have come together. Many have grown tired of this war and have never cared to acquire more power. More have tried to take Izrazyk down by every means imaginable. He has built enough immunity to the dark power that he is undefeatable in Hell."

We went to the stables, mounted our horses, and rode into the night. Willa led us through the back roads out of the city as it would have taken longer to go straight through. The people celebrated in the streets as word of their master's victory spread throughout the kingdom.

They thought they were safe inside the city walls, but it was all a lie. The Hedrix thought they'd killed more Necros warriors this day and sent them fleeing for safety. But how could they have destroyed any without the only proven method that works?

The Hedrix were not necromancers, but Izrazyk had them believe they'd gained the upper hand, having consumed the Necros's blood. The Sevifk still had some trace of necromancer blood flowing in their veins. Therefore, they could weaken the Necros.

The Sevifk began to fake their deaths on the battlefield, only to change sides. Those who remained loyal to the Hedrix master did so out of fear that their loved ones might meet the same fate.

Willa's power made the dead rise so Izrazyk could send the Sevifk to the living realm through a doorway unlocked by a portal key master. As for Willa's parents, it just so happened that they stumbled upon Tara's power shining like a beacon over Gina's body on All Hallows Eve when the veil was thin.

I was particularly interested in gaining access to this portal key master. If I could find a suitable body, I could return to Bren. I'd need a male of the right age and reasonably attractive for Bren's sake. I couldn't show up before my love as an old, wrinkled fart with weak muscles and brittle bones, could I? I would need a necromancer's power to make it stick permanently, and I happened to know a few powerful necromancers.

The other issue was the only portal key master within a thousand-mile radius was in Izrazyk's possession, hidden and locked away. But, as luck would have it, Willa knew her location. If we could get her to cooperate, I wouldn't have to wait till next Halloween. No, I didn't want to wait that long to return to my love.

Time seemed to drag on forever in Hell. How long have I been gone from the living realm? The pain my brother must be going through made my chest ache with grief. I missed being close with Dean. But, something deep inside me knew my death was coming. It struck me when we visited the old lady, and she gave Bren something. What was it?

I couldn't remember, but at that moment, I knew I'd give my life to save Bren. I wasn't sure when that time would come or how it would happen. I just knew it would. And I never said anything because I didn't want to upset anyone or have them think they could do something to prevent it.

We were riding our horses now beyond the city's walls for hours when a light flashed in the distance. The thundering of our horse's hooves echoed through the open terrain. Willa flashed a light toward the other, communicating in code. We slowed to a trot as we got close, then stopped.

"What are we waiting for?" I asked.

"The Sevifk on the other side," Willa replied.

"How?"

"Only a Sevifk can breech both ways and only for a short time. It must be from a grave at the witching hour, and they can pass Tara's gift through the blue orb's light."

A light flashed again, and Willa dismounted. She handed her horse's reigns to Domonique. "Stay here and keep watch."

"Yes, Mistress."

I slid down from Perseus and handed him over to Saharah.

"What are you doing?" she whispered.

"I'm going with Willa," I replied.

"She said to stay and keep watch!"

"What if it's a trap, and she needs my help?"

"Our mistress is no fool, and she doesn't need your help! Get back on your horse, vampire!" Saharah whisper-shouted. I ignored her and went after Willa into the darkness. She disappeared into the forest, and I pushed through some dense thorny brush. I didn't get scratched with my thick leathers and gloves as I silently moved. I was in a graveyard and saw an eerie blueish glow in the distance.

I moved stealthily toward it and saw a group of hooded figures standing before a ring of dim light. A hand passed through it from the other side, but I couldn't see anything beyond it. I thought this must be a portal, so I circled to get a better view.

After the hand placed a dark object in Willa's, she and the cloaked figures bowed to their knees, and what my eyes saw made me gasp in shock. I lept from my hiding place and ran toward the portal as the cloaked figures turned around and pulled their swords.

"Who are you?" I shouted. Those standing on the other side looked up at me with the same surprised expression. I focused on the man who looked just like me. But, in my haste, I ignored what was coming as cloaked figures plowed me over, and I growled as swords pointed at me from every direction. I strained to see the man on the other side, but as the portal faded, the last face I saw was my brother's.

Chapter 10
DEAN

A Grave Exchange

Tara's blood sparked with electricity coursing within the pendant as she punctured her hand with the sharp pin. Richard placed the glass vessel in a black container with the concealment vigil he and Tara designed and marked with the necro claw.

Tara prayed. "Keep this gift I give far and free from the hands of all who seek to do evil. Deliver it safely to those I wish to bless with Airmed's gift. May it find the Necros people by the hands of those I trust, and may you keep them safe on their journey."

Tara said these words for a second time when we reached the graveyard with Richard and Jeremiah, who wished to see one of his compatriots rise. He was the most eager to help in this transaction because he hoped to receive any good word he could bring back to his people at The Roost.

George opened the gate, and I stopped. "Good evening, George."

"Hello, Dean." I handed George the roll of money.

"Thanks. I have to say it's been crazy around here lately," George said.

"What's happening?" I asked.

"Well, about three weeks ago, I was walking the grounds and noticed quite a few graves had been disturbed."

"In what way?"

"It looked like the corpses had dug their way out of the ground. I'd counted thirty graves with the soil pushed outward and muddy footprints walking away. I couldn't believe my eyes. But I think the kids who sneak in and party sometimes get pretty creative. They're all into that zombie apocalypse shit. It's all a sick joke if you ask me. But it's still creepy as hell."

Jeremiah barked a laugh from the back seat, and George looked at him. "You wouldn't happen to know anything?"

"No, sir!" Jeremiah straightened with a serious expression. Tara held her hand over her mouth to hide the smile I knew was there.

"We'll keep an eye out, George," I said.

We drove around the large circle, looking for a sign. We weren't sure from which grave the Sevifk would rise, and it could be a crypt, for all we knew.

Tara slipped the necro claw onto her hand. "Be it thy will, and show us the way, to the grave or the crypt, where we make this fair trade."

Tara's hand rose, and she pointed. "Keep going this way."

"That is amazing," Jeremiah said.

"The necro claw listens to all commands made by Airmed's blessed so long as it's with good intent and a pure heart," Richard said.

"Oh, I thought we were screwed for a second there," Tara said.

"Why would you say that?" Richard asked.

"Well, I thought you might say a pure person, and I'm far from that," Tara joked.

"Cursing and having sex doesn't count," I said.

Tara blushed. "Dean! Not in front of my dad and Jeremiah!"

"You brought it up first," I said.

"I may have, but you didn't have to spell out what that implied."

"Sorry, my sexy potty-mouthed songbird!" I teased.

Richard and Jeremiah laughed.

"You have a pure heart and soul, Tara. Sure, you could clean up your language a bit, but you never use those choice words against anyone who doesn't deserve them, and you and Dean are in love and dedicated to one another," Richard said.

"Thanks, Dad. Can we move on now, please? Turn left!" Tara pointed with the claw.

I turned and saw an eerie blue light in the distance. I parked the truck, and we climbed out. We met around the front and looked in every direction to ensure our surroundings were safe.

"It's a quarter till three, and we need to find out if that light leads us to the right place," I said.

"The claw is pulling me towards it. It must be this way." Tara's hand was in the air, and it looked like someone was pulling her forward by her arm. Richard and I walked on either side of Tara with Jeremiah watching our backs. We came armed if, by chance, we had any unexpected company.

"George certainly keeps the place looking nice. There's scarcely a dead leaf on the ground, and the stones look in tip-top shape," Jeremiah said.

"George has a lot of respect for the dead. I've never seen a man more dedicated to his job. Of course, it helps when Tara and I come along and make it more worthwhile."

"You come here often?"

"We have lately. Lyle, Gina, and Asher's graves are here. We had to do a scavenger hunt in Lyle's to find evidence of his innocence. We figured out where to find Richard and learned how the Hedrix had a hand in Tara's predicament all this time."

"The Hedrix is an asshole! He took my Adria from me. Then he lied to me about giving her back. He nearly sucked me dry and turned me into a demon. I'd like to repay him for everything he did to Adria, my people, and me."

"His time is coming," Tara said. As we approached, the glowing blue light grew from behind a stained-glass window inside a crypt.

"It's inside there." Tara pointed.

There was a lock on the door, and Jeremiah pulled a lock-picking kit from his jacket pocket. "I've got this. I broke into a lot of places when I was younger. Times were tough, so my family and I had to do what was necessary to feed ourselves."

"You robbed places?" Tara asked.

"We were like Robin Hood's band of merry men. Stealing from the rich and giving to the poor." Jeremiah got down on his knee and pulled out a few picks. Within a few seconds, he opened the door.

"Ladies first!" He held the door open and gestured with his arm through the doorway. Tara walked through, and the blue light moved.

"There are some stairs going down. The light is going that way," Tara said.

We followed her, and the light orb, like a spirit, guided us down the pitch-black stairwell. It illuminated the descending steps that twisted like a spiral, and the passage became tighter the further we went.

We reached a landing, and on either side were open crypts along the walls. From here, we could see a hall that stretched onward before us, and the light continued down the pathway.

"Ahh!" Tara screamed as a skeletal hand reached out and tapped at her. She batted it away, and it dropped to the ground, breaking into pieces.

"What the hell?" she cried.

"You're a powerful necromancer. You draw the dead to you," I said.

"Well, can someone explain to them that I'm not available? I'm already happy with you!"

"It may be the necro claw along with her energy. Perhaps you should put it away," Richard said.

"Whatever helps!" Tara removed the claw from her hand and put it inside the leather case Richard made. Tara wore it on a strap from her shoulder and crossed her torso.

"Necro claw at my side. Keep the long-dead peaceful and satisfied."

"You're getting good at your commands. They rhyme and work well," Jeremiah said.

"Thanks. It's like someone is typing it all and hitting the enter button. They just come to me," Tara said.

"Wouldn't it be funny if we were all characters in some elaborate fantasy book and some crazy woman made up our fate as we went along?" Jeremiah asked.

"If that were the case. I wish she'd hurry up and kill off the Hedrix master so we could live happily ever after," Tara said.

"I'll second that," I said.

"Sounds good to me," Richard said.

A loud crack of something falling at Tara's feet made her yelp and jump back. The blue light halted and waited for us. I shined my flashlight down at a skull. I picked it up, looked for a skeleton missing its head, and shined the light across the name of the person who'd lost it.

"Oh! Here you go, Misty Dawn Tackett. You can have your head back. Sorry, it's all cracked up. Hmm! Interesting!"

"What is it?" Tara asked.

"Says here she was an author. Maybe she's behind all this!"

"Well, she lost her head, and now it's cracked. Perhaps she is. Thanks for all the hell you've put me through. Could you please make my life a little easier from here on out?" Tara pleaded.

"Here's something else written above her name. *If you keep moving forward, you are always on the right path.*"

"How inspirational!" Tara replied with sarcasm. "She probably had it easy sitting on her ass dictating the fate of her characters."

"Think of it this way. Maybe you are her hero and inspiration. Why else would she jump at the opportunity to land before your feet?"

"So that she could put herself in my story! I might consider allowing it if she can get me out of this mess. Moving on!" Tara walked ahead, and the blue light continued leading the way until we reached a dead end.

"Is this where we find some hidden lever or a button to push? Or do we step through the wall like in Danny's mountain?" Tara turned on her flashlight and looked around. Jeremiah, Richard, and I did the same. The blue light hovered before the wall, waiting.

"I don't see anything," Richard said.

"What time is it?" Jeremiah asked.

I looked at my watch. "It's two-fifty-seven."

"The light isn't moving. Perhaps this is the place," Richard said.

"But isn't there supposed to be a Sevifk meeting us on this side?" Tara asked.

We all turned around and shined our light down the passage. Our beams crisscrossed back and forth as we illuminated the dead in the walls' crypts. There wasn't a sound or movement. Maybe Misty would come to join us.

"Wait! I hear something," Richard said. He shined his light further down, but we didn't see anything.

"I can hear it too!" Jeremiah moved his light around and, low to the ground, ten or so feet away, a pair of beady red eyes halted, and a loud squeak came from a rat, which quickly turned around and ran the other way.

"I guess that's not the Sevifk we're waiting for," Tara said.

A loud crack sounded from the wall behind us, and we all jumped. The blue orb wedged inside, and a circular portal opened. Several cloaked figures stood on the other side, staring at us.

Graves and dead cragg-haggardly trees surrounded the cloaked figures, and the sky was a deep dark crimson haze. This was Hell! It wasn't a resort destination, but it wasn't lakes of fire filled with screaming souls of the damned.

The people in cloaks dropped to their knees and bowed their heads. They pounded their fists to their chests and hooted. "Hail, Queen Tara! Airmed's blessed daughter."

Tara shook her head in her hand. "I don't know if I'll ever get used to this! You may rise!"

The group rose to their feet.

"Our liaison has not met us on this side," Tara said.

"He is already among you, Queen!" one man responded.

Tara looked back at us, confused.

"But we were told a Sevifk would rise and meet us here."

"A Sevifk has risen, and you have freed his soul. But he can still pass your gift through the portal," they replied.

"Jeremiah?" Tara questioned.

Jeremiah stepped forward. "I guess they're right. My soul has been to Hell and returned. I may pass through but only for a short moment."

"Alright." Tara removed the black container marked with the concealment vigil from her jacket, whispered another prayer, and placed it in Jeremiah's hands. He moved ahead of Tara and waited for her to command him to proceed.

The people were startled when a sound from the trees made the group turn. I expected the portal to close as this may have become a trap, and we'd have to turn and run.

"Mistress!" They all bellowed as one and kneeled.

The figure approached wearing a red cloak and walked with sure steps indicative of an authoritative presence. The group parted for the person who came to stand directly before us. Hands reached up and pulled their hood back far enough to reveal their face.

"Willa?" Tara questioned.

"Hello, Tara." Willa smiled. She looked as Alma described with her raven hair and violet eyes.

Jeremiah bowed his head. "Mistress!" He held the case out to Willa, and his hand passed through, barely disrupting the portal light.

Willa smiled and accepted it. "You honor Airmed by bequeathing this gift to the Necros. She is smiling upon you, blessed sister!" Willa kneeled, bowed her head, and the people behind her followed.

"You are very welcome. I am honored to help," Tara replied.

"Who are you?" a man shouted as he broke away from the trees and ran at the people kneeling before us. He was looking directly at Jeremiah. My eyes widened in shock. The man looked just like him. But, he also looked like someone else.

The people turned, pulling their swords, and knocked the man to the ground. Tara panicked and reached out, and her fingers grazed the portal. She yelped as if it had burned or stung her. Jeremiah grabbed her hand and pulled it away.

The light faded, and the portal closed. The last thing I saw was the man's dark eyes looking at me as he strained to look past the capes of the people who held him, surrounded with the tips of their swords aimed and ready to strike.

One name escaped my lips. "Zane!"

"Did you see that man? He looked just like me!" Jeremiah said.

"He also looked like my brother!" I said.

"This is insane! We always thought you looked like Dean and Zane, only with dark features," Tara said.

"How is it I landed a body from this graveyard with the same physical characteristics as you and your brother?" Jeremiah asked.

"Maybe he was an ancestor," Richard said.

"With that strong of a resemblance?" I asked.

"It happens more often than you might think," Richard replied.

"What if that was, Zane?" Tara asked.

"You think it could have been?" I asked.

"Well, we have no idea where his soul went. Abigail and Willa said someone would die, and I wouldn't be able to bring them back. That, someone, was Zane, and he didn't stick around for me even to attempt to revive him."

"You couldn't have. Zane's heart turned to ash," Richard said.

"And that's why you couldn't bring him back, Tara," I said.

"I didn't realize there were limitations," Tara said.

"You can use this body," Jeremiah said.

"What?" Tara and I questioned.

"This body has a strong heart, and I look like his doppelganger. If it is Zane and he finds a portal key master, you could pull him back, and I'd gladly allow him the space."

"Wait? Where would you go?" I asked.

"We could be bunkmates," Jeremiah said.

Tara looked away, and I knew she knew something that I didn't.

"Spill it, Tara!" I demanded.

"It's not a big deal. It worked for Alma, Gina, Esaw, and Asher. It may work." She shrugged.

"Why couldn't Zane just come back and bunk with me? His brother?"

"Because you are not smitten with Bren."

"What? Ohhh!" I slapped my head.

Richard and Tara laughed.

Jeremiah smiled sheepishly. "Do you think Zane would be cool with it?"

"Zane was cool with sharing women with Dean in the past. Not me, of course, but Bren is Zane's woman. I don't know. You'd have to discuss it with him," Tara said.

"My body would become his body. I think it could work," Jeremiah said.

"Have you mentioned this to Bren?" I asked.

"I did. I made the offer to Bren first."

"Are you so in love with her that you're willing to make that sacrifice? Zane is a hard ass. The two of you couldn't be more opposite," I said.

"Bren has a beautiful soul, and I would be honored if she would have me. She told me you and Zane served in the war. Which infantry?" Jeremiah asked.

"Fourth Infantry. You?"

"Second. We may have crossed paths at some point. I'm sure Zane and I could share some war stories."

"Were you killed by another necromancer in the war?"

"No. But I surrendered to the Hedrix, who stole my Adria, then dragged me to Hell. You probably know what happened next."

"Can we talk about this in the truck? I'd like to get out of here before the author of this shit show makes all the corpses jump us," Tara said.

We made our way out of the crypt and back to the truck. We drove past George, and I stopped and backed up.

"See anything strange?" George asked.

"Nothing we aren't already used to," I replied with a grin.

"You pay me to go grave exploring. I imagine you've seen some crazy shit."

"You aren't lying. Take it easy, George." I chuckled. I drove out the gate and watched from the rearview mirror as George closed it.

"Do you think Zane is okay? I mean, if it was him?" Tara asked.

"You know Zane can get out of sticky situations. I have renewed hope. If that was him and he can get to the portal key person, we can get him back."

"I want to tell Bren, but I'm not sure I should get her hopes up just in case," Tara said.

"It would be nice if we knew for sure."

"I'll ask Alma what Willa knows. If she were the one to mention someone dying in the first place, she should know if that was Zane or not."

Tara knocked on the door to the new cabin. Everyone pitched in to build two more over the past few weeks out of pre-fab kits Uncle Woody picked up from a local tiny homes builder.

Gina opened the door. "What's up, buttercup?"

"Hi, Gina. How are you and Asher settling in?" Tara asked.

"It's too cramped for Asher and me, but Alma and Esaw love it. Would you like to come in and see the touches Alma and I have made?"

"Sure." Tara walked in, and I followed.

"Hi, Gina. Where is Asher?" I asked.

"He's out with some of the guys. He and Esaw are getting along famously with the others. There aren't as many women, and they seem a bit standoffish. But I don't blame them. I just can't relate. Alma mostly talks when they're around."

"I'm sure you can relate to them with what you've been through," Tara said.

"It's easier to talk with Alma. She's very motherly and tells me everything about her daughter. Willa sounds pretty badass."

"I saw her this morning," Tara said.

Gina's eyes turned violet.

"You did?" Alma asked. "How was she? How does she look?"

"She looks just like you. Willa is a commander in her own right, and the people we met bowed to her."

"Oh, my baby has grown up! She has the favor of our people. She never tells me these things. She just passes information and lets me know she loves her papa and me."

"Are you able to reach her whenever you want?"

"No. Willa contacts me when she has something relevant to share. Do you need me to ask her something? I can the next time she reaches out."

"Yes, please. The portal closed before we had a chance to ask any questions. But there was a man who showed up and saw us give the gift to Willa. He wasn't as concerned with that as he was when he saw Jeremiah."

"Why is that, I wonder?" Alma asked.

"Because the man looked just like him. They could be twins, and we thought he might be Zane."

"But Zane looks like Dean, does he not?"

"Is it possible Zane's looks may have altered in Hell?" I asked.

"I suppose. People are capable of changing their appearance by artificial means just as they do here," Alma replied.

"So, someone could have dyed and cut his hair, and he's wearing colored contacts?" I asked.

"Colored contacts?" Alma looked confused.

"Lenses people put in their eyes to see better or change their eye color," Tara explained.

"Oh, yes! These things they can do, but only the wealthy have such means to do so," Alma said.

"Willa looked as regal as she sounded and held herself. Do you think she has sway with people of high standing?" Tara asked.

"If the people bowed to her and called her their mistress, that can only mean one thing."

"What is that?" I asked.

Alma looked at me. "Willa is the mistress of the Hedrix master."

"What?" Tara stood abruptly.

"Have we been tricked?" I asked.

"On the contrary. My daughter would have the Hedrix master wrapped around her finger, and she has tricked him."

"You are certain?" Tara asked.

"My Willa would not consort with such a monster without a plan to take him down." Alma sounded offended by Tara's question.

"I'm sorry, Alma. Too much is at stake here. We have to be sure."

"Though my daughter was taken by the Hedrix at such a young age and trained under his tutelage, she most certainly remembers from whence she came! Her alliance rests with her people and you, Tara. Do not doubt my Willa!"

"I do not. I have many people relying on me, and I have been lied to, tricked, and manipulated all my life. I trust your word, Alma. But you must see where I'm coming from. I have only learned about all of this over the past few months, and I could no more tell who is or is not on our side in Hell than anyone else. Please don't fault me for asking questions! Even ones that might evoke your motherly ire."

"I do not fault you, Tara. All I ask is that you do not doubt Willa's loyalty. She has been a prisoner for more years than I care to count. She has suffered abuse at the hands of the Hedrix master, and it must have taken her a great deal of time to gain his trust. She has done this so she can aid the rebels and feed false information back to him.

She continues to do what needs to be done, no matter the cost. And because of this, the tides have turned. And with your gift in her hands, we now have the greatest chance than we've had in centuries."

"Dean?" Tara asked.

"Yes, love!"

"Do we have any humble pie in the kitchen?"

I laughed. "No, dear. But I'm sure Alma can make you one."

Alma looked at us with a puzzled expression. "What is a humble pie?"

"Tara's saying that you've put her in her place," I said.

"Oh! I do not mean to kilter your fighting spirit, Tara. You have done so much for our people, and we are eternally grateful. Willa knows the sacrifices you've made, and she knows well of your plight."

"Thank you, Alma. And please tell Willa how grateful I am for everything she's accomplished. I couldn't imagine the hell she's been through. If it helps, she looks strong, healthy, and like a top-notch kickass warrior. And I'm proud to call her my sister."

Alma smiled. "I will tell her, and I will remember to ask her about Zane."

Tara bowed her head. "Thank you, Alma."

"You are welcome. Now, I will ask your mother how to make a humble pie for you." Alma smiled and winked.

"I am sure she remembers all the ingredients by heart," Tara replied.

Alma and I laughed. Someone was knocking on the door. Alma went to answer.

"Hello, Alma," came Bren's voice. "Jeremiah told me Tara and Dean were here. May I come in?"

"Did you bring humble pie?" Alma asked.

"No!" Bren chuckled. "Did you just put Tara in her place?"

"She did!" Tara called. Bren laughed as she stepped inside. She carried the shoulder bag with Zane's ashes in the blue jar.

"I thought you were letting him hang out in the camper?" Tara asked.

"I was. I mean, I had. I wanted to show you something." Bren pulled the double-bubble-wrapped jar out of the bag and carefully unraveled it. She set it down on the table and pointed.

"Do you see anything?" Bren asked.

"I see a blue jar with dirt and ashes," Tara said.

Bren picked it up and held it out to Tara. "Look closer! Real close!"

Tara held the jar to the light and turned it in her hands. I came to stand by her and looked as well.

"Do you see it?" Bren asked.

"What am I looking for? Oh! Wait! Are those worms?" Tara asked.

"No!" Bren sounded disgusted. "Look closer!"

"You're going to have to fill me in here, Bren. I'm not getting what you're. HOLD ON! Are those?" Tara sounded astonished.

"What?" I asked. I couldn't get a good view at this angle and with Tara's hands in the way.

Tara handed the jar to me. "Look, Dean!" I held the jar where I could see better, and it took me a moment to realize what Bren and Tara were saying. But then I saw it! My eyes widened.

"It can't be!" I said, astonished.

"What is it?" Alma asked.

"Those aren't worms! Those are veins! Zane's heart! It's growing back!"

Chapter 11
ZANE

My Ass Is At Stake Here

The sharp metal tips dug into my flesh, and I felt my skin break and bleed. These hooded bastards meant business, but I was too beside myself to care. Willa needed to explain what I had just witnessed.

"Put your swords away! He is my first guardsman!" Willa cried. I breathed a sigh of relief as the people obeyed and sheathed their weapons.

"Why would he approach in such a dishonorable manner?" A deep male voice asked.

"He must have seen something that concerned him for my safety," Willa replied.

"What was it you saw, guardsman?" the man asked.

I looked at Willa. "Who was that man?"

"I do not know," she replied. "But he was a converted Sevifk. Otherwise, he would not be able to pass through the portal."

I stood up and came closer, but a sword was held before me, halting my advance. I ignored the flat side of the metal pressing against my chest.

"And you didn't notice something oddly familiar about him? Like, I don't know! That he looked just like ME!"

"Lower your voice, guardsman!" the man commanded.

I looked at the asshole. "Was I talking to you?"

The man stepped toward me, throwing his cape aside, and gripping his sword's pommel like a 'real' Musketeer. How very, not impressive! I stood in place and yawned at his menacing approach.

"Enough!" Willa demanded. The Muske-douche halted.

"Artus. Thank you for your service. You may take your men and ride on to Marcascus, and I will send word to you in the days ahead."

"Yes, Mistress!" All the caped people bowed their heads and pounded their chests.

I smirked at the asshole who roughly bumped into my shoulder with his as he passed. He and the rest of the Judas Priestly gang departed, and Willa walked past me, and I grabbed her arm and pulled her back.

"Are you going to explain to me what I just saw?" I asked.

"A coincidence!" Willa pulled her arm free from my hand.

"I saw my brother, Dean, and Tara! What did she give to you?"

"I already told you! It is her gift to the Necros people. I cannot say anymore till we reach Ardromezor." Willa walked into the trees, and I followed her.

"Can you be certain that what you are carrying will remain safe? What if one of Izrazyk's men intercepts it and brings it directly to him? We'd all be screwed!"

Willa pulled the container from her cloak. "What does that look like to you?" she asked.

"It's a container," I replied. It looked like one of those hard-shell pencil boxes with a snapping lid.

"That's not what I see," Willa said.

"What do you see?"

"It is a chalice." Willa held the box oddly like she was holding a cup.

"It's not a chalice. It's a black box!" I tapped against it with my finger.

"Do you see the markings?" Willa pointed and moved her finger like she was reading the ingredients of a food label.

"I don't see anything! But a box!" I smirked.

Willa rolled her eyes. "It is a concealment vigil. Everyone who looks at it will see something different. Something mundane, ordinary, and no one will suspect what it is."

Will slipped the container inside her cloak. We made it out of the thickets where Willa's friends waited. Saharah scowled at me, and I bared my fangs back at her as I walked and took hold of Perseus's reigns. We mounted our horses and rode to Ardromezor.

I had no idea which direction we were going. All I had to do was keep up with Willa. She rode her horse like she was sailing on a tempest wind. She looked like an avenging warrior angel with her cloak flying behind her. She was a glorious sight to behold.

Alas, my thoughts always came back to Bren. Did she know that man who looked like me? I had a nagging feeling he might try to move in on my woman. The more I thought about it, the more it pissed me off. I needed to bite someone and drain them dry, starting with him.

Being in Hell was starting to suck balls, and riding this damn horse for hours on end was making mine go numb. I couldn't take any more of this constant life-or-death melodrama! I needed to get back home. I don't understand why I ended up here!

Okay! Maybe it was because of all the people I killed, but they were assholes, and the majority were the enemy on the battlefield. I fought in wars and defended my country, and those guys came at me first. If someone was going to shoot me, I needed sustenance to heal my wounds. It was probably an unfair advantage, but I didn't ask to become a vampire.

And now, in Hell, none of it mattered. Here I was, the low man on the totem pole, a mistress's foot soldier. I suppose it could be worse. I could be dancing in a sheer toga with a feathered boa for some flaky dipshit who might want me to do other lowly down-on-my-knees tasks. I'd more likely bite it off than blow it. I wouldn't make a very good harem boy. I'd be hanging from chains in a dungeon by now. I suppose I owed Willa for bailing me out of that pre-dick-ament.

The dark red sky changed into a light red sky as we arrived at Ardromezor.

"Welcome, Mistress!" A soldier took hold of Willa's horse as she dismounted. Domonique, Adria, and Saharah walked with their hoods up behind Willa. I watched for any suspicious activity in the crowds. More soldiers were present than the civilians who ran businesses that supplied food, drink, and other essentials.

There wasn't a shortage of work for the metalsmith forges as the sound of iron striking iron rang out in the dismal air. Red hot metal hissed as a smith submerged a blade into a water trough and steam billowed into the air as we passed.

The smell of human blood made my fangs itch for someone to bite. The soldier led us to a private tent, where I waited patiently while the women ate bread and drank wine. All the while, my head and stomach were burning, and my fangs descended and dripped with saliva.

My blood lust was becoming unbearable without the help from Tara and Dean, and I'd never gotten my second helping of Saharah's blood that Domonique offered last night. Adria saw my distress and came to me first, offering her wrist. She winced as I sank my teeth and drank enough to calm the ache inside me. She then provided her other wrist to Domonique and then ate some more to replenish herself and rest.

Willa nudged Saharah, who left her side with hesitancy. She eyed me warily as she approached. "I can sense your blood lust, vampire. You'd better take more so you maintain control." Saharah held out her wrist, and I brought it to my lips.

"Thank you, Saharah." Her blood was the most delectable I'd tasted aside from Bren's. There was a peculiar yet enticing quality that I could no better describe than blissful satisfaction. I only took slightly more from Saharah than I had Adria. Sated, for now, I licked her wounds closed and let go of her.

I sipped some wine as the women rested. Willa tossed and turned fitfully. She must always find herself in battle, even in her dreams. I wondered if she slept well a day in her life. I didn't require much rest, but I sat and put my feet up for a moment. There were guards stationed outside our tent, but I wasn't taking any chance of dozing off.

Willa's cape served as a blanket draped over her body. She turned, and it slipped to the ground. I went to place it back over her when I felt a knife dig into the underside of my chin. I dropped the cape and held up my hands. Wild violet eyes stared into mine.

"It fell. I was just picking it up," I said.

A breath of relief left Willa. "Survival habits."

She didn't remove the blade right away, and I cleared my throat. "Are you still planning to kill me?"

"Oh! Sorry!" She put the knife away and sat up.

"Do you always sleep this way?" I asked.

"One never knows when an enemy will strike."

"You haven't slept long. Perhaps you should lie back down."

Willa threw her cloak around her shoulders. "I'm fine. What about you?"

"I'm good. I mostly needed to feed."

"Is it different for you here?" she asked.

"Everything is. I can't say I'm enjoying it much, but I suppose it could have been worse. I want to thank you for saving me from becoming a harem boy. I'd hate myself for betraying Bren that way."

"It could have been much worse than that. You could have been a bucket boy toting around piss every day."

"That's a thing?"

Willa smiled. "That and much worse."

I bowed my head. "Then I owe you a great deal. To go from a life of prowess and dominance to a piss pot toter or a shit shucker would demoralize my soul."

"You have come to serve a greater purpose, Jeremiah. You understand self-sacrifice more than most. You gave your life for the woman you love."

"And I would do it again! But, isn't sacrifice supposed to buy you brownie points with the big guy upstairs?"

"Better people have done a tour in Hell after they died."

"So, what am I? A martyr? A sacrificial lamb? I didn't sign up for this, just like I didn't sign up to be a vampire."

"Still, here you are." Willa gestured around the tent's interior. "I never asked to be taken away from my parents when I was a child by a demon who brought me here. Nor did I ask for everything he has put me through since. I cannot change the past, but I can make the best of my future. It is why I fight. Whether I rise or fall, at least I know I have made a difference."

"Okay. I see where you are going with all your inspirational mumbo-jumbo. Whether I like it or not, I'm here, so I'd best get used to it and make the most of it. If I get my ass in gear, I can help make a better life worth living. Yada. Yada."

Willa looked at me like I was nuts, which essentially, I was after dying when I thought I'd never die. And waking up in Hell didn't contribute to a clean slate of mental health. My ass was on the line, and my nuts were in a vice, but it didn't mean I had to like it. Still, I was a team player, and I enjoyed winning.

"Your words are rather odd, vampire. I do detect a note of sarcasm. Is that your go-to when things become overwhelming?"

I threw my hands up in the air and shrugged. "You got me! So, when will this commander guy show up so we can get this show on the road?"

Willa's brow furrowed in question.

"So, we can finish what we came to do," I reiterated.

"Oh! The commander will send word when he is certain there is no suspicious activity afoot."

"Can you communicate with him using your gift?"

"Using that power requires going into a deep meditative trance, and I must stay vigilant in this environment. I have a question for you, Jeremiah. Do you know Tara's brother well?"

"Rudy? He's a nice guy and an athletic powerhouse."

"What does he do?" Willa asked.

"He plays football. It's a game where the players run, kick and throw an oblong-shaped ball up and down a field, scoring points by getting the ball to either end. They have to keep the ball away from the opposing team."

"What is the point in that?"

"Fun. Entertainment. Many players go on to professional teams and play for wealth and fame. It's a big deal in the part of the world I used to live in."

"And Rudy wants wealth and fame?"

"No. Rudy plays because he loves the game. He enjoys being part of a team and working hard. He cares about his friends and family. He's one of the most authentic people I've known. I admire him and don't say that about many people. But I would never tell him that."

"That is good to hear." Willa smiled.

"You like him, don't you? Wait! Aren't you related to him?"

"I do like his kind voice. Rudy and I are more than seven generations apart, so officially, we are not related."

"Still, you are both alive today. It seems a bit weird."

"Once you've passed a fifth cousin, you are no longer related, and it is okay to pursue them as a potential love interest."

"But your people live longer and share the genetic markers of your power. Does that not count?"

"Rudy did not inherit the power from his father's side. He is human, like his mother, with her receptive tendencies. His blood and mine are not a crucial matter."

Saharah yawned and sat up. "Who are you talking about?"

"Tara's brother, Rudy."

"He sounds interesting. What's he look like?" Saharah asked.

"Why? Are you planning on putting yourself in the running?" I asked.

Saharah rolled her eyes. "Are you concerned about never being considered?"

"I already have a woman who loves me. I don't care if another woman finds me attractive or not."

Willa laughed.

"What?" I asked.

"You should have seen yourself posing on the market stage for all the women bidding. You looked like a pompous Adonis flexing your ass cheeks!"

I couldn't help but grin at Willa's prodding. "I did that to make sure I'd go to the highest bidder, and it worked, didn't it?"

"That's because I was already looking for you, and I had to make sure you didn't fall into the wrong hands. I was looking out for you as a favor to Tara."

"So, you knew I would die and come here?"

"Yes! How else would I have known to come to the market to save you from a fate worse than death? You are in Hell because you died. It was foretold."

"By whom?"

"Fate, of course."

"Of course! Fate brought me here! It's the predictable explanation for when everything goes to shit!"

"You are going in circles, Jeremiah! Moving forward is the best direction. Stop feeling sorry for yourself. It will only drive you mad. And going mad in Hell is a thousand times worse than losing your mind while alive."

"I told him this already," Saharah said.

"Okay. For everyone's sanity, I will try to maintain a positive attitude. But my blood lust is becoming more of an issue, and I have needed to feed more since coming here."

"Just let any of us know, and we will find you a source," Willa said.

"Thank you. I appreciated it."

A soldier poked his head inside the tent. "Mistress, the commander asked you to meet him at the Northern front. It is but a short walk from here."

"Very well. Domonique, Adria, wake up! It is time for us to move," Willa ordered.

Both women yawned and stretched.

"Awe! I was having a good dream," Adria complained.

"You can dream all you like when our work is done," Willa said.

"That will never happen," Domonique said.

"Now look who's being a negative Nancy," I said.

Domonique pursed her lips. "At least you have the better gig, Jeremiah!"

"Enough bickering! Time to move, ladies!" Willa commanded.

I sheathed my sword and pistol and buttoned my cloak. We walked through a city of tents where soldiers looked worn to the bone as they tried to find comfort in the little things. Some tended to wounds they could no longer heal from their drained power, while others ate their rations. The luckier few sat around smoking pipes and playing card games.

Weary eyes looked up at me as I passed. Regardless of their status, every soldier stood and saluted as Willa passed.

"Mistress!" They bowed their heads.

Willa stopped before those with the worst injuries and pressed her power into them, giving them enough boost to recover somewhat. She could not heal others the way Tara or Woody could, but the men cried and kissed her hands in gratitude.

"Thank you, Mistress. May you be blessed for your kindness!"

"There are no blessings in Hell!" the man next to him muttered. Willa paused and looked at the man.

He froze and looked ashamed. "I beg your pardon, Mistress. It has not been easy as of late!"

"I agree. It has not. What is your name, soldier?" Willa asked.

The man tried to stand, but Willa pressed her hand to his shoulder, and he bowed his head. "Eseph Mikivi, Mistress. I apologize."

"Do not apologize, Eseph. You and your friend, come with me."

Willa looked at me. "Sergeant Vansbrie! Assist these men!"
I bowed my head. "Yes, Mistress!"

I had no qualms with aiding these men to their feet and allowing them to lean on either side of me as we walked. I had done this a thousand times before with my brother, helping our fellow soldiers stand in one way or another.

They were filthy and smelled, but I paid this only a fleeting moment's notice because I knew a soldier's dignity was not defined by their hygiene or appearance but by their dedication to a cause greater than themselves. These true heroes fought, so their families remained safe from monsters who sought to destroy their people. As we passed more soldiers, whispers of words flooded my ears.

"Our mistress! Look at the vampire helping her."

"The vampire, vampire, vampire." The word echoed like it had taken on a new meaning. The notoriety made me feel like my presence was making a difference. Maybe this was part of fate's plan all along. It starts with one person taking a stand, and here I was, a lowly creature at the bottom, being noticed for a simple act that carried much weight. Hats came off, and heads bowed as we walked past the entire encampment.

Inspiration was Willa's true power. I was blind before, but now I could see. Being what I was on a battlefield was no longer for kicks and getting a blood fix. I was no superior here. Any one of these men could have been someone I'd sent here, so perhaps I did deserve to be in Hell after all! I had to do my part and make things right! Because no one deserved to live this way, not even in Hell!

Your final death is coming, Izrazyk!

Chapter 12
TARA

Growing A Vampire Heart 101

My family was fascinated as they looked through the blue-tinted glass of the old mason jar. Bren stood by nervously as Dad passed the jar to Uncle Woody, then he handed it to Danny, then Cannon, and so on to the next person.

"I've never seen anything like it before!" Dad said enthusiastically. Bren kept throwing her hands out, ready to catch it. She bit her lips against protest as they casually moved the fragile container around.

"You said this came from that lady, Abigail?" Danny asked.

"Yes. Abigail gave it to Bren and told her she'd know what to do with it when the time came," Dad replied.

"There has to be something in the soil that's making it grow," Danny speculated.

"Abigail said she had a secret garden," I said.

"Where?" Danny asked.

"I don't know! Inside her house somewhere! She went to a room filled with clutter and disappeared. Then Dad and I turned around, and she was standing in the hallway holding the jar."

"Maybe she's a fairie, and her garden is in the fae realm," Danny said.

"I don't know about that. Abigail has a gift for making things grow, but a vampire's heart?" Dad questioned.

"Have you heard any other instructions?" Woody asked Bren.

Bren shook her head. "No. I was setting Zane in the sun, but then I set him out under the full moon the other night, and I woke up to these sprouts the next morning."

"Have you opened the jar since you put Zane's ashes inside?" Dad asked.

"No. I'm afraid to do that. Please don't!" Bren jumped with her hands outstretched.

"I wasn't going to open it. But it is interesting how anything can grow without air," Dad said.

"Well, essentially, vampires don't need air to survive. But Zane was no ordinary vampire," Woody said.

"He did breathe and have a heartbeat," Bren said. She jumped again when Dad turned the jar in his hand.

"We did share lungs, and I had to breathe. Zane's heartbeat was much slower, but it was always there." Dean's hand went to his chest. I put my arm through Dean's and leaned my head on his shoulder as I recognized his grief. Bren looked at Dean with sorrowful eyes.

"I have tried to call Abigail, but she has a recording on one of those old answering machines. I left messages, but she hasn't called back," I said.

"What does the recording say?" Dad asked.

"She said not to worry about her. She has worked diligently in her secret garden, preparing for something outstanding. She said not to bother stopping by because she wouldn't be available."

"I still think we should go and check in on her," Dad said.

"I would love to see Abby again. I have missed her," Mom said.

Bren was extra quiet as she watched and listened. She shifted often but relaxed as Dad set the jar on Woody's desk. She went to pick it up when Danny picked it up again.

"WOULD YOU ALL STOP!" Bren shouted.

Everyone froze and looked at her with their mouths agape. Bren walked over to Danny, grabbed the jar with both hands, and hugged it to her chest. She rolled out the bubble wrap on Woody's desk and carefully rolled the glass container till it was covered and doubled. She put the mass of plastic back inside her shoulder bag, hugged it to her chest, and walked out of the room.

Everyone's eyes followed her, and we heard the entrance door to the bar open and slammed closed.

"Did I do or say something wrong?" Danny asked.

"No, Uncle Danny. Bren has been handling that jar with kid gloves since Abigail gave it to her. It's become her lifeline, and she's scared to death of it getting broken."

"Well, shit! I suppose we weren't being very sensitive," Woody said.

"I'll go talk to her," Dean said.

"I'll come with you." I took Dean's hand.

"Would you tell her we're sorry?" Danny asked.

"I will." Dean and I walked outside and went to the camper. He knocked on the door, and we waited, but Bren didn't answer.

I knocked again. "Bren! Are you in there?" I opened the door and stepped inside while Dean waited at the steps. I looked around, but Bren wasn't there.

"Where do you think she went?" I asked.

"I think I know," Dean replied.

We walked through the woods and found Bren sitting at the tree where Zane died. She was clutching the bag to her chest and crying. Dean went to her, sat down, and put his arm around her.

"I miss him, too." Tears trailed down Dean's face.

Bren sniffed. "I know."

I came to sit before them. This spot was the same I'd been when the Hedrix snatched me, but that didn't matter right now. Bren held the charred branch in her hand that pierced Zane's heart. Why it hadn't burned to ash, too, I couldn't explain. But, there was always something magical about the trees here. Ever since I explored these woods with Mom, Dad, and Rudy when we were younger, I had felt it.

I don't know if it had to do with our family being supernatural, but I remember Dad telling me that Uncle Woody felt drawn to this land when he purchased it years ago. He said that it had felt like a haven, and I didn't understand the full extent of what that meant until recently.

Yes, we were attacked, and people have died here, but this land was our camouflage, our cover from discovery away from the world. No one set foot on these grounds unless Woody approved it, and intruders have fought and lost every time. So, yes, I believed these trees were our guardians. The lake and I needed to have words, but that would have to wait.

Dean kissed the side of Bren's head, and she hiccupped and sniffled. We sat there in silence, and I was aching to tell her that Dean and I thought we'd seen Zane on the other side in Hell. But, again, I didn't want to create false hope because what if I was wrong?

"Did I ever tell you how I knew Zane was a part of me when we were little kids?" Dean asked.

"No, but I'd like to hear it," Bren said.

"I was two when I first heard his voice inside my head. I didn't know what to make of it; this was long before most children were diagnosed with a mental disorder like schizophrenia. But, the first word Zane said to me was 'mine' while I was playing with a little toy horse I called Percy."

"Like Horsy only with a P?" Bren asked.

"Kind of. Our dad used to read the penny comics to me, and there was one with a man on a horse named Perseus, like the Greek hero in mythology."

"That's cute," Bren said. "So, did your parents know about Zane?"

"They did in a way. When I started speaking to Zane out loud, they assumed I had an imaginary friend like most children my age. They never realized he was here, inside me." Dean put his hand on his chest.

"That must have been hard for Zane not to be acknowledged by your parents," Bren said.

"Oh, believe me, he tried to get their attention!" Dean chuckled.

"What did he do?"

"Mostly got me into trouble, but when he found his voice, and it came out of my mouth for the first time, our parents took us to the doctor. He said it was probably early hormone fluctuations. But that wasn't something quite heard of for a four-year-old."

"I imagine not. What did your parents end up doing? Did you try to tell them about Zane?"

"I did, but they became upset and told me I was taking things too far, and if I didn't stop, they'd have to take me away to a special home where I had to live away from them."

"You never told me that," I said.

Dean looked at me. "I recall different things at different times, and this just happened to pop up now. Sorry, Tara."

"It's alright, Dean. You know me. I suffer from CRS."

"CRS?" Bren asked.

"Can't Remember Shit. It's one of Uncle Woody's favorite sayings."

Bren chuckled. "That's me too. So, how did Zane get his name?"

"Tara can tell you that one," Dean said.

Bren looked at me, and I smiled. "Dean used to get bullied a lot by other kids for talking to himself when talking to his brother. They called him all the names a kid would come up with when telling someone they were crazy. Well, one name stuck, zanny. Zane said he liked it when Dean shortened it to just Zane. So, it stuck. I don't know if I told it exactly right. Dean told it much better."

"No, that was a good version. I liked listening to you tell it," Dean said.

"But yours was more entertaining."

"True," Dean agreed.

"Hah!" I gently punched Dean's arm.

"Don't hold back on me, Tara. I might be sad, but I'm not fragile," Dean smiled.

"Okay, maybe later. Is there anything else you'd like to know?" I asked Bren.

"Did Zane have a first crush? Did you both ever like the same girl?"

"He did," Dean responded.

"When we were thirteen, he was smitten with a girl named Alice Neads. I thought she was alright. She was pretty and nice enough, but Zane always made me shout, 'Alice, I Needs You!' She became so annoyed that one day after Zane said it, Alice came up and decked us in the eye."

"Ooh! I bet that hurt your eye, ego, and Zane's heart," Bren said. She tightened her hold on the bag and looked down at it.

"As we got older, women became our biggest struggle. We hardly ever agreed. We didn't have the same preferences. It wasn't till I first saw Tara that Zane approved. And when he saw you for the first time, he swore you were the one. I didn't believe him at first, but he was never so committed to winning a heart like he'd done yours, Bren."

Bren sniffed and wiped at more tears as they sprung from her eyes. "Thank you, Dean. Zane was everything I never knew I'd wanted and more. We only had a short time together. But, to me, it was everything. I could never love another the way I did, Zane."

"I know! He was a pain in the ass, but he was our pain in the ass," Dean chuckled.

Bren laughed, took the bubble-wrapped jar out of the bag, and unraveled the plastic. She held it up to the light beaming through the trees. "Look! I see some more veins."

Dean took hold of the jar and looked. "No, I think that's something else. Look, Tara."

He passed the jar to me, and I paid mind to handle it with care. I looked closely, though it was difficult to make out through the blue glass in the single ray of light. But what I saw did look different.

"That might be an artery. It's a bit larger. Perhaps the aorta?"

"That's the main artery, right?" Bren asked.

"Yeah," I replied.

"He's trying to come back to us. Where ever his is right now," Bren said.

"I believe he is," I agreed.

"I do, too," Dean said.

"Where do you think he is? What do you think he's doing right now?" Bren asked.

"I'm not sure, but wherever he is, I'm sure he's stirring up hell," Dean said.

"I can see that." Bren laughed.

"I think I know what is making Zane's heart grow," I said.

"What?" Bren asked.

"Your love. See? That little bit wasn't there before now. I think talking about Zane and your love and warmth is the catalyst that sparked it."

Bren looked at the jar in my hands. "Studies have proven that when people speak nicely or play soft, classical music, it helps plants grow and thrive. Maybe I'll play some nice music for him."

I picked up a dead leaf from the ground, and it instantly turned green with life. I held it up to the light and looked at the veins that ran through it. I passed it to Bren, and she accepted with a smile.

"That's your power, Tara," Bren said.

"My necromancy?"

Bren turned the stem of the leaf between her finger and thumb. "No. It's your love."

I looked at Dean, and he smiled at me. I passed the jar back to Bren. "Bren, my dad and uncles wanted me to tell you they're sorry for being insensitive to how they handled things back there."

"I know they didn't mean any harm. I just panicked," Bren replied.

"Are you okay now?" Dean asked.

"As okay as I can be." Bren kissed the jar. "I love you, Zane. Wherever you are, I hope you heard that."

"Let's all say it together," I said. I placed my hand on Bren's, holding the jar, and Dean stacked his hand on mine.

"On the count of three. One, two, three!"

"We Love You, Zane!"

I hoped that our voices carried beyond the veil with all my heart, and Zane heard and felt us. I prayed we'd have an answer soon from Willa confirming what Dean and I thought was true. I wanted to tell Bren with certainty that we knew where Zane was and that he was safe. Please let it be so!

Chapter 13
ZANE

Rock It Launch

A wave of an echo struck me like an arrow to my heart, in a good way, making me pause. I put my hand on my chest and felt a distinct thump. Bren, Dean, and Tara came to mind. I felt sorrow, then joy and love. It was like that feeling one would get if someone talked about them. One's nose or ears would itch or whatever. I wasn't sure. But I felt it inside of me. It changed my whole demeanor. I was a cocky bastard at one moment and a sympathetic man with a heart at the next. Add that with the change of environment with the soldiers surrounding me now, and I felt my walls of uncertainty crumble.

Willa approached a man who looked like a higher-ranking soldier, though his uniform didn't look much different. Aside from his hat, he didn't have any metals, patches, or rank markings. He bowed his head.

"Mistress, thank you for coming."

"Commander Koh, I'm glad to be here. I have a gift for you." Willa reached inside her cloak and pulled out the black pencil box. She held it out in her hands before him.

"A rock?" Koh asked.

"It is much more than what you see, Commander, I assure you," Willa said.

"What is it?"

"Take it, and you will see." Willa placed the box in Koh's hand, and he inspected it for a long moment. He continued to look puzzled.

"I'm not sure I can see what you are talking about, but I feel something." Koh paused.

"How about I take a look at it," came an unwelcome familiar voice.

Weapons rose in the air, and suddenly we were surrounded by Hedrix soldiers that came out of nowhere. The men at my sides gasped and shook with fright.

"All is lost now!" The men moved away from me and fell to their knees.

Izrazyk smiled with victory gleaming in his eyes as he approached Willa, who froze in shock. But then she scowled and looked around for the traitor in our midst. Izrazyk grinned, then beckoned for someone behind me. Domonique swayed past me and went up to the Hedrix master. She bowed to him.

"You have done well, love," he praised her.

Willa looked pissed, but she bit her tongue. Izrazyk pulled Domonique into his arms and kissed her. She ran her hand across his chest.

"I will do anything to please you, Master."

"I can see that, and I wish to reward you for all to see." Everyone was frozen. I had my hand ready to draw my sword, looking at Izrazyk.

"How could you?" Willa cried. "I was your friend! I'd saved you from a life on the streets as a common whore."

"But a whore I am still. Am I not?" Domonique asked. She strode toward Willa with her long, colorful braids swaying like a mass of slithering snakes. She was a treacherous snake.

Domonique traced a finger down Willa's face. "I have grown tired of watching everyone bow to you. My master has promised me to become his new mistress, and we will finish this war together. You have gone behind his back for too long now, Willa. You have lied to and manipulated our King. Luckily for you, I have asked that he spare you and bestow a proper place amongst his harem where you will service him every night till he grows tired of you."

Willa's jaw clenched as she stared Domonique down in challenge. Her hand rose to strike Domonique's face, but with the vampire's quick reflexes, she caught Willa's wrist before making contact.

Izrazyk laughed. "Domonique. Come back to me, my love."

Domonique smirked and turned away. Her braids flew up and smacked Willa's face. I growled, and Izrazyk's eyes found mine. He smiled wickedly and winked at me. Domonique purred as she rubbed her body against her master, but then he fisted her braids roughly, and she yelped. Izrazyk shoved her away from his side, still gripping her hair, and she cried.

"Do not forget your reward, Domonique. You have done me good service, and I will repay you for that. But, in doing so, you have also betrayed your mistress."

"What? I don't understand! I told you what you asked me to know!" Domonique cried.

"Which is why I will not kill you."

The Hedrix master tugged her hair. "Snakes of treachery. Turn back and bite the one who caused my mistress's plight."

Everyone gasped as Domonique's long braids transformed into snakes. They slithered and hissed, and Domonique screamed. The snakes began biting her face, neck, and shoulders. She threw her hands up to protect herself and fell to the ground rolling and screaming like she was on fire.

Blood poured from hundreds of puncture wounds. The snakes were relentless in their attacks. No one moved to save her from her fate as Domonique continued screaming and crying. Bloody welts rose from Domonique's once silky-smooth skin.

Domonique cried till she could cry no more. She passed out, the snakes slithered away free from her head, and she was left bald. Her hands had fallen away, her face was bloated and grotesque, and her eyes had swollen shut.

"Oh, don't worry about her! She's a vampire! She will heal soon enough," Izrazyk said.

"You're a fucking monster!" Willa cried.

"I'm a monster?" Izrazyk stepped over Domonique's body and rushed at Willa. I drew my sword but found myself surrounded by Hedrix soldiers with spears.

Izrazyk grabbed Willa's face with his hand, squeezing her cheeks. "You betrayed me! I have loved you and given you a good life, and you have thrown it back in my face! I trusted and was lenient with you, and you have lied to me all this time! You have stabbed me in the back and broken my heart, Willa! Why?"

"Look around you, Izrazyk!" Willa cried. Everyone gasped at her using his name. He didn't correct her or punish her for doing so. He released her face and let her speak.

"Look at the destruction you have caused and the lives you have taken! These people are drained, weak, and in misery! They did not ask for this war! You have taken and taken more, and you are never satisfied. The necromancer power will never work for you! When will you figure it out?

When every last one of the Necros and Airmed's children is gone, then what? You will rule over no one and nothing. You will land right back where you started, and your throne will be nothing be a pile of ashes and bones!"

By the expression on his face, Willa's words struck a chord with Izrazyk, but they did not achieve the results she had hoped. He grabbed her again, brought her face closer to his, and stared into her eyes. His voice shook with rage as he spoke. "You think you know everything. BUT YOU DON'T!" Izrazyk screamed. "Do you want to know why I want this power, why I deserve it? Do you?"

Willa pulled at Izrazyk's hand as he squeezed her face harder. I growled louder.

"Let her go!" I shouted.

"Shut your mouth, Zane Perrish!" Izrazyk commanded.

I froze, and he smiled at me.

"Yes, I know who you are! Vampire brother to the Necros born of the living world, Dean Perrish. The man who stole my queen. YOU ARE IN HELL! You no longer have a say! I OWN YOU NOW!" Izrazyk roared.

I felt my hope draining down the shitter. I could see myself emptying his chamber pot while he tortured Willa in his bed. No, I couldn't let this happen!

"NEVER!" I cried. I pushed forward, but a spear pierced my gut. I groaned and fell to my knees.

"ZANE!" Willa cried. Adria and Saharah cried out behind me. I held my hand to my stomach as I bled. I felt the wound knitting back together, but it was slow. Izrazyk smirked at me, then looked again at Willa.

"If he makes another move, I will personally remove his head and stick it in his ass. Now! Whether you like it or not, you are coming back home with me, Willa, but first, you will give me whatever you just handed to Koh."

Willa shook her head. She looked at Koh, who looked defeated as Hedrix soldiers held him at spearpoint. He held up the pencil box in his hand.

"A rock?" Izrazyk questioned. I was surprised that he saw the same thing as Koh.

"Take it!" He nudged Willa forward. Willa shook as she reached out and took hold of the black container. She looked at Izrazyk as he held his hand out in expectancy. Willa lowered the black box slowly, hovering over the Hedrix master's hand.

"Let it go!" Izrazyk commanded.

"I'm trying!" Willa cried. Her hand trembled, and Izrazyk pushed his hand upward, but Willa's hand rose higher.

"Stop playing games with me, Willa!"

"I am not!"

His hand went higher, and hers went higher still. Izrazyk growled. He grabbed her wrist with his other hand and jerked Willa's hand down. The black container launched like a rocket, flying up over the encampment, and a bolt of lightning cracked across the sky. The lightning burst like an exploding transformer, and sparks of white light scattered and rained down. Everyone screamed and ducked for cover, but it happened so fast that it was too late as a mighty wind gust knocked everyone down like an atomic blast had hit us. My body felt plastered to the dirt.

I lifted my head and looked around when it became more of a gentle breeze. Everyone around me was doing the same, and the sparks of light drifted and began landing on the Necros and Sevifk soldiers. Their bodies absorbed the light, and their lungs pulled in deep breaths as if someone had revived them.

I stood up and watched as the whole encampment rose to its feet. The soldier's eyes flashed with brilliant illumination, and their faces rejuvenated. Their bodies became strong as their muscles filled out their uniforms.

Everyone looked up as the sound of something falling came from the sky. Willa reached up, and an object landed in her hand. And I watched as she punctured her chest with a long needle. Izrazyk's eyes widened, and he looked frightened as Willa's eyes flashed.

Every Necros and Sevifk soldier turned their eyes on the Hedrix master, who cried out, "Hedrix soldiers! Fight for your master!"

Battle cries rang out, and I dove for my sword, snatched it up, and rolled as the Hedrix soldiers launched their spears at me. I stood swinging my sword, and metal crashed against metal. I cut off a man's arm, and he screamed. Another came at me, and I plunged the blade into his gut.

My feet moved swiftly, and my sword deflected every strike with precision as I took on three fighters at once. I launched myself into the air as all three men lunged forward, only to impale one another. I landed on my feet, and I heard Willa scream with rage.

She launched with the object in her hand with a needle pointed at Izrazyk. His eyes widened as he blocked her before she could pin him in the chest. The pin's tip scratched his arm, and the Hedrix master bellowed in pain and then roared in anger.

The glow of power coming from her palm enclosed the object with the pin sticking out between her knuckles, and suddenly I knew what Willa was holding. It was Tara's brooch!

Tara's power was inside and had detonated and rooted into the Necro's and Sevifk soldiers, giving them the vital recharge they needed. Tara had delivered the gift of Airmed's power, and it was the power that ran through her veins. The tide had turned, and I screamed a battle cry and continued to fight. I stabbed, disemboweled, dismembered, or decapitated each beast that came at me as I charged at Izrazyk.

Adria and Saharah had their swords fighting against the enemy, and I passed them by as they needed no help from me. Willa engaged Izrazyk with the brooch, and she had her knife in her other hand as the two moved swiftly and parried each other's strikes. I ran into the fray, and Izrazyk jumped back as I intercepted his next blow.

The muscle memory of all those years Dean and I fenced and beat every opponent now quickened as my vampire speed took over, and I wickedly smiled as Izrazyk began grunting a breaking a sweat. I was gaining the advantage, and Willa had turned and blocked as another Hedrix came at me from behind. The Hedrix soldier screamed, and I heard an explosion with a shatter of light in my periphery.

Izrazyk's eyes widened in horror, and he turned to run. A portal opened up, and Izrazyk and a handful of his soldiers jumped through. It closed before I reached it, and I cursed.

Cries of victory rang out as the Necros and Sevifk chased the remaining Hedrix soldiers out of the encampment, with only a few getting away unscathed.

Willa ran up to my side. "He escaped!"

"Unfortunately!" I replied.

"Fuck!" Willa cursed. "I wish you hadn't jumped in like that! I almost had him!"

"I'm sorry! I was just as set on killing the bastard like you!" I argued.

"And now he has the opportunity to regroup and try to create more demons out of unwilling souls," Willa said.

"But now, we have the upper hand! Willa, look around you! Tara has gifted the Necros and Sevifk with a mega energy boost. There is hope!"

"I know! But we could have finished this today if Izrazyk hadn't gotten away."

"He's on the run, and most likely, you know where to find him."

"I can think of a few places he might go to lick his wounds." Willa pinned the brooch to her cloak, and the glass vessel swirled with energy. Saharah and Adria ran up to Willa. "Mistress! This day is ours! We have taken down the Hedrix army!"

"There is no need to call me by that title anymore. Please, just call me Willa!"

"Yes, Willa!" They bowed.

"And stop bowing! We are all equals here!"

I smiled. "You sound just like Tara."

Willa smiled in return. "It will be good to get to know her better."

Willa walked through the camp, and the Necros and Sevifk soldiers cheered. Commander Koh approached and bowed his head.

"Thank you, Mistress! You have saved us all!"

"It wasn't me! It was your new Queen, Tara."

"I have heard that name! Where is she?"

"In the living realm, and she is still in danger. Izrazyk got away and still intends to take her for his prize."

"What can we do to help?" Koh asked.

"I will need your Sevifk soldiers," Willa said. "I can send them through to the living realm."

"Considering it done!" Koh bowed and walked away.

"Willa. I think Domonique is dead! Come and see," Saharah said.

We walked to where Domonique's unmoving body lay. Willa knelt and touched her with tears in her eyes. She pressed her hand to Domonique's chest, and Domonique's eyes opened. The swelling had gone away, and the bites had healed. Domonique's hair regrew, but it was no longer in braids. Instead, she had short, colorful curls. Domonique sat up and threw her arms around Willa, who hugged her back, and I was confused as hell.

"Sister!" Domonique cried, and Adria and Saharah joined them in their embrace.

"I'm so sorry, Domonique! I didn't know he'd do that to you." Willa touched Domonique's face and kissed her cheeks.

"I'm okay, Willa! It was better that I take the fall than our sisters. They would not have survived."

"What the? I thought that she betrayed you!" I said. These women had just pulled off the most badass coup I'd ever seen!

"She did! But we planned it that way," Willa said.

"You are an evil genius!" I smiled.

"I learned something from Izrazyk during all those years. Strike first!" Willa said.

Chapter 14
TARA

You May Proceed

Someone was pounding frantically on the door, and Dean groaned as I moved his arm from my waist and sat up. I pushed my feet into my slippers and pulled on my extra fluffy robe. It was getting colder outside, and we were due to have snow this week.

"Tara! Open up!" Hearing my mother's frantic voice made me panic. Were we under attack? Dean jumped out of bed and ran ahead of me to open the door.

"What's wrong, Lydia?" Dean asked.

"Woody has called a meeting in the bar. Something has happened!" Mom stepped inside, shivering in a light jacket, Dean closed the door, and we started getting dressed.

"What is it, Mom?"

"He didn't say. But I saw him and your father talking with Alma and Esaw. Everyone is gathering in the bar now."

"You could have called and saved the trip in the cold weather," I said.

"I was already outside when Alma approached, but I was returning from a walk, and Woody told me to come to get you."

"Mom, you shouldn't be out in this weather!"

"I'm fine, Tara. I'm a grown-ass woman capable of making my own decisions. Now, cut me some slack and get your ass in gear, young lady!"

Dean laughed. "Where have I heard that line before?"

"Like mother, like daughter." Mom smiled.

"That's what Richard says." Dean chuckled.

"Alright, you two." I huffed.

We walked outside, and a frigid gust of wind hit us.

"Holy! Mom! You were out walking in this? Are you nuts?"

"A judge and jury of my peers thought so. Mighty as well go with it," Mom replied.

"Well, screw this!" I ran the rest of the way to The Roost and sighed in relief as I made it inside. A roaring fire heated the room in the vast fireplace between the two main windows. I ran over to it and held my hands before the screen.

"Ahh!" I sighed happily. Dean came up behind me and wrapped his arms around me, pressing his cold body to my back.

"Get off me! You're freezing!"

Dean laughed. "Big baby! I thought you were tolerant of the cold?"

"Not that shit out there! It felt like a Sub-Arctic blast! Mom must be having some crazy heat flashes to withstand that! I can't wait till we go on that beach vacation. I'm tired of these cold mountain winters."

"Well, let's hear what Alma has to say. Hopefully, it's good news, and we may go on that vacation sooner than you think."

Everyone was sitting as Mom, Billie, Bren, and Martina passed out hot chocolate and coffee. Bren had returned to toting the bag around with Zane's ashes, but no one questioned her as she smiled graciously, handing out cups.

Uncle Woody stood up and cleared his throat, and all the chattering died down. "Alma has received some news from her daughter, Willa. She didn't tell me any details because she wanted to share it with all of us at once. Alma." Woody gestured for her to take the floor.

Alma stood and smiled at the crowd. "I'll cut straight to it. The package arrived safely at the Necros and Sevifk camp in Ardromezor."

Everyone began cheering.

"Hold on! Settle down! The gift Tara provided aided them with what they needed to turn the war around, and they defeated the Hedrix army."

My brothers and sisters collapsed into each other's arms with cries of joy. Many hands reached out to pull me up, and I received tearful words of gratitude. I thanked God and Airmed with ecstatic laughter.

"This victory is much to celebrate, but there is more to tell!" Alma called. "During the battle, the Hedrix master and a few of his men got away. They escaped through a portal, and Willa doesn't know where they are now."

Everyone voiced their disappointment, and my heart sank. The Hedrix is a coward. Of course, he'd fled and left his men to fend for themselves. With his army defeated, the Necros and Sevifk had a chance, but he could still retaliate. He's somewhere in hiding, licking his wounds and scheming.

Alma continued. "Which means we still need to be prepared for an attack. Willa told me the Hedrix is still after Tara, and he will remain relentless in his quest."

Hands reached out and squeezed my shoulders and arms. Jeremiah stood up and shouted. "We won't let that happen! That asshole has another thing coming if he even thinks about stepping foot on this land!"

Boisterous voices cried out with agreement, and I stood up. Hands clapped, and lips whistled in encouragement as I went to stand by Alma's side and speak. "I want everyone to stay encouraged as we face this obstacle. The Hedrix held me captive; he thought He is a coward who prizes himself above all others because he is a vain, sadistic blowhard that believes he has the upper hand. Well, guess what? Willa just handed his ass to him and sent him running like a big fat chicken!"

Everyone cheered and made chicken calls.

Jeremiah jumped up and shouted. "Hell, yeah!"

Bren was smirking, and I laughed.

"I do not doubt that he will show his face here, and we will be ready! My brothers and sisters! Are you ready for a fight?" I cried.

"YEAH!" Everyone shouted. Jeremiah and Rudy picked me up and tossed me like I'd just scored the game-winning goal. I yelped and heard Dad, Dean, and my uncles laughing.

Rudy started chanting. "Tara, Tara, Tara, Tara!"

Everyone else joined in.

"Stop! Stop! Put me down!" I yelled.

They laughed and ignored me.

"I'M GOING TO BE SICK!" I shouted. That worked.

The guys immediately set me down. I wasn't feeling sick, but it was getting annoying, and I wasn't a little child who might enjoy getting tossed like a rag doll. At least no one drowned me with a cooler of icy sports drinks.

Alma came up to me and hugged me. "I have something else to share with you, but in private, and Dean can come along."

I looked at Dean and waved him over. He joined us, and we made our way to the billiards tables. I was anxious to know if our suspicions about Zane were correct.

Bren was talking with Jeremiah, and they were both smiling and laughing. Bren still hugged the bag to her body like her favorite childhood safety blanket.

"I asked Willa about the man you saw, and she made the confirmation," Alma said.

"Really?" I asked excitedly. "It's him?"

"Yes!" Alma smiled.

I squealed like a girly lunatic and hugged Dean like an over-enthusiastic spaz high on a case of energy drinks. Dean laughed, and I kissed him. His eyes were brimming with tears.

"And he's safe?" Dean asked.

"He is. He helped Willa take down the Hedrix army. He fought the Hedrix master before the portal opened, and he got away. Willa told me he fought well. But there is something else you should know."

"Okay," I said.

"Your power is extraordinary, Tara. It shook the Hedrix to the core. Not only had your power restored the Necros and Sevifk army, but there was still some left when Willa stuck herself in the heart to recharge it.

She battled the Hedrix master hand to hand before Zane stepped in, and she scratched him with the pin, which caused him great pain. And when Willa stuck the pin in another Hedrix, the soldier exploded into ashes, and that frightened the master and sent him running."

"Holy! Are you saying my power combined with Willa's blew a Hedrix to ashes?"

"No, Tara. When Willa pierced her heart, your power did not discharge, nor did hers go into the glass vessel. Your power alone destroyed an evil demon."

"Wait! What?"

Alma nodded. "I believe you alone must take the Hedrix master down."

"Then we must devise a plan. But, first, I want to know if it's okay if I tell Bren the good news?"

Alma nodded. "Now that things look brighter, Willa is okay with it."

I hugged Alma. "Thank you!"

"Oh, and Tara!"

"Yes."

"You'll never believe the name Willa gave Zane as his secret identity."

"What was it?"

Alma's eyes looked over to Jeremiah standing with Bren. My eyes widened. "Are you for real?"

"I tell you the truth."

I kissed Alma's cheek, then Dean and I went to Bren and Jeremiah.

"How's it going?" Jeremiah greeted.

"Better than expected," I said.

"Do you mind if Dean and I borrow Bren for a bit?"

"I'm not invited?" Jeremiah pouted. He must be feeding off some vibes because he was starting to sound more like Zane.

"Bren can fill you in later. We need to talk to her first."

"Very well!" Jeremiah conceded.

"Sorry, Jeremiah. I promise to get with you later," Bren said.

Jeremiah smiled. "Okay."

I took Bren's arm and led her toward the door.

"Where are we going?" she asked.

"Wherever you'd like to go," I said.

"Your cabin is probably warmer than the camper."

"Alrighty." I smiled.

We stepped out into the freezing wind, and we huddled together. I didn't run this time, keeping in mind Bren's fear of breaking the jar. We made it safely inside.

"BRRRRR! It's colder than Hell froze over out there!" I chattered.

We sat at the kitchen table, and Dean went to make more coffee. He always made it better than anyone else, and I didn't get to finish my first cup, so I was grateful.

"Any new development with Zane's heart?" I asked. Bren took the double-bubble-wrapped jar out of the bag. It looked like she put some fresh packing material on it. The older plastic was getting a bit ragged. She unrolled it and set it on the table.

"There's more happening in there," Bren said. I lifted the jar and held it up to the light, and sure enough, there was the beginning of muscle tissue growing around the aorta that had doubled in size since the day before.

"That is fascinating! I'll never get over it! It's like magical medical advancement in a garden jar."

"I've been playing music to him and singing." Bren smiled.

"Looks like he's listening."

Dean set our coffee down and joined us at the table. He looked at the miracle in the blue mason jar and smiled. "That's my brother for you. Too stubborn to quit! He's a fighter."

"Is Jeremiah still behaving himself?" I asked.

"He is a perfect gentleman, but I'm noticing he's acting differently. Maybe he's starting to loosen up more as he gets to know everyone better," Bren said.

"Maybe." I pondered.

"So, what did you bring me here to tell me?" Bren asked.

I looked at Dean, and he nodded.

"Bren. When Dean, Jeremiah, Dad, and I went to the graveyard to meet with Willa on the other side, we saw a man who had an uncanny resemblance to Jeremiah."

"Wow! Really?"

"Yes, and Willa had called him by the same name. Jeremiah Vansbrie. But it was a cover for his true identity."

"Who was he?" Bren asked.

Dean took Bren's hand, and his voice choked. "It was Zane."

Bren's lips trembled, and she burst into tears. "Oh, Oh my god! I can't believe it! Is he okay?!"

"He is more than okay. He helped win the battle against the Hedrix army."

Bren broke into a sobbing fit. I got up and put my arms around her. The jar on the table began to rattle, and we looked at it. The tiny bloom doubled in size, and a whole heart molded into existence before our eyes. It began to beat, and we all gawked at the vessel that housed Zane's vampire heart. His heart still had much more growing to do, but would it outgrow the jar before it developed fully? And would Bren carry it around for the rest of her life before she ever had a chance to see Zane again?

"Oh my god!" Bren cried.

"We will have to find a body to house his heart before it outgrows that jar," Dean said.

"I'm afraid of opening the lid. I have a strong feeling it shouldn't be opened at all," Bren said.

"As long as it doesn't outgrow the jar overnight, we still have time," Dean said.

"Jeremiah offered his body, but a physical heart is different than spiritual energy. So, I'm not sure how that would work. We might have to pay a visit to Rosco and do some shopping," I said.

"Who's Rosco?" Bren asked.

"He's the coroner who helped us with Asher."

"No!" Bren shook her head. "Something tells me to hold out just a little bit longer."

"Like a voice in your head?"

"No. More like a feeling," Bren said.

"Are you going to talk to Jeremiah about Zane?" Dean asked.

"Yes. I think, in all fairness, he should know. Jeremiah has been very supportive." Bren repacked the jar and put it back in her shoulder bag.

"I'll walk you back to the bar," Dean offered.

"I'm staying here and drinking my hot coffee," I said.

"Thanks, Tara." Bren hugged me.

"I'm so happy for you. And Dean."

"And you?" Bren asked.

"Yeah! I've missed him too! I'd be happy to have Zane around again, so I have someone to terrorize with threats of bleeding on him." I grinned.

"That's not nice, Tara!"

"If you knew how Zane tormented me, you'd be on my side."

"I'll take your word for it. See you soon." Bren hugged the bag with a serene smile as she turned to leave.

Dean kissed my cheek. "Be back in a few."

They went out the door. I sipped my brewy bliss and sighed.

"Please come back to us, Zane. I miss you, brother."

Chapter 15
IZRAZYK

Narcissistic Rantings

Two thousand years flushed down the bowels of Old Hades in a matter of minutes! All because of a woman I trusted with my secrets and life.

"ROARRRR!" I released my rage. It didn't alleviate the painful scratch on my arm. The darkness seeped from my wound, and the thin line of light kept consuming it, making me feel weaker by the minute.

It wasn't supposed to work that way. The darkness should shield the light, not get devoured. But this was the Necros's power, and Tara's light charged the Necros. Why was it reacting this way to me? Because of HER, that's why! Damn HER and HER curse!

The Hedrix soldiers who followed me through the portal had run in fear after seeing one of their brothers burst into ashes from my queen's power. They ran now due to my rage. The only two who remained with me were my closest confidants. Malichi and Demetrius.

"Master. We did not know the weapon would have that effect. The harem girl."

"I no longer care about what that bitch told you, Demetrius! My mistress outright betrayed me and did so with the help of my queen! I practically raised Willa from a small child, sparing her from the pain most of her kind suffered. Ungrateful woman!"

"Master. We have lost the loyalty of the Sevifk. Perhaps if you had returned upon your promises sooner."

"Do not lecture me on what I should have done, Malachi. I should have killed those I held captive long ago. Anyone who betrays me will pay in blood!"

"And what of our Mistress?" Demetrius asked.

I could not kill Willa. She was too valuable an asset. I provided her with an elite education and trained her with the best teachers in combat and strategy. I suppose I taught her too well. And perhaps I was somewhat proud that she almost defeated me. Still, I was pissed, rightfully so, because she outwitted me. With the help of my queen, she had turned the tables and taken down most of my army.

"Willa is to be captured along with her coconspirators. I will gut the vampire, hang him by his entrails, and gag Adria and Saharah to death on my rod! Those ungrateful bitches! Have I not provided them a life of luxury? I have spared them servitude within lesser stations, and they too, turned on me. And the vampire!"

"The vampires should have never been allowed to rise as high as you've allowed, Master. You've grown soft since the death of their queen. It was a mistake to allow them such prominent positions as guardsmen," Malichi said.

"You forget who took out their queen. I did my people a favor. Her death sent those vermin scattering like cockroaches, and the citizens of my kingdom slept better at night, no longer in fear of a vampire attack."

"And still, you gave them a position to rise again," Demetrius said.

"I will not stand here and argue with you about my decisions. Now we must focus on capturing my queen! She is our last hope of regaining the advantage to win back the Sevifk."

"Master. We were all there! The Sevifk will not turn on the Necros! They have decimated our numbers, and we haven't the backing needed to defeat them," Malichi said.

"They will change their minds once I have my queen. I will have access to her power, and we will sway them together. Both Sevifk and Necros will bow to us."

"How do you plan to capture the queen? The last attack upon her people resulted in the loss of thirty Sevifk. And we lost several more of our brethren while you were off playing mind games."

"If all you plan to do is remind me of my failures, Malichi, then I no longer wish to speak. Why don't you and Demetrius make sure this location is secure while I think."

"Yes, Master!" Malichi bowed.

He and Demetrius left my private chamber. They were the only men close enough to me who I would allow to voice their opinions in such ways. Anyone else who spoke to me in this manner would become my new bedpost head ornament.

My portal key master, Beatrix, sat in her cage, growling like the bitch she was. She may not like me, but she did her job. If she ever wanted to be free of the witch's curse, she'd behave herself like a good dog and open and close portals when I called for her to do so. I would relieve her when I captured another key master.

She wouldn't give up any of the other's locations, choosing to live out her fate as my lap dog. I should have had the witch turn her into a mule for how stubborn she's become.

I kicked her cage. "Stop that incessant growling! I have offered you your freedom time and again! It is your fault you choose to remain this way!"

Beatrix morphed into her human form and smirked as I winced at the painful throbbing scratch on my arm.

"You know why. I will never betray my family and have them suffer this way. Perhaps you will let me be on my way once you have your queen."

"My queen wishes to travel to see all the realms with me. I will still require you even then. I also have matters to discuss with the vampires of the living realm."

"Perhaps if they knew who murdered their queen, they would no longer have dealings with you. They would have your death."

"If you or anyone speaks of this to the vampires, I will have your death first, Beatrix. Then I will still find your family and have them under my control."

"Ha! Go ahead and kill me, then. It will be the first thing I do when I get the chance. The vampires have no loyalty to anyone but their kind. They are as vain and selfish of creatures as are you!"

"Selfish? Have I not given my people a haven behind my walls? They have lived in peace and harmony while I kept the war far away from my city. I have given a good life to all who have turned their backs on me. I promised to return the Sevifk to their families upon victory over the Necros. We were so close! Everyone would have their freedom and a better life!"

"You seek rights to power, not yours to hone, Hedrix master. You have stolen from and tormented Airmed's children and the Necros. It is no wonder many have turned against you. Your greed blinds you from the truth."

"THERE IS ONLY ONE TRUTH! From the start, that power was MINE! It was stolen from me! Stripped away by the one person I once called beloved. And see what it does to me now?

I held up my arm for Beatrix to see better, and she rolled her eyes like I was acting like a baby, but this shit hurt!

"SHE punished me! All because I proposed a better way to use the gift for all of creation. She took what was mine, sent me away, and cursed me never to have my power returned."

Beatrix crossed her arms beneath her ample breasts and scowled. "And you think it right to steal it from someone else! You who felt the hurt of losing your gift. You turned your pain on the innocent and took all your hatred out on the Necros! They did nothing to you! You are to blame for all that has happened. You.."

"ENOUGH! You are in no position to challenge me! I will have what is rightfully mine! Tara will be my queen and give me her power, and my original plan will succeed. Then she will see I was right all along!"

"You have grown too dark with the Necros power. There is no balance in you. It was never meant to be this way. Your selfish ambitions have turned you into a monster."

Beatrix was right about one thing. Little by little, my darkness grew, but I still needed the light to create balance and have total control. I siphoned Airmed's children, but the light never clung. Not like it did now on my skin where it did me no good eating away at what power I had.

It was part of the curse she placed upon me. And her children always fought because they never understood the bigger picture. It was selfish of them to keep their gifts all to themselves.

I had to take what I deserved and share it with those more worthy. My Hedrix brethren understood my goals. When I was cast down thousands of years ago, I fought tooth and nail to rise to my status. It took me years of blood, sweat, and tears to build a loyal following. I raised my army, rewarding them well. And my city grew, thriving in riches and beauty.

I made thousands of promises to Airmed's children to gain their loyalty. I gave them new life and a form more fitting for survival in Hell. They would have claimed their prize if they had just seen this war to completion. They would have shared in the spoils and become nobility in my court with land and titles. I am a very generous man who repays loyalty.

But, somewhere along the way, many accused me of scorning them because I had not yet fulfilled my promises. Lies spread about me, holding the Sevifk and their family prisoner and hanging threats over their heads. Rebellion reared its head and bit at me like a viper. I had to turn it all around. I had to be the one to strike first. And it was then I became forced to make my threats into reality.

It's a lonely existence when many want to be your enemy. I gifted many fine young women and men a grand home filled with luxuries in exchange for a bit of company, and I pleasured them, asking little in return. Dammit! That was another thing! I'd lost three of my best harem girls. I was frustrated, and I could use a little comfort right now.

I looked at Beatrix and considered her for a moment. She was a beautiful woman, but she despised me. It was apparent in her scowl every time my eyes met hers. I had never forced a woman into bed. If one displeased me or didn't want to engage, I'd shove them away, take one who was willing while making the other stand and watch what they were missing.

Ultimately, their lust betrayed them, and they all returned, pleading to let me take them. I would make Tara and Willa see how generous a lover I was. But before they received their treat, I would take them over my knees and punish them first. Their soft rounded bottoms would receive a sting from my hand they would never forget. Ungrateful women!

How could my mistress and queen do this to me? They knew how much I desired them. I would give them everything in exchange for the tiniest bit of their light. Even if I could never wield it myself, their reward would be more significant once they saw my plan achieve fruition. I could no longer stand around and wait.

"Beatrix! You have one of two choices. You can give me your body to lavish into sweet ecstasy, or?"

Beatrix sneered at me in disgust, which worked to my advantage because I knew she wanted nothing to do with me that way.

"Or what?" she spat.

"Or, you make a portal where I can fully enter the living realm in my true form. Once I have my queen, I'll grant you some freedom and remove your curse."

"When do you desire this, Master?" Beatrice asked sweetly.

Oh, now I've piqued her interest enough to earn the title of Master from her lips! I just needed to give this little bee a taste of honey.

"I wish to go tonight, along with my brothers, and you will allow them the same passage."

"Very well, Master I will send you and your fellow Hedrix through safely, but you will remove my curse before you make your leave."

"You are full of demands! But, very well. I will do this, and upon my safe return with my queen, I will give you a wider breadth to roam with a private chamber, yet you will remain guarded at all times. Does this satisfy you, Portal Key Master?"

Beatrix bowed her head. "It does, my lord."

Chapter 16
WILLA

By Blood And Mud

There was no time to stop and celebrate. I knew Izrazyk would go for Tara next. She was his last hope to bring the Sevifk back to his side, and I couldn't allow that to happen. This was why every Sevifk soldier stood at attention as I addressed them in the war-ravaged field. Most of these men and women fought for Izrazyk under false promises of a better life for their families. He'd sold them on the idea when times had fallen tough in the living realm.

They'd seen many wars amongst the human race and tried to help them. They brought many lives back so they could return to their loved ones. But Airmed had stopped this practice; sighting humanity had to learn to solve their problems without resorting to violence.

She had told of a man called Yeshua who gave his life in sacrifice so there would no longer be a final death. He had walked the living realm and taught the people how to live a life in peace and harmony.

Izrazyk thought this was ludicrous and wanted to overthrow Airmed's decision. He argued that the establishment of peace amongst all creation was possible had they the option to live eternally in a realm of their choosing. There was no reason to fight if no one died, and they would learn to live together under a singular leadership.

That leadership being Izrazyk as the king of all life.

Should there be a dispute, he would choose each party's fate. He would decide who was right or wrong or who lived and died. And he'd use Tara and me as his pawns to establish himself a just king over the realms.

Izrazyk was already a totalitarian tyrant in Hell. He'd taken down three leaderships and gained the support of his fellow Hedrix because they wanted a piece, a governorship in a realm of their choosing. He didn't understand that he was stripping everyone of their freedom and right to make their own choices.

I stood before my people and gave them a choice now.

"My brothers and sisters. Time is of the essence. With the Hedrix master's escape, he plans to enter the living realm and kidnap Airmed's blessed daughter Tara Raybrook. She is the one who sent her power this day to turn this fight in our favor. I will need volunteers to fight the Hedrix who enters the living realm and the rest to remain here to aid in her rescue if he should succeed. Raise your hands, all who wish to go to the living realm."

Every hand went up in the air, and I didn't blame them. Unfortunately, I would have to make the tough decision to narrow it down. There were still many here with families held prisoner, and they, too, would need help escaping.

"How many of you have family trapped here by the Hedrix?"

More than half raised their hands. They would need to stay and help one another with rescuing their families, leaving several dozen men and women plus the thirty others in the living realm to fight.

"Those of you who have family here will remain until you have helped one another find and free your missing family members. The rest will come with me now."

They talked amongst themselves, heads nodding in agreement. A few of them raised their hands, and I pointed to a female Sevifk.

"Mistress," she began.

"Willa," I interrupted. "I am no one's mistress here."

The Sevifk soldier bowed her head. "Willa. After ensuring Tara is safe and finding our families, will we return to the living realm and have our old lives back?"

"Once we have found the portal key master to open the door to the living realm, I will make sure you return to your lives. I will remain here with you until this happens. I only go to the graveyard to send the rest to aid in the fight. My mother, Alma, has told me that the place of refuge can only accommodate so many of us at a time, so we will have to take turns in smaller groups till a plan for all our benefit comes along. Much has changed since our times, and those before us agreed to teach the ways of the modern world. It will take time for them to help us with the resources we'll need to pass as mortals."

I was thankful no one questioned me on the matter. Everyone discussed it and seemed to understand my reasoning. My mother told me space and resources were limited. Many of my people came from times less complex than the world today. I would stay here until the threat no longer existed. And I would remain until the last of Airmed's children stepped back into the living realm. And what a glorious day that will be. We never belonged here.

Zane, Domonique, Adria, and Sahara stood at my sides. Many of the Necros and Sevifk came and thanked them for their help. We mounted our horses and began heading back to the graveyard in the forest from the night before. Eighty Sevifk followed as we made our way through the camp.

"I have heard many people talking about the vampire race. I heard the Hedrix murdered their queen. I didn't know about this before now," Zane said.

"No. You wouldn't have known. And many didn't know about you. Having shared a body with your necromancer brother concealed your existence from the vampires in the living realm. Should you return and claim a body, the vampires will know. They will find you, and you will have to join a coven."

"Is that why the one who sired me never returned? Because Dean shielded me? But Dean and I have encountered other vampires. Why didn't they say anything?"

"Probably because they didn't recognize what you were or were rogues." I touched the pin on my cloak. There was still enough of Tara's power to give that extra bump to send the eighty or so Sevifk through the graveyard should mine run too low.

Zane looked at the brooch. "Your power looks a lot like Tara's."

"That is Tara's power."

"But I saw you stick yourself. Didn't Tara's power go in you or your power go in there?"

"No. But I guess Airmed made it that way to contain enough of Tara's power to boost her children and the Necros. Once Tara's power is used up, I can charge it."

"It's amazing! Tara charged the whole army, obliterated a Hedrix demon, and there was still some left?"

"She's more powerful than she realizes. The scratch on Izrazyk's arm caused him a great deal of pain. I can only imagine what might have happened if I'd stuck him in the heart."

"That other Hedrix exploded into ashes. You don't think the same could happen to Izrazyk?"

"No. Izrazyk has too much dark power inside. It would take an overload of light to affect him that way. It would have weakened and made him ill by eating away at the darkness inside, but there's not enough to accomplish his destruction."

"Why? If it charges the Necros, why does it ill affect Izrazyk?"

"He has complained that Airmed cursed him, and some have heard him say that he used to be one of us. He opposed one of Airmed's decrees and tried to overthrow her decision, and she stripped his power and cast him from her realm."

"Airmed stole his favorite blanket." Zane laughed.

"What does that mean?"

"It's an expression referring to an adult taking something special away from a child, and the kid throws a tantrum. He's a big baby upset because Airmed stole his favorite blanket."

"You have a strange way of explaining things, Zane."

"There are many more euphemisms you'll have to learn to understand the modern world, Willa. The world consists of three types of people: mostly bullies and crybabies. The rest are the mediators. If it weren't for the fact that I drink their blood to survive, I'd question if humanity is worth saving anymore. But then I see people like you, Tara, my brother, and Tara's family and recognize that there's still hope."

I shook my head. Maybe that was true. I hadn't seen the living realm for two centuries. I'm sure it will be a shock to see how much the world has changed.

We cleared the camp, and we rode faster to the graveyard. Not all the horses were fresh enough to go fast for long, and some had double riders. Still, we had to get there as fast as we could. The night was falling soon, and I needed to get the Sevifk through in time to make it to Tara's family's land.

When we made it just before dark, the Sevifk followed into the forest and gathered before the Plemming Stone. Sedgwick Plemming was a powerful sorcerer who'd left behind his energy to open portals by a scarce few with a specific type of gift. One of those was necromancy, but not all could pass.

A necromancer could send those who have traversed both realms for a short time. Once these Sevifk reached the other side, they had two weeks to find the means to free themselves of their demonic bindings, or their borrowed bodies would decay, and they'd return to Hell.

Tara freed my mother and father, but she could not reveal how. Tara's advantage depended upon maintaining this secret. It was best if I didn't have this knowledge. Even under duress, I wouldn't say a word. But in Hell, there are many ways to make a person speak.

Instead of using the brooch, I cut myself with my blade. I'd hold onto Tara's power for a rainy day. I marked the Plemming stone with the sigil of passage and called the blue orb. One by one, I pressed my power to the Sevifk before they passed through the blue light.

They already had instructions on where to go and what to avoid. The Sevifk were swift and fierce warriors. Izrazyk commanded the Sevifk to perform vile acts, and they obeyed upon penalty of a fate much worse than death. Nothing was worse than the threats he'd made against their families, and he'd made good on his word at one point.

He'd made an example of one poor soul having them tortured in every conceivable way for all to witness with their family front and center. Afterward, Izrazyk ordered the whole family disemboweled, drawn, quartered, and beheaded. It was a gruesome and bloody day.

It was also the day I decided enough was enough and began scheming to take him down. Alliances weren't hard to find. My ladies listened to whispers in the dark, and I tested those people to ensure they weren't double agents—many who'd be damned if not for my intervention.

Nearly forty years passed, and our plan finally paid in full. If I had stuck the pin into Izrazyk's heart, Tara's light would have made him drastically weak, and I would have cut off his head. He never stayed in the living realm long enough to build a tolerance to the light, and we had Tara's mother to thank for that.

"That is the last, Willa. It is time to reach out to your mother and let her know," Saharah said.

"Wait!" Zane said.

"Why?" I asked.

Zane moved his hand toward the blue light.

"I wouldn't do that if I were you," Domonique said.

"What's the worst that can," Zane's hand touched the portal.

A loud buzz of energy sounded, zapping Zane and, "AAAHHH!" His body flew backward into a tree that broke into thousands of splinters, and he burst through two more before landing in a muddy cesspool.

My ladies and I strode casually to Zane's sprawled form and grinned at him. He lay and groaned while smoke plumed off his body. Adria giggled, and Saharah smirked.

"Told you," Domonique said.

"Why did you do that?" I asked.

"I was curious," Zane groaned.

"About?"

"I want to see Bren, even if only for a minute."

"I'm sorry, Zane. You can only get through a portal made by a portal key master."

Zane pushed himself up, and he looked like a roasted swine. I offered him my hand but gave him a look of warning. If he dared try to pull me into the mud with him, I'd take him for another zap at the Plemming stone. Zane smiled devilishly and took my hand, but I pulled hard and fast before he could even think about tipping me his way.

"Until we find the portal key master, you will travel with my ladies and me. Word has already spread fast of the vampire who aided in taking down the Hedrix Army. And it will change the opinions of many about the vampire race. You have done a service for my people, the Necros, and yours by your acts of courage. It was all in the cards of fate."

"I am glad to be of service. Now, is there a place we can go where I can get this shit off me and a drink? Blood preferably."

"Yes. There's a tavern east of here."

<><><>

Adria and Saharah went with Zane to help him with his clothes and a bath. Domonique watched over me as I sat on the floor of our rented room.

I closed my eyes as the room around me faded away. I envisioned my mother's eyes, and I felt pulled into a dark void where I stood surrounded by galaxies of light. I reached out and touched the one I knew well with my fingertip. It knew where I needed to go as it zoomed in on the sun and planets and continued until I reached my connection.

"Mother!" I waited a moment. Sometimes it took her a few minutes to realize I was there.

"Willa! What news do you bring?"

"I have sent forth eighty Sevifk to aid you. Tara may not have time to free them before Izrazyk comes. Our people should be there any moment now. You must prepare. It won't be long till the portal opens and the Hedrix arrives."

"Okay, Willa. I will." She stopped speaking.

"Mother?"

"Willa! They are here! I have to go! I love you!" Her voice sounded panicked.

"Mother? Who's there?"

I lost the connection.

"Willa?" Domonique touched my shoulder. I opened my eyes, and she was before me with a concerned expression. Domonique took my hands in hers. Zane, Adria, and Saharah walk into the room.

"What's happening?" Zane asked.

"I just contacted my mother. I told her help was on the way, and she told me they were there."

"Oh! That's good!" Zane sounded relieved.

"No, Zane! You misunderstand! Izrazyk is on his way too. I was cut off before my mother confirmed who had arrived, and she sounded panicked."

"Oh!" Zane sat on the bed. "I wouldn't worry, Willa. We know they have been preparing for this. Whether Izrazyk or the Sevifk show first, your mother, father, Tara, and everyone there is ready for this fight."

Tears sprung from my eyes, and I felt Zane's fingers grasp my chin. Zane tilted my head up and met my eyes with his silver that shined like armor reflecting the sun. He gave me a hopeful look, and I knew he was right.

"Have faith, Willa." I swallowed and nodded. There weren't many Hedrix who could have crossed over with Izrazyk. Still, they were a force to be reckoned with, and I didn't know what skills Tara's people had.

My mother had reassured me that they were excellent fighters. One of which was called Cannon, a demon slayer and Roman gladiator trained by Spartacus once upon a time. And Tara had bested him in her first training round.

There was hope. All I could do now was sit, pray and wait.

Chapter 17
TARA

Queen Of Hearts

The commotion that started outside the bar an hour ago died down. I sat in a chair with my wrists shackled to the table, defeated and in despair. I awaited the monster from my nightmares to come and collect his prize. We had put up a good fight, and now all was lost. Endless tears dropped onto the hard wooden surface where my family sat around me dead. Their hearts torn from their chests lay in a circle like a roulette table of death. Their bodies slumped in their chairs while their glazed eyes stared at their hearts in disbelief.

My father and uncles were no doubt fighting their way back from Purgatory to come and save me. But it would be difficult with their hearts outside their chests in a circle around me like a roulette table of death. Their bodies sat slumped in their chairs while their eyes stared at their hearts in disbelief.

I couldn't believe they'd turned on us. As soon as word got out that the Hedrix demons were coming along with their master in the flesh, the people we saved and called our friends attacked us. I knew it was out of fear of the master's retaliation, but why would they cower to him now with the news that his army was defeated in Hell? It just didn't make any sense.

I wanted to bang my head on the table to wake up from this nightmare. The problem was that I was wide awake. At least Danny had gotten away with Billie, Bren, and my mother. He'd taken them away on Neveah to hide them in the dream realm. I had no clue how he did it. I was just relieved to know they were safe.

I wish I had telekinesis so I could place my father's and uncle's heart back in their chests. I couldn't heal them without putting them back first.

After the fight outside and the slaughter that had ensued here, the people I once called my friends fled. The entrance door screamed on its hinges, and HE walked inside. His eyes went straight to mine, then my dead family seated around me, and he smiled.

"Hello, Tara! Having a rough night?"

I held his gaze but did not answer. What did he want me to say? *Yeah! Care to join me for a drink? Not happening, asshole!*

But then the Hedrix walked behind the bar and began making drinks. What would he make pray tell? Ahh! How predictable! Yep! I guessed it. Two Bloody Mary's! Fitting for such a time as this!

When Uncle Woody made it back, he would be pissed. There was blood everywhere. Two more Hedrix walked inside and took in the bloody scene. They spotted their master behind the bar and went to sit on barstools.

"Uh! Bartender! I'll take a double shot of whiskey on the rocks. He threw a pair of eyeballs on the bar, and the other demon beside him laughed.

"Good one, Malichi!" He patted him on the back like old pals having a night out on the town, then stood and went to the jukebox. He stopped at the table and looked at me with mascara running down my face and my hair disheveled. He poked at my father's heart, then the gaping hole in his chest, and sniffed his finger. He didn't say anything till he looked back at me and smiled.

"Why do you look so blue? This night should be the happiest one of your life. You are our queen, and you get to come back to Hell with us and begin your rule. Just look at that handsome man behind the bar making you a drink. He's the best guy I know and good with the ladies."

"Leave her be, Demetrius. She's grieving. It will take her some time to come around," Malichi said.

"How thoughtful of you to speak up for me, Malichuck! I never took a Hedrix for the sensitive, caring type," I spat.

The Hedrix master smirked as he poured whiskey for his buddies while Demetrius continued to the jukebox.

"That's my queen for you, Malichi! She has a sharp tongue. I'll have a fun time taming it."

"Lucky bastard!" Malichi spouted, and his master laughed.

"Tell me, my queen! Who do we have the honor of thanking for murdering your friends and family?" Malichi asked.

"That would be the Sevifk heathens your master sent the last time. We had captured most of them, but some got away and came back tonight to free them and take us out. Word must have gotten out about your arrival."

I wasn't about to tell these bastards that I had set the Sevifk free from their demonic curse, only to befriend them, train with them, feed them and teach them the ways of today's world. All that, just to have them turn on us and run at the last minute.

"And where are they now? Surely, they know that their master will reward them," Malichi said.

"I don't know! They chained me to this table, murdered my family before my eyes, and wished me luck with my king. Fucking assholes!"

Demetrius laughed. "You think she'd be more upset!"

He made a few song selections, and, You Make Me Feel Like Dancing began to play. "Man, I love this song!" Demetrius began to sing and dance along like the 70s had returned.

The Hedrix master rolled his eyes. He came around the bar and set my drink with a straw before me. He shoved Woody's body out of the seat and sat down.

"Drink up, love. I made this one special for you." He winked. The Hedrix waited for me to take a drink. I glared at him, and he set his glass down.

"Something wrong, Tara? Talk to me, sweetheart. I'm a good listener."

"What's there to talk about? My dead family and friends? Being taken against my will? To Hell, no less. Not my dream destination, by the way. At least take these damn shackles off my wrists!"

"Promise you won't run?"

"Where in the Hell am I going to go? Oh! That's right! Hell! With you! You've just made this night better! You showed up after the Sevifk made the job easy for you. And you made me a drink? How thoughtful!" I sneered

Demetrius came over, picked up his drink, tossed it back in one go, and sucked the air between his teeth. "Whoo-Wee! That's just about as snippy as she is!"

Malichi sipped his whiskey slowly and chuckled. Their master smiled at me. "My queen is displeased. I can take you anywhere you want to go, my love. Just name a place, and we can go right now."

"Purgatory! I'd rather be there with my family than go anywhere with you." I jerked on my shackles, making the table wobble and the hearts shift.

"Come now, Tara! You haven't even given me a chance! The world is our playground. You've been stuck in this miserable, backwoods town all your life, haven't you? Where would you like to go? Paris? Cairo? Tokyo? Honolulu?"

"The beach sounds nice," Demetrius said. He hiccupped and smiled. He began to giggle and wiggle his fingers in the air.

"What's wrong with you, Demetatrous, Demaruous, Demitree?" Malichi laughed.

The Hedrix master looked at them like they'd lost it. "I guess it's been a while since they've consumed alcohol in the living realm. My friends can't hold their liquor."

The Hedrix picked up his drink, took a sip, and then set it down. "Aren't you going to try the drink I made you?"

I looked at my shackles and tugged the chain for emphasis.

"Oh, yes! Of course! Let me get that for you, love!" The Hedrix slapped Woody's heart to the floor, and I winced.

He saw my reaction. "Sorry. Demetrius! Pick that up!"

"Yes, Master!" Demetrius got down on his knees, cupped his hands before Woody's heart, and made a forward scooping motion, pushing the organ and making it tumble away. He scooted on his knees and tried again with the same result.

The Hedrix shook his head. "Just pick it up, Demetrius!"

"I got it, Master!" Demetrius paused. "Ooh! Look at all the pretty little naked dancing fairies!"

Demetrius grinned and began to sway. He swiped at the air and then fell forward, face-planting on the heart with a sickening splat. Malichi laughed and nudged Demetrius with his foot.

"Get up, Demetritis!" Malichi slurred. He took another sip of his whiskey and barked out a laugh.

The Hedrix master reached across the table, tugged at my cuffs, and the shackles popped open. He took my wrists in his hands and rubbed them with his thumbs.

"As long as you are loyal and stay with me, you'll never be shackled again."

Even though he was tender, and it alleviated the soreness, I felt disgusted by his touch. I tried to refrain from pulling my wrists free from the Hedrix's hands.

Instead, I looked at him. "Might I inquire about my king's name?"

"You wish to call me by my name?"

"I do." I smiled.

He smiled back. It was dazzling. But, seeing past his beautiful cover, I knew what he was and what he's done, and it made my stomach churn.

"My name is Izrazyk."

"Iz-rah-zick?" I enunciated.

He nodded and smiled. I slipped my wrists free from his hold.

"Thank you, Izrazyk. It's nice to put a name to a face."

Izrazyk sat. "You're welcome, Tara. See how pleasant this can be for the two of us? You are a brilliant conversationalist. I imagine we will have many wonderful things on which to converse."

"Do you mind if I stand, Izrazyk? I've sat here for hours, and my ass has gone numb."

Malichi burst out in laughter. "Ass-numb! Frairies dancing!" His eyes wandered about as he looked up at thin air and sang, "Doo-da, doo-da, do!"

Another song came on the jukebox—a slow song, and I gulped as Izrazyk looked at me. He offered his hand. "Dance with me, my queen."

I nodded and slowly stretched my arm out to offer my hand. Suddenly the sound of a motorcycle pulling up outside made me pause. Izrazyk looked toward the window.

"Malichi! See who that is and send them away!"

"Yes, Master." Malichi stood up but then collapsed back into his seat. "Is someone on a motorbike."

"You didn't even see," Izrazyk said.

"I head, ur, heard though." Malichi began to sway.

The door burst open.

"THE ENTERTAINMENT HAS ARRIVED!" Martina sing-songed as she entered the room. She had on a honey-colored curly wig. Her sparkling purple jumper hugged her curves, and her rhinestone high-heel boots sparkled. She had on a red rouge and glossy painted lips.

Izrazyk's and Malichi's heads turned, and their jaws dropped. Martina looked our way and screamed. Her thickly long-lashed eyes widened in terror. Martina saw me, and she cried, "TARA! Oh, honey! You're alive!" Her heels clip-clopped across the floor as she ran toward me.

"You know this, woman?" Izrazyk asked.

I nodded and rose from my seat. Martina wrapped me up in a hug. "Oh, baby girl. Aunty Martina is here!" She backed away with her hands still on my shoulders and looked at me. "Are you alright?"

My lip quivered, and I nodded.

"What happened here?" Martina looked at my dead uncles and dad. She shivered and looked away from the carnage.

"We were attacked. Everyone is dead."

"Oh no! Oh, God! Oh!" Martina held me as I cried. She sniffed as she patted my head. Izrazyk cleared his throat, and Martina let go. She turned to look at Izrazyk and purred.

"Well, hello!" She eyed him up and down with an appreciative gaze and smiled seductively. "Aren't you a tall, gorgeous drink of Evian? Your mama and daddy must have been angels because you look like you fell from Heaven!" Martina walked over to Izrazyk, and he smiled at her.

"Sorry to disappoint you, sweetheart, but I came from the other direction," he said.

"Ooh! Well, I do love a bad boy!" Martina purred as she ran her long shimmery dark purple fingernail down the front of Izrazyk's shirt. He grabbed her wrist and pushed it away.

"I am here for my queen!" Izrazyk looked at me. "But I have an opening in my harem if you wish to join us."

"A harem?" Martina laughed. "Baby! I'm a queen too, and I just happen to have an opening I'm sure I can fit you in." She suggestively replied while eyeing Malichi, who tried to stand but fell back again.

"I'll be your harem, boy, baby!" He smiled.

"Oh, you'll do nicely!" Martina walked around Izrazyk as if he no longer mattered. But he smiled as he watched her ass sway. She grabbed a glass and the bottle of whisky and poured a drink.

Martina walked back toward us and winked at me. She swirled the contents in her glass as she stood before Izrazyk. Her tongue darted out, licked the glass rim suggestively, then pressed it to her bottom lip. She began to tilt the glass slowly to take a drink when Izrazyk swiped it from her hand, turned the glass so it touched his mouth where hers had been, and knocked the whiskey back in one go.

"Mmm! I appreciate a smooth drink as much as a smooth woman," Izrazyk purred. He grabbed Martina by the waist and pulled her flush to him. My eyes widened in shock as Martina laughed and wrapped her arms around Izrazyk's neck.

"Want to dance with me, sugar?" She smiled.

Izrazyk looked over at me, and I sat down.

"I'm not going anywhere, my king," I assured him.

Martina took Izrazyk's hand and led him out on the dancefloor. They assumed a traditional slow dance position. His other hand went around her back, pulling Martina close again. They began swaying together as one song ended and another began. Malichi pranced his fingers in the air and hummed along with the music.

"Pretty little fairies! Hmm, hmm, hmm!" He sang this repeatedly. Halfway through the fifth round, he slumped in his chair, unconscious.

Every so often, Izrazyk's eyes would look over at me. I put my elbow on the table, leaned my chin on my hand, and watched without a care as he continued to slow dance with Martina. She pressed her finger to his chin and turned him to look at her.

Izrazyk smiled. "You are a powerfully persuasive woman, Martina. I could use a lady like you in my court."

"Baby, I already told you I am a queen with my own court. My people love me."

"I am sure they do! Perhaps we can form an alliance. I may require your assistance in this realm. A favor from time to time." Izrazyk pulled Martina closer, and she gasped.

"Oh my! Aren't you a big boy!" Martina purred.

Izrazyk paused and grinned. "I feel you are hiding something from me, sweet Martina." Izrazyk's hand came down and groped Martina between her legs. Martina yelped, and the deep masculine undertone in her voice became apparent. She slid her hand down to take Izrazyk's and pulled it away.

"It seems you found out my secret, lover boy. Does it bother you?"

"On the contrary. I enjoy mixing things up from time to time."

"I can tell you do, sugar!" Martina batted her eyelashes, and her hand groped Izrazyk between his legs more forcefully.

He jumped, then laughed out loud. "Do you like what you feel?"

"I've never felt anything like it before. Shall we continue this dance in my boudoir? Martina purred.

My eyes widened, and I slapped both hands over my mouth to keep from dying of laughter. My eyes were watering with tears. Izrazyk looked over at me but more than likely mistook my tears for betrayal. He took Martina's hands and gently pushed them away.

"I'm afraid we must wait for another time, Martina. My queen has not had the pleasure of my company first, and I dare not disappoint her." Izrazyk stroked Martina's cheek and gave it a tender kiss.

"Too bad! I would have rocked your world, sweetheart." Martina scraped her nails along the rough stubble of Izrazyk's face. She pecked him on his lips and walked back toward me, smiling victoriously.

"Got him!" She mouthed silently.

I put my head down in my arms on the table and burst into laughter. From Izrazyk's perspective, it looked like I was sobbing. I knew this when I felt his hand rubbing my back in soothing circles. "Calm yourself now, my love. I would never be so unkind toward you."

What a dipshit! Everything he did to my family and me was horrendous. Not to mention all the poor souls he screwed over in Hell! Izrazyk was so blind that Noah's Ark must have crashed into his face and left one big ass splinter in his eye. When was he going to give already?

Izrazyk giggled, and I paused with hope at the sound. He chuckled again, and I lifted my head to see his fingers prancing in the air. Martina came up beside me, and I looked at her. She grinned at me and winked. "Any moment now!"

Izrazyk started cooing. "Ooh, little fairies. I'm going to get you! Yes, I am! Pinchy, pinchy, I got you're little sparklies!"

Martina counted. "One, two, and," Izrazyk toppled to the floor like a tower of bricks.

"Uhg! Finally!" I huffed. I stood up from the table and yawned. Dad, Woody, and Cannon stretched and groaned. Woody rose from the floor. Dad and Cannon stood up from their chairs just as Danny and Dean ran through the entrance.

Cannon clapped his hands and rubbed them together. "Well, folks! Who's up for shish-ka-bobbing some demons?"

Chapter 18
TARA

Never Bet On Red

The City Coroner van pulled up to The Roost in the early afternoon. Dean and I met Rosco as he opened the vehicle's back doors. There were three styrofoam coolers, and he passed the one to Dean and me and carried the third.

"Thanks for pulling through for us again, Roscoe. You're a lifesaver!" I praised.

"I'm not even going to ask what weird thing you're doing this time. How's the fake dead friend?"

"Alive and moody as ever."

We went inside and turned into the kitchen, setting the coolers down. Trey was putting the finishing touches on the prosthetics for the chest pieces my dad and uncles would wear.

"What are you working on?" Rosco asked Trey.

Trey turned around, looked at Rosco, and smiled. "You're the guy from the morgue, right?"

"Yep, Nice to meet you. My name is Rosco Bell. And you?"

"Trey D. aka Martina Dollyounce." Trey's deep voice rose several octaves whenever making introductions this way. Dean always thought it was funny because it reminded him of the fateful day they first met, and they've been best friends since.

Roscoe's eyes lit up. "Oh wow! I saw your video performance. You are stellar!"

"Thanks, sugar. As you may already know, Martina is great at theatrical makeup, but I'm having a tough time figuring out how to make a hole in a chest look authentic. Care to help?" Trey asked.

"I'd love to," Rosco said.

"Well, you two have fun. Dean and I are making the rounds to check on everyone," I said. As we left the kitchen, Rosco talked excitedly, giving Trey pointers, and they started laughing. I had a feeling there was a budding friendship in the works. Trey and Martina had a way of drawing people to them like a magnet. Or, in Martina's case, a moth to a flame.

Woody and Danny worked behind the bar while Stella and my mom were sprucing up the floor, moving the tables and chairs back to their original places.

"Is this a good spot?" Stella called.

Mom looked up at the hidden camera behind the bar and pressed her hand to an earpiece, listening to Billie's instructions. "Move it a little to the left."

"Hey, Mom." I went to hug her.

She wrapped her arms around me. "Hey, sweetpea. How are you feeling?"

"I'm good. Dean and I are going around checking on everyone." I looked over at Dean talking with Woody and Danny at the bar. Everyone seemed chipper today as we prepared for our unwelcome guests.

Mom looked skeptical. "Is that what you're telling everyone, Tara?"

I released a breath of pent-up anxiety. "I'm doing the best I can despite the situation. I think we have a good plan, and we'll pull it off."

"I can't help but worry about the worst-case scenario. I'm your mother; that's what I do. I have a lot of faith in you and everyone here."

"It will be okay. I'll be fine. I know it's not the ideal situation a parent could imagine for their child, but you taught me to be strong."

Mom kissed my cheek. "I love you, Tara. I believe you'll do a terrific job. We'll be breathing a sigh of relief and celebrating tomorrow."

"You're right. We will!"

Stella came and put her arms around us. "Billie just told me all the cameras are good to go, and she can hear everything we're saying. You're going to do good tonight, Tara. We've gone over every possible scenario, and every checkpoint is covered. There's no way you're going anywhere with that asshole."

"Thanks, Stella. Dean and I will see what it looks like on Billie's end." I walked to the bar, and Dean put his arm around me. Woody cut up some celery sticks, and I took one. Woody snatched the celery back and glared at me.

"Those are for the guests," he growled.

I tried to hold a straight face as he glared at me, but I burst into laughter. Woody chuckled and shook his head. He set out vodka, tomato juice, lemon juice, Worcestershire sauce, and other ingredients.

"Are we making Bloody Mary's?" I asked.

"Cannon said that demons like to mock people's grief. What better way to toast our deaths than with a Bloody Mary?"

"Sounds fitting," Dean replied.

Danny was straining the roots he used to make his fairie juice, then he added something smokey to it and restrained it. He cackled like an old witch and crooned. "Come along a have a drink, my little pretties! Eeh, hee, hee, hee!"

Dean and I laughed.

"Is that going to be strong enough to do the job?" Woody asked.

"I'm adding a neutralizer to remove the taste and smell. It won't affect the potency. And once I add it to the alcohol. The effect will hit those pesky little demons harder than little Tommy's baseball through the glass window next door," Danny said.

He put a funnel in the whiskey bottle, poured the root juice, and swirled it around. He sniffed it and smiled. He held it under Woody's nose. "Do you detect it?"

Woody took a whiff. "I think you did good, Danny boy! Hopefully, it won't take too long to knock them on their asses."

"Does everyone know not to touch that bottle?" I asked.

"I've got this." Dean typed a message on his phone and sent it out. Everyone had an alert app on their phones, so we could reach out with updates and send the alarm when the time came for the Hedrix's arrival.

Dean and I went to the cellar where Billie and Bren set up the audio/visual equipment. Billie watched Danny on the monitor and listened with headphones cupped over one ear.

"How's it going in here?" I asked. Billie held up a confident thumb as Bren chewed on hers nervously.

"We've got every angle covered, and we'll need to do a final soundcheck before tonight," Billie said.

"Are you okay, Bren?" I asked.

"Yeah, I'm fine. Just a bit nervous."

"Everything will be fine. We just need to work out the last few details. Everyone is doing a great job pulling this together."

I looked at the live feed on the monitor. The table where I'd sit was optimal for every camera angle. It was strange seeing the bar back to its original space again after everyone had removed their sleeping cots and personal belongings.

"I'm sorry, I will not be here for showtime. All the sights and smells will make me sicker than I already am," Billie said.

"Oh no! You're sick?" Bren asked.

"I've just been getting ill in the mornings," Billie replied.

"You're pregnant!" I blurted out. Billie smiled and nodded. Bren and I squealed, and Dean had to cover his ears. Bren and I hugged Billie.

"I'm going to have a baby cousin!" I cheered.

"This is so exciting! When did you find out?" Bren asked.

"Four days ago. I woke up violently ill, and Danny ran to the store to buy some pregnancy tests. They all came out positive." Billie said.

"What did Danny say?" Dean asked.

"He's ecstatic! He wants to go shopping for a minivan and add a sidecar to his motorcycle with a baby mobile of little Harleys hanging over it." Billie laughed.

"Have you talked about names?" Bren asked.

"Grayson Tyler for a boy and Thelma Louise for a girl."

"Like the two ladies in that movie where they die at the end?" Bren asked with a doubtful expression.

"No. I get it. Ride or die. But, just keep moving forward," I said.

"Exactly! Little Grayson or Thelma will ride with us everywhere we go. Our baby will be a traveler like their daddy," Billie said.

"Well, congratulations, Billie. Does Danny know you were going to tell us?" Dean asked.

"I told him. But don't tell anyone else. We're going to make an official announcement next week."

"Our lips are sealed." I hugged Billie.

Dean and I went to see Gina and Asher next. I could hear them arguing, which was their norm.

"Those aren't going to pass for human eyes, Asher. Here! Give them to me!" Gina leaned over to grab Asher's hand, and he turned, leaning away and extending his arm out of her reach.

"Just let me finish them, Gina! You're always taking my shit and telling me it's not good enough! I was good at making this stuff for Halloween when I was a kid!"

"That's the problem, Asher! It looks like something a kid would make!"

I interrupted their quarrel. "Hey, guys, just checking on everyone! I didn't know you were making props. I thought Martina had that covered?"

"She already has too much to do with your uncles and dads. Asher thought it would be a good idea to throw these out as a distraction," Gina said.

"That sounds like a good idea," Dean said.

"See, Gina! Dean agrees," Asher said.

"I never said I disagreed. I just think you should take them to Martina for some help," Gina said.

Asher got up. "Fine! I'll go. Happy?"

Gina smiled sweetly. "Very!"

Asher grumbled as he walked away. "The damned woman thinks she can criticize everything I do!"

"Asher, hold on," I called.

He turned around. "Yeah?"

"Rosco is helping Trey in the kitchen. You can ask him for help."

"I guess he would know better than GINA!" Asher said loud enough for Gina to hear.

"Whatever, Asher!" Gina flipped him off.

Asher jacked his fist up and down in the air. "I know you want me, baby, but you'll have to wait till later!"

Gina rolled her eyes but laughed.

"How are you two?" I asked.

"Getting along as famously as ever. Asher's such an asshole! I don't know how you dealt with him."

"The both of you are bullheaded, Gina, but I can tell he adores you."

"He's got a funny way of showing it. Why can't he act more like Dean? You got lucky, Tara!"

Dean laughed. "I have my moments too. Tara can tell you."

"Yeah. Dean has become full of himself when it comes to coffee." I laughed.

"Why is that a problem?" Gina looked confused.

"I'll explain it later. Did Alma go over everything with the group this morning?"

"Yeah. We have the app on our phones synched and ready to receive the alert when it's go time. Everyone knows where to go, and we will already be in position as soon as the assholes arrive."

"Perfect!"

"Oh, yeah, Tara! Alma wants to speak to you!"

"Okay. What's up, Alma?"

Alma's violet eyes flashed. "Tara. I wanted to help you prepare your mind for the Hedrix's arrival."

"Okay."

Alma took my hands. "You'll need to create a dialog in your head and convince yourself that your brothers and sister turned on you. They did so out of fear of the Hedrix's arrival. You will tell him of their betrayal, and we will provide the proof. The more you've convinced yourself, the more believable you will be."

"Okay. I can do that."

Alma froze and zoned out. Willa must be contacting her. He can't be on his way already? Can he?

"Tara!" Dean whispered. "There's rusting in the trees. Someone is here."

"Oh shit! Alma!" I shook her.

"Alma!" I tapped her cheek.

She blinked at looked at me. "I know, Tara. I just told Willa. It should be the Sevifk she just sent through."

"She sent more?"

Dean started typing on his phone and sent the message. "How many?"

"She said around eighty," Alma said.

"Eighty? We can't possibly get them on board with the plan in such a short amount of time!"

"Several people walked out from the trees covered in dirt."

A female Sevifk spoke. "We didn't realize it would still be daylight on this side when she sent us through. The others are still gathered and waiting back at the cemetery."

I sighed in relief.

"It's alright. We can make this work to our advantage," Alma said.

"What should we do?" the Sevifk asked.

Alma looked at me, and I shrugged.

"Let them come at dusk," Dean said. "We can split into groups and pretend to fight one another. We will need bodies to scatter around for the Hedrix to see and set traps to capture them."

"And what about the original plan?" I asked.

"We will proceed with that," Alma said.

She addressed the Sevifk. "Go and tell your companions this plan. The Hedrix master and his two higher guardsmen will not be captured. We already have plans for them. But first, we will put on a show for them."

The group of Sevifk bowed and took off through the trees.

"I had to cut Willa off. She must be fraught with worry," Alma said.

"Eighty! How will we accommodate eighty more Sevifk?" I asked.

"We'll figure it out after this is all over," Dean said.

"There will be hundreds more," Alma said.

My jaw dropped. "Hundreds?"

"Don't worry, Tara. They will not come all at once. Willa understands that accommodations and resources are limited. She will send them through a few at a time, and it will take time to find all of the lost," Alma explained.

"Oh! Phew! Well, that helps. I want to make sure they all make it home. Willa must be overwhelmed!"

"She is handling it well."

"I don't feel fit to be a leader like she is."

"But you already are, Tara. You may have had different experiences, but that doesn't make yours trivial. You were put in this place for a reason. And your role is just as important, if not more so. Never doubt yourself," Alma said.

"She's right," Dean agreed.

"Okay. I think we should tell the others it's crunch time. We need to be ready before dusk," I said.

Martina had an apron on as she helped my dad put his chest piece on. The shirt went over his head, and the gaping hole had to be adjusted to sit in the right place. But it looked right once dad pulled the long-sleeved button-up shirt over his shoulders. Rosco stuck around and was having a ball with Stella, and they got Cannon and Woody ready.

"Maybe we should put Woody under before we start splattering the blood everywhere," I suggested.

"If it's gonna look like I put up a fight here, I will spill my blood to make it believable," Woody said.

"I've seen loads of crime scenes and can tell you what looks real," Rosco said. He went into the kitchen and took out the containers of blood. Rosco passed out medical gloves, and everyone got to work creating a battle scene with the bar as our canvas. Blood spattered in patterns where it looked like fights had taken place. We made puddles and drag marks from those to the chairs and footprints trampled through the blood running out the door.

"Where should we put the hearts?" Martina asked.

"On the table in front of us. It adds insult to injury, and the demons will love it," Cannon said.

"That's brilliant," Roscoe said.

"Roscoe. You'd better go. Things are about to get real, and I don't need you getting caught up in the cross-hairs," Woody said.

"You're right. It looks like you all can handle it from here." Roscoe picked up the containers.

"I'll help you out with your supplies," Dean said.

Martina put on my mascara and filled my eyes with artificial tears. I followed her instructions. "Keep blinking, baby. Now rub your eyes up and down with your hands. Good! This will sting a little."

"What?" I asked. She dabbed something in my eyes, and they started burning.

"Ahh! What the hell was that?" I cried.

"Just a tiny dab of hot sauce! Your eyes can't be clear now, can they?"

"That shit burns, Martina! Get it out!" I cried.

"Baby girl! You need to look like you've been crying your eyes out! You'll have them bloodshot and tearing, and it will wash out. Now! I've got to get my glamour on, and I'll be here when the time is right. You've got this, Tara!"

Martina messed up my hair and then kissed my head. She grabbed her garment bag and went out the door. I hear her start up her Trike and drive away. Dean came in as Dad, Woody, and Cannon positioned their hearts before them. They poured the rest of the blood into the holes on their chest and dribbled it on the table, seats, and floor.

"It looks like we lost at Death's roulette table, boys," Dad said.

"Never bet on red," Woody said.

"I love you all! Thanks for doing this for me," I said.

"We would hug you, Tara, but." Woody gestured to his gruesome-looking chest. Martina and Rosco did a phenomenal job. Eat your hearts out, Hollywood horror prop masters!

"See you on the other side," Danny kissed my cheek, ruffled my hair, and headed out the door. I went around the table and kissed Dad's, Woody's, and Cannon's heads, and they smiled at me.

"You've got this, kiddo. We're here for you," Dad said.

I sniffed as real tears sprung from my eyes and nodded. "I know, Dad!"

"Ready?" Alma asked. She got them into position and began the hypnosis session. She dropped a crystal hanging from a chain above the table's center and swung it around in a circle. "Keep your eyes focused on the crystal and hear the sound of my voice. Good! As soon as I snap my fingers, you will fall into a trance and do as I say."

Cannon grinned. "I gotta say, Alma. Hypnosis has never worked on m...." Alma snapped her fingers, and Cannon zoned out. I looked at Dean, who snickered, and Alma continued.

"You will hold your eyes open and go into a deep sleep. Slow your breathing. Again, again, once more. Good! Your heart rate is decreasing. Again, again, once more. Good! If Tara should need your assistance, she will say the word 'nightingale' twice, and you will wake and jump into action. Otherwise, you will not wake till she says the phrase Uhg! Finally!"

My father and Uncles sat staring at their hearts with lifeless glazed eyes. The blood glistened from the gaping holes in their chests. It looked so real that I told myself it was in my mind, and I began to cry.

Alma guided me to my chair and shackled my wrists. "You are defeated, Tara. Your brothers and sisters have turned on you and murdered your family. Your father and Uncles cannot return from Purgatory with their hearts outside their chests. Some of the Sevifk that the Hedrix sent before got away and returned to free the others this night. A massacre takes place. NOW!"

A commotion of screams and fighting began outside.

"Good luck with your king!" Alma laughed evilly and kissed my head. She took hold of Dean's hand and pulled him away.

"I love you, Tara!" Dean yelled desperately.

The door closed behind them.

I screamed in agony.

Chapter 19
DEAN

It's Show Time

Leaving Tara behind felt like my heart ripped out of my chest. Alma pulled me through the door, and I heard Tara scream. It made me want to turn around and take her away and hide. But I knew she had to do this. Should the Hedrix try to run with Tara, her father and uncles would fight to the death. The dead would rise from the forest all around and circle them. I would jump through the portal to Hell and follow them.

The Sevifk fought Airmed's saved, and it was easiest to make out the newly risen covered in dirt and grime. Both sides could survive significant wounds, but they made superficial lacerations, shallow punctures, and deeper gashes. Alma ran into the fray, and I ran around back and came through the cellar door. I locked it behind me and took a chair beside Danny at the command center. I put in my earpiece, and we listened and watched the battle ensue. The Sevifk and Airmed's armies clashed and ran and chased each other, making loud battle cries. Many began to fall out.

I looked over at the screen where Tara sat sobbing and tugging at the chains of her cuffs. A U-bolt held the chain down to the heavy wooden top, so Tara could only move if she pulled the table with her.

"She will be okay, Dean," Danny said.

"I know."

"Look!" Danny pointed at another monitor.

A pinpoint of light pierced the darkness. It stretched into a vertical line, then out, like a doorway. The first Hedrix stepped through, followed by a dozen more. I waited on bated breath for the one fitting Tara's description, but two more came and gave a command. The first twelve took off in different directions.

"Where is he?" I asked.

"You're kidding me? Is this guy too much of a pussy to lead his troops?" Danny asked.

The last two stood guarding the portal, waiting as the others found the Sevifk and attacked. The odds were against them as the soldiers encountered groups with seven or more Sevifk to one Hedrix. They were ferocious fighters and took down some of the Sevifk before more came to aid those fallen. But the Hedrix became overwhelmed.

They ran, and the Sevifk made chase. They traveled beyond camera range, so Danny and I could see who was left. Bodies lay scattered everywhere. I couldn't make out Alma, Esaw, or Jeremiah amongst them, but I recognized a few of our people. Most of the bodies playing possum were the newly arrived.

"He's here," Danny said.

I looked at the screen where the Hedrix master finally stepped through the portal. He stood and surveyed the carnage with a smile and declared his victory. "This is our moment, brothers. Now I go to claim my queen! Check the grounds. She may be anywhere."

The portal closed behind them as they spread out to search. There was no movement around the three Hedrix as they stepped over, on, and around bodies. One of the demons picked up the fake eyeballs and chuckled. The master walked ahead and entered the bar.

He saw Tara sitting and crying, surrounded by her dead family members, and the smug look on his face made me want to smash it in with a sledgehammer.

"He's going to the bar. YES! We called it! He's making the drinks!" Danny held his knuckles up, and I fist-bumped him. The other two came in, and we watched the scene unfold. We had these fools convinced that Tara was the lone survivor of this massacre, and the Sevifk left her waiting for them on a silver platter.

The two lapdogs began laughing after one tossed the fake eyeballs down. They engaged Tara in conversation, and she had them eating out of her hands with the lies she fed them. Music played, and the first took the bait.

"Ha! Yes! One down! Two to go!" Danny clapped.

"He just drank it. It's not working yet," I said.

"It will. Just keep watching."

The Hedrix master set a Bloody Mary before Tara. Danny didn't spike its ingredients, so if she did drink it, she wouldn't succumb to the fairies' dance, but neither would the master.

The master pushed Woody out of his chair, and Danny and I cringed. We worried about the chest piece moving. If one of the demons turned him from his side, it would become evident that it wasn't real.

Tara kept focused, not giving anything away. Her performance was concise and so convincing that she had me believing everything she said. Danny was so impressed that he kicked back and watched the show grinning like a Cheshire cat.

"He's not taking her anywhere. We've already got his lackeys down for the count. Ha, ha! Look at the moron!" Danny laughed.

It was comical watching the first Hedrix called Demetrius trying to scoop up the heart only to faceplant on it instead. Danny and I were cracking up with tears brimming from our eyes.

Then Martina showed up, and her performance had us dying. The one called Malichi was just moments away from tipping while Martina played the master with her persuasive, seductive techniques. Her wicked mind tricks had him taking the bate with gusto.

"This is too good to be true!" I laughed.

"What fucking idiots!" Danny wiped at the tears as he struggled to contain his glee.

"Tara was right about him. He's the typical jackass, showing his cojones by knocking back a drink like some Don Juan De Gigolo. His balls must be bigger than his brain."

"Oh, look! Martina has our boy out on the dance floor," Danny pointed.

I laughed but then looked back at Tara as she sat at the table, bored and waiting for the fairy juice to kick in. The Hedrix groped Martina, but then she returned the favor, and her words had the idiot drooling like the dirty dog he was.

Tara laid her head in her arms and looked like she was sobbing, but I could tell she was laughing. Danny and I were rolling, nearly ready to fall out of our chairs.

The Hedrix dared to come and comfort Tara after his abhorrent display. He had no idea of what love or fidelity was. He only sought to satisfy himself.

The master suddenly toppled over, and Tara groaned, "Uhg! Finally!"

Richard, Wood, and Cannon woke up and began moving. I jumped out of my chair and ran back to Tara with Danny still laughing behind me.

Danny sang as he pulled the oars through the water.

"Row, row, row your boat.
Gently through the lake.
Shish-ka-bob, shish-ka-bob,
Shish-ka-bob, shish-ka-bob.
With demons, we will make!"

Cannon was feeding a thin metal cable between the Hedrix's cuffed wrists and ankles. The boat's bow bumped into the middle wooden cross Alma had erected while in her Sevifk demon form. We still hadn't figured out how she accomplished it, but it came in handy now.

Woody strapped the climbing spikes onto his boots and threw a strap around the tree trunk. He fastened it around himself and then climbed swiftly to the top. Woody towed the line with him, fed it through the pulley, and pulled it taut, letting the slack tumble down to Cannon, who began drawing the cable. Izrazyk's feet lifted, followed by his body.

Once, he was hanging upside down with his feet where Woody's had been when the Sevifk hung him; Woody wound the line around the cleat, then climbed back down, stopping to clamp the chains of the cuffs on the heavy-duty bolts that went all the way through the trunk. We looked up from the boat at Izrazyk dangling.

"I think that's a good place for him," Cannon said.

"Sweet dreams, lover boy," Danny called.

"Who knew shish-ka-bobbing demonic asswipes would be so fun," I said.

Danny laughed and patted my back. "Stick with us, kid. There will be many good times ahead."

"Since meeting all of you, I can honestly say these have been the best and worst days of my life," I replied.

"We understand. This is not our first rodeo dealing with monsters, but we're happy you and Zane came aboard," Woody said.

"Ditto," Cannon clapped my back. He anchored the boat up to the next cross.

"I believe this was mine," Danny said.

We repeated the process with Malichi, hanging him right side up, then moving to the last cross, hanging Demetrius the same way. Danny rowed the boat back to shore, where Tara, Richard, and Martina waited.

"You think that will hold them till sunrise?" Tara asked.

"They will be out for at least two days," Danny said.

"We'll do rotations keeping watch. I will set up camp and stay the whole time," Cannon said.

"We should decorate," Martina said. "You know! Wouldn't they look adorable with flower crowns and lays? Maybe some sparkle! Ooh, I know! I can make some mums! Those great big over-the-top ones like the high school kids do for homecoming."

We all started laughing. I could picture it now as I looked at the three demons hanging from their posts. They deserved much worse for the hell they put Tara and her family through. Especially the bastard in the middle. I wanted to be here when Izrazyk woke, but it wasn't part of the plan. I hated that Tara was going through this next phase mostly by herself, but everyone had their place to take to make it all come to completion. Martina would be with her and hopefully continue to keep the Hedrix subdued with her charms.

I held Tara to me, thankful that this night went perfectly. She was still here, safe. We returned to our cabin, and I made her some coffee and a loaded omelet. Afterward, we took a shower and relaxed in each other's arms.

"This night could have gone so differently," Tara said.

"But, it didn't. You, Alma, and Richard came up with a brilliant plan and executed it to perfection. You had me sold, and I don't fall that easily."

"I'm happy that everyone is okay."

"You're so selfless, Tara. You always think about everyone else first, and that's why they give their all for you."

"Dean. Do you notice how I always look to you when someone asks me a question?"

"I do. And I know it's not about you seeking my approval."

"It is, though, in a way. Mostly, it's because you are the best part of me. I don't believe I could have done any of this without you by my side. You're so supportive in everything I do and every decision I make. And I look to you because we are a reflection of each other's souls. My mind is already made up most of the time, but I still look at you, my reflection, to check myself. And when you nod, I know I have made the right choice every time."

"Tara. You are my inspiration, and your soul is what mine aspires to be. Everything you say or do fascinates me. I may be older than you in this life, but I believe your soul comes from another place and time where the wisdom of the ages has touched and blessed you."

"It must be because I'm Airmed's blessed." Tara smiled and averted her eyes in a way that struck me with curiosity.

"What?" I asked.

"I didn't want to believe it at first. But now, I've come to a point where I have finally accepted who I am. Dean, I know we were destined and mated to one another, but I want to ask you a question."

"You can always ask me anything, Tara. You know that."

Tara sat on her knees, took my hand, and looked at me, smiling with her beautiful Charlie brown orchid eyes. I adored this woman. She was everything to me, and there was something I wanted to ask her too.

"Dean Perrish! Will you marry me?"

I smiled. "I will answer your question, Tara, with a question of my own." I moved and pulled her to the side of the bed, then got down on one knee before her. I took my red ruby ring off my pinky finger and held it before her ring finger. "Tara Raybrook! Will you marry me?"

Tara's eyes watered, and she nodded. I slid the ring on her finger. "Then yes, Tara, I will marry you."

"Oh, Dean!" Tara cried. She threw her arms around me, and we kissed.

"You are my queen and no one else's. You rule over my heart, Tara. What is your first command?"

"My king. My first command is that you make love to me right now."

"Yes, my queen."

Chapter 20
IZRAZYK

Worst Hang Over Ever

My queen was a vision of beauty in a white fitted dress. She floated along in the boat, surrounded by water lilies and white orchids. I could smell the flowers now like they surrounded me. She sang with her beautiful voice like a little songbird.

"Mmm. Come to me, Tara."

She looked at me, smiled, and crooked her finger, beckoning me to her instead. I happily obliged. Wait! Something held me back! It was at my back, and I couldn't move.

"Wakey! Wakey!" her lovely voice called to me. I cracked my eyes open, and bright light blurred my vision. I blinked, and my eyes watered.

"Uhg, my head!" I rasped. My head felt like all the blood rushed to it, like the worst hangover ever! It felt like the world turned upside down, and when my eyes cleared and focused, I realized I was upside down.

"Ohh," I groaned. This was agony. What happened? Who did this to me? There will be Hell to pay once I stop hurting and figure it out.

"Yoo-hoo!" A feminine voice rang. I looked for the source, but all I could see were upside-down trees, the shoreline, and water.

"Down here, lover boy!"

I arched my head back and saw her. It was that woman from last night. The self-proclaimed queen. What was her name?

"Martina? What have you done to me?"

"Hello, baby. I thought you'd appreciate a romantic time out on the lake. Tara told me you showed her such a fabulous time here, and I thought I'd return the favor. You see, I am a jealous queen. How dare you take her out here before me!"

"Martina! Cut me down, and we can talk about this. I'm sure you'll understand once you see things from my perspective."

"Understand? Baby, I understand, all right! You want my sweet baby niece to go to Hell with you when you could have had me instead. A real queen!"

"Blazes, woman! You are not a real queen! Now get me down from here!"

"Oh, but I assure you I am. I can prove it to you too. I have over a million followers on all social media platforms. My people come to court and scream my name, excited to see me."

"Fine! I believe you! Pardon me, Queen Martina. Let me down, and I'll bow to you and kiss your feet. It is imperative that I find Tara. Time is of the essence. If I don't show my people their queen, my kingdom will fall to ruin—I, Uhg! Oh, my head! Please help me. My head feels like it will explode."

"I can't."

"What? Why not!"

"This is an Haute Couteur Qweenie original, and I would ruin my custom-made Louboutin's." Martina motioned to her off-shoulder, tight-fitted, multi-colored dress and matching high-heeled shoes. The sunlight bounced off it in a sparkling display, hurting my eyes.

"Dammit, Martina! Help me, and I'll buy you every damn dress and pair of shoes you desire!"

"You can't replace this dress! I told you it was an original!"

"AARGH! I DON'T GIVE A FUCK! JUST GET ME DOWN, YOU CRAZY BITCH!" I shook with rage.

Martina put her hand to her chest. "WOW! Don't you have a temper? I brought you out here for a nice time, and you dare to yell at me this way? Nope! Uh-uh! I'm out of here! You can tell your friends to help."

Martina pointed to my right and left and began rowing the boat away. I looked to my right and saw Demetrius hanging upright on a tree, then to my left was Malichi. They looked like they were dead.

They had crowns of orange roses with white baby's breath on their heads and large clusters of orange and white flowers, beads, and ribbons reading 'Go UT' hanging from silken cords around their necks. It was obscene and completely distasteful!

Martina's boat was farther away, approaching the shore. "Wait! I'm sorry! Martina, my love! Come back!"

She let one ore drop inside the boat and flipped her middle finger at me. Her long shining purple fingernail mocked me. Martina took off her shoes, stepped out of the boat, waded in the water, and pulled the line to dock to the boat onshore.

"Unbelievable!" I groaned.

Martina was cold and heartless and the kind of woman I could use on my side. I heard her speak to someone. "I can't deal with him anymore! He's all yours, baby!"

And that's when I saw her! A vision of beauty in black stepped out from the trees with her dark blond, sun-kissed hair flowing in the breeze. She had something in her hand. No, on her hand! And it shimmered in the light. She held it up, extending her forefinger before her lips in a hushing gesture, and she smiled. It was a piece of hand armor with a claw, a golden gauntlet claw.

"Tara!" I whispered.

Tara stood on the shore alone. I was desperate to go to her. I pulled on the chains at my wrists. The shackles were not like the ones I used. These were much stronger, slimmer, and more like a woman's bracelet. I struggled with them, but they had no give. A larger link went through them and an odd-shaped nail hammered through the tree. These were much more advance than anything the blacksmiths forged in Hell.

A strange break in the link had me curious. I molded my fingers around it, tugging. Then it occurred to me that it was a hinge. I pushed, and it collapsed inward. I was able to unhook it from the nail, and I laughed. My arms swung free, and I could lift them back toward my torso.

"What is that?" I felt with my hands, arched my neck, and saw a heart-shaped patch of orange and white flowers hanging in front of the crotch of my breeches. Martina must have done this! Her sense of humor might be hilarious if I weren't the brunt of her amusements.

I engaged my core muscles and slowly rolled my torso up, catching hold of a wooden crossbeam. The same linking mechanism held my ankles to another nail, and a metal rope fed through the chain.

"Izrazyk! What takes you so long, my king?" Tara called from the shore.

I smiled. My queen wishes to play games with me. I looked back at her standing on the lakeshore, watching me. I must make haste. I curled the rest of the way up, took hold of the metal rope with one hand, and unhooked the link.

I pulled myself up, taking hold of the rope with one hand. I unwound it from the cleat and gripped it tight as it became slack. I lowered myself, but there wasn't enough rope to make it all the way. Letting go of the remainder, it zipped through the pulley's wheel, and my body dropped fast, plunging headfirst into the water.

I righted myself and kicked my feet till I broke the surface. I lie on my back, floating and allowing blood to flow throughout my body. The pressure in my head subsided, and I felt relieved. I was a strong swimmer, so I had no problem kicking my feet simultaneously as I stretched my arms ahead.

I made it to the shallows quickly and stood. Looking back at Malichi and Demetrius still on their crosses, I had no time to help them. Nor could I with these confounded cuffs on my wrists and ankles. I would need to find a way to remove these, and then I would need to capture and detain my queen. I would send help back to my brothers.

I hopped the rest of the way out of the water and collapsed in exhaustion on the rocky shore. I'd never felt this tired before. What was in that drink? Looking up to the heavens, I saw an angel come to stand over me.

"You made it!" Tara smiled.

"I did! Well played, my queen. I suppose I deserved this for what I did to you before."

"So, you admit you went too far? It seems I have years of catching up to you for all the shit you put me through, Izrazyk. And since we'll have eternity together, there is no better time to get started than the present. Wouldn't you agree, my dear?"

"Alright! But first, would you happen to know how to remove my restraints?" I lifted my wrists to her; her laughter was melodious and sweet.

"Tsk, tsk, my king! You must abide by my rules now. No, I think you will wear those for a while. You'll grow to like them for what I have in store for you." Tara smiled mischievously.

She pulled out a slim device from her back pocket, pressed it with her fingers repeatedly, and then put it away. A loud engine came from the forest, and Martina appeared riding a motorcycle with a sidecar attached. She had changed into a tight black leather pantsuit with rhinestone boots.

"We are going on our first trip," Tara said.

"May I change out of my wet clothes?" I asked.

"Honey, you'll dry on the way," Martina said.

"Very well. Does this mean I'm forgiven, Martina?"

"It's not me you have to worry about, baby."

I pushed myself up to my knees and then stood. I hopped over to the sidecar, jumped in, and then slumped down into the seat. Martina put a helmet on my head, and Tara linked my wrist cuffs to a bar in front of me. Tara winked and blew a kiss, and I smiled at her. I'd play along for a little while if it pleased my queen.

I'd taken her father, held him hostage for years, and drained him repeatedly. I made the doctor my puppet, took her blood, and performed dreadful experiments on her. Then, I tested her with abysmal nightmares and made her friend shoot herself. Lastly, I sent my Sevifk demons to murder her family. I supposed I owed her this little moment of vengeance.

There was nothing she could do to me that would cause lasting damage, and I still planned on spanking her ass to a bright cherry red once we made it home. Then she'd play by my rules.

Tara got on the motorcycle behind Martina and put a helmet on. We took off through the forest, past the bar, and down a long drive that led to the open road.

Music played in my ears from my helmet. A man kept singing about his black magic woman, and I looked at Martina. She was undoubtedly magical. This song had to be about her.

"Where are we going?" I shouted.

"You don't have to yell. We can communicate through our helmets." Tara's voice came through like she was speaking into a microphone.

"Well?" I asked.

"We're going to see an old friend," Tara responded.

"Who are they?"

"Her name is Abigail."

"And she is an old friend or just an 'old' friend?"

"Does it matter?"

"I'm just making conversation. I want to know about the people in your life."

"You killed most of them."

"Is it too late to apologize? There's still a chance you can bring them back. If we can reach an understanding, I will allow it."

"How gracious of you, my king."

"I am nothing if not generous. You will see. We can overcome our differences in time, and you will come to love me, Tara."

"I suppose since I no longer have a choice in the matter."

"You will have many choices, my love. Once I show you the magnificent picture of the future we will have together, your power will be the element that binds us and builds trust between us. We will create a better world."

"How much say do I have in our grand conquest?"

"My dear, you hold all the cards. I merely mean to teach you which ones to play."

"I love a good card game. But I'm capable of playing my hand the way I see fit, and right now, this queen is dealing with her king in the same manner."

"Ooh, so witty! You must be the queen of hearts. You are certainly holding mine in your hands."

"Nope. I am the queen of aces. I rule over the whole deck."

Martina laughed. "Whoo-wee! My baby girl got that sharp tongue from her auntie. You tell him, Tara."

I laughed. I hadn't had such a stimulating conversation in ages. Perhaps I was overdue for a vacation. I enjoyed watching a good battle, and sparring with Willa was fun, but Tara sparred with me with her sharp tongue, and I couldn't wait to have a taste.

Chapter 21
IZRAZYK

Time To Wake Up

After an hour's worth of slapstick banter, we arrive at a little blue house with a bright yellow door. The front garden had a multitude of flowers thriving in the cold weather. Someone had a mighty green thumb, indeed.

Tara came around to me. "I will release your feet so you can walk. Once inside, you will sit, and you'd best behave yourself in front of Abigail. She may look frail, but she is a special lady and dear to my heart. She is off-limits! Understand?"

I bowed my head. "No harm will come to your friend."

Tara produced a small key, unlocked the cuff from the bar, and released my ankles. We walked beneath a trellis, up a path, and reached the yellow door. Tara brushed past me with her body and pressed the doorbell.

"I'm coming!" an elder-matronly voice called.

The door opened and a petite old-aged woman wearing a blue housecoat and pink rollers in her silvery hair smiled.

"Tara! Oh, honey! I'm so happy to see you. Oh, and you brought new friends to visit. Come in. Get out of the cold."

Tara hugged the lady. "Thank you, Abigail. It's good to see you. I was worried when you didn't answer your phone the last time I tried to reach you."

"Well, you see me now, and I'm fine! Come in and have a seat. Tell me who your new friends are."

Martina and I sat on a dated couch, and Tara sat in a chair opposite the wooden rocker, where Abigail creaked and groaned as she sat down. I smirked because humans were pathetic beings who lived short insignificant lives and grew old and grotesque in such a short time.

The old woman looked at me and seemed puzzled. "Do I know you from somewhere?" she asked.

"I am afraid not. I'm not from around here."

"Abigail, this is Izzy and my auntie Martina," Tara said.

I scrunched my brows together. "Izzy?"

Tara laughed. "Yes, Izzy!"

"It's nice to meet you, Izzy and Martina. Are the two of you a couple?" Abigail asked.

Martina looped her arm through mine. "Why yes! Yes, we are! And I am so pleased to meet you, Miss Abigail! Tara has told me so much about you."

"How kind of you to say, Martina. And might I say you have quite the flair for fashion, dear. You exude class and fine taste, and you've fetched yourself a most handsome and dashing man."

I flashed Abigail my megawatt smile. "I can see why our Tara has taken such a liking to you, Abigail. Your eyes see very well."

"For an old lady, I suppose they do. But these eyes see more than you could ever know, Izzy. Tara, if you don't mind, I'd like to show your friend something interesting."

"No, I don't mind at all, Abigail. May Martina and I come with?"

"Of course, honey. I know you'll love this too. I'm sure you'll get a kick out of it," Abigail chuckled.

Abigail got up and shuffled along in her yellow slippers. We followed her down a hallway, and she turned into another room. Tara, Martina, and I piled into a heaping landfill of old junk.

"Over here," Abigail called from inside a closet, and Tara went inside.

"Come on! All of you!" Abigail motioned with her hand, waving at us to join her.

"Why are we going into a closet?" I asked.

"I don't know, honey, but I came out of mine a long time ago." Martina grabbed my arm and pushed me ahead, and we squashed together like sardines.

"What is this?" I asked. The old lady didn't answer when she reached up and pulled a string and the light shut off. It was so dark that I couldn't see anything in front of me. It became quiet, and I felt alone with no one around me.

"Hello! Where is everybody?" Crickets chirped, and stars and constellations appeared in a vast night sky. I remembered seeing these a long, long time ago. A bright moon appeared as if someone had flipped on a switch, and I stood in a garden.

Memories flooded in, and I remembered a little boy running around and chasing away the rabbits that would nibble upon the leaves of the different plants. The fragrant smells hit my nose, and I knew where I was.

"NO!" I shouted.

"Yes! Hello, Izrazyk," came a voice I remembered from ages ago.

"Mother?" Abigail appeared before me, and I was confused. But then her appearance changed. She grew young and beautiful and gained a few inches in height. Her hair turned dark and dropped down in long loose curls. Her eyes, like mine, glowed with an ethereal sparkling blue. Her robe and slippers morphed into a regal blue, flowing gown and shoes made of silk with embroidered green vines and yellow flowers.

I fell to my knees in shock.

Her hand pressed down upon my head. "It's time to wake up, Son."

"But I am awake!"

"No. You are not! WAKE UP, wake up, wake up…….." Her voice echoed and became Tara's. My eyes cracked open, and I moaned. My arms and legs stretched outward, my wrists and ankles restrained, and something wrapped around my waist, holding my torso bound against a hard surface.

Tara was standing in front of me. Behind her were the men who'd been dead at the table, and I recognized Tara's father. The men crossed their arms and smirked. Behind them were a crowd of people and Sevifk demons occupying recently risen flesh. They all glared at me with malice and vengeance in their eyes.

"Enjoy your trip?" Tara asked.

"Where am I?"

"On my family's land. Did you have pleasant dreams, Izrazyk?"

"My mother."

"Is not here. I can see the appeal of invading someone's subconscious, snaring their minds with trickery. Although, I've gone much easier on you than you did me."

"Fine, Tara. You made your point, and I went too far. I thought we reached an understanding."

Tara crossed her arms and gazed quizzically at me. "What understanding did we reach, Izzy? It was your dream, and it seems you made my mind up for me. I don't think I've truly had my say in anything. Look around you! Everyone here never had a say, either. You took something from all these people you see before you."

I looked at the crowd gathered in a semicircle around us. Two voices were yelling, and the crowd parted as Malichi and Demetrius were rolled toward us from either side, mounted and shackled on a wooden X the same as I. We'd been tricked! Our drinks were tainted with something powerful enough to knock out demons. I would applaud my captors, but.

Tara began to speak. "Today, Izrazyk, Hedrix Master of the Syadestese Kingdom, stands accused of tyranny and war crimes, usurping power from Airmed's children and the Necros, premeditated seizure of the realms, murder, kidnapping, theft, torture, slander, public executions of the innocent, trickery, and forced mental trauma. How do you plead?"

I smiled. "You think your little trick will have me pleading for mercy, Tara? I haven't taken anything that wasn't mine from the beginning. Your goddess stripped away my powers. I was only reclaiming what was mine."

"So you say. But does that give you the right to start a war and steal power from others? You admitted you went too far."

"With you, Tara. I went too far with you. Everyone else is inconsequential."

Growls and shouts came from the crowd behind Tara. "GUILTY! MURDERER! THIEF! MONSTER! HE MUST DIE! KILL HIM! KILL THEM ALL!"

"It seems the jury has spoken." Tara walked away from me and approached her father. He opened a purse, and Tara reached inside. She pulled out a golden object and slid it over her right hand. I remembered seeing it before. Where?

She turned around and held her finger up to her lips in a hushing motion, and I remembered. I thought I'd been awake, hanging upside down from the cross on the lake. She stood on the shore and made the same motion wearing the golden gauntlet claw.

"I call forth my witnesses. The Sevifk soldiers forced to fight against their will in a war, not of their making. All because, Izrazyk, the Hedrix Master, took away their families and threatened their lives."

"It wasn't like that!" I yelled. "I made a deal with them. Once the war was over, I promised to return their family members and give them land and titles. They grew impatient and turned on me."

"Was that the way of it?" Tara asked.

A Sevifk woman stepped forth. "He lies! He stole everything from us! The only deals he made were in his favor. He took our children and threatened to torture them if we did not bow and fight for him. He turned us into demons against our will and drained most of our power. We never wanted to be like this!"

Shouts of agreement rang through the crowd, and Tara quieted them down by raising the gauntlet in the air. "Today, I will free you from your demonic bindings, brothers and sisters. Step forth and let your master see!"

"No one can undo the spells I cast except me," I said.

Tara turned her head and spoke with an authoritative tone that brokered no argument. "Let me show you what I can do, Hedrix Master."

I smirked at her. Whatever display of tricker she planned wasn't going to sway me in the slightest. The Sevifk came forward. There were eighty who formed a circle around Tara and kneeled. They bowed their heads, beat their fists to their chests, and hooted in salute to my queen. I didn't mind. I would have them do this myself.

Tara raised her gauntleted hand to the sky. "By the power vested in me by the Goddess Airmed, I now free every soul before me of their Sevifk bindings.

The Hedrix Master no longer holds them or their loved ones captive. All shall be free by the first blood I draw with this claw!"

Tara approached the woman who spoke against me. She would be the first to die by my hands.

"I ask that all place your right hands on the shoulders of the person next to you," Tara said. They did as she asked, creating a complete connection around the circle.

"Place your left hand in mine," Tara instructed the female Sevifk. The demon obliged, and Tara pressed the claw's sharp blade to her flesh, making a small scratch. A golden light entered the woman and surged throughout her body. It then traveled to the next demon and zipped around the circle in seconds. All of the bodies jolted, and they gasped as dark matter escaped their mouths like a horde of gnats, which fell to the ground dead.

I was shocked beyond belief as I watched my Sevifk soldiers transform. Their auras glowed with a brilliant light, and their demonic features disappeared. They looked fully human once more, and I realized that the other people behind them were from the first wave of soldiers I'd sent when I took Tara the last time.

I was furious when I realized Willa must have sent these Sevifk soldiers through. They were part of the ruse, the battle on Tara's family land, and the dead bodies scattered amongst the forest before I entered the bar. It was all a trick, and I fell for it. I was ashamed of myself for being such a fool, blinded by my beautiful queen in her moment of feigned despair.

And Martina! She was as good as dead!

I heard Malichi and Demetrius whimpering in fear. I looked at them, and they gave me a wary look. The transformed people rose to their feet and gathered around Tara, praising her and kissing her hands. They went back out to rejoin the others.

Tara's family came back to stand behind her as she approached Demetrius next. She raised the claw to his chest, and he broke down like a weak, sniveling child. Tara spoke. "You have stood by your master and committed crimes by his command and name. How do you plead?"

Demetrius sobbed. "I'm sorry! Please spare me, my queen! I will bow and serve you. I will go and make things right."

Tara seemed to consider Demetrius's words for a moment before saying, "If I free you and send you back to Hell, the Sevifk and Necros will hunt you down like the vile pig you are. Is that what you wish?"

"Please, my queen! Give me a chance!"

"You are a coward, Demetrius!" Tara shouted. "You wouldn't be brave enough to stand before all you have wronged and apologize. You would run for your life. What good would that do anyone?"

Demetrius looked to the crowd. "I am sorry! To all of you! I vow from this day forward to make things right! Please spare me! I beg of you!"

The people booed and spat at him.

Tara cupped her hand to Demetrius's cheek. "Why so blue, Demetrius? Now that you see your death before your eyes, you now wish to make amends? You never provided this kindness to those in your current position. Why should they spare you now?"

"Because you are a benevolent queen. You are kind and merciful! I seek to do as you command. I pledge my allegiance to you and all of Airmed's children. Please!" Demetrius cried.

Tara looked into Demetrius's eyes. "I will do you this kindness and spare you from an eternity of misery, Demetrius. You will begin anew and become the seeds of forgiveness and healing. You will spread far and wide. Fruit will grow from your branches, and the people will partake of your generosity. They will smile and give thanks as they pluck your offerings."

"Oh! Thank you, my queen! Please! I wish this so. I will do this for you and your people." Demetrius bowed his head.

"That is very gracious of you, Demetrius." Tara kissed Demetrius and then pressed the claw's blade to his forehead. Light entered through the small cut. Demetrius's body jolted, and he looked up to the sky as the light surged and glowed through his veins. He screamed just before his body burst into thousands of golden seeds that rained to the ground. The people ran and scooped the seeds with their hands, cheering and laughing with glee.

Malichi screamed in terror and struggled against his restraints. My heart was slamming inside my chest. Was this to be my fate? Tara's eyes watched mine as she walked toward me. I looked at her and shook my head.

No! Please! Do not stop before me!

Tara had the power I craved, and my mother had given it to her. As she came closer, I felt an emotion I had never felt before.

FEAR!

My queen has the power to destroy me!

But she did not stop before me. Instead, she continued to Malichi, who shook his head and cried. His trousers had become wet from pissing himself in fright.

"No, oh, oh, oh!" Malichi cried pathetically.

"And what say you, Malichi?" Tara asked.

"I am guilty, my queen. I am not worthy of being the dirt beneath your feet. I pledge my allegiance to you and your people. I will go forth before them and make my apologies. I will help rebuild their communities with my hands. I will make things right."

"And who will go forth with you and witness you fulfill these promises? If you choose one from the crowd willing to go and vouch for you, I will set you free to do so."

Everyone froze, and Malichi looked at the crowd. His eyes scanned with pleading desperation, but no one held his gaze. They turned their backs to him, and he began to sob.

"I think the people have spoken. It seems they distrust you and your word. Have you ever made such promises to them before this day?"

"You are right, my queen. I have not. I am truly sorry."

"No, you are not!" I growled. "Before today, you sought the same as I, Malichi. You hungered for our victory. You wanted a realm of your choosing to govern so the people would bow and snivel at your feet! How dare you stand against me now?"

"Those are the first words from your master's mouth, I believe," Tara said.

"Izrazyk is no longer my master! I DENOUNCE YOU! DO YOU HEAR ME? My allegiance is to my queen! Please! I beg of you! Spare me! I will hold to my word."

"You're a fucking coward and traitor, Malichi! I hope she kills you!"

"Is this what your wish, Izrazyk? For me to kill your friend?"

"I see what you're doing, Tara. And I commend you. Go ahead and kill, Malichi. You'd be doing everyone, including myself, a favor."

Tara whipped her head dramatically and scowled at me. "I feel we've reached an impasse. As much as Malichi's pleas tug at my heartstrings, maybe I should take into account the time you made my best friend kill herself. Perhaps I should repay the favor!" Tara held the golden claw up and drew closer to Malichi. He began panting and shaking his head.

"NO! NO!"

Tara stopped. "No?"

"I'm sorry, I'm sorry, I'm sorry!" Malichi trembled.

"Fucking coward," I smirked.

"Hmm! No, Malichi, I won't kill you, but I will show you something. Then I will send you on your way back to Hell, where the people will decide your fate." Tara lifted her gauntlet before Malichi's face and prayed. "Goddess Mother, let Malichi see. With my touch, be it so times three."

Tara pressed the claw to the bridge of Malichi's nose between his eyes. The light entered him, and his body jolted and constricted. His eyes glazed over with a white film, blinding him to the world around him. The muscles and veins in his neck strained and popped, and he let out the most deafening and terrorizing scream I'd ever heard. His body shook, and he foamed at the mouth, groaning in so much pain that I wished she'd just kill him already. Was this what she would do to me?

Eventually, he stopped and slumped unconscious. Then instantly, Malichi poofed away, followed by the echoes of his screams. The crowd cheered, and I growled and snarled at them.

I looked back at Tara. "Is this to be my fate?"

Tara moved to stand before me and slowly shook her head. "You know, Izzy, I planned to kill you, but I received a phone call yesterday from my friend Abigail. She implored me to spare her son. I didn't know what she meant at first. My father knew her son, who had passed long ago. But she explained something to me. It seems this wasn't her first son, but he was her first and only born in this realm. She admitted she had another she'd lost due to his grave betrayal.

Izrazyk, you did come with me to Abigail's house, and we did go to her secret garden, where she revealed her true identity. I didn't realize it would be this. That she was the one who knew who I was all along. She was the one who blessed me and the many generations before with our gifts. The gifts you sought to have all to yourself and use for the wrong purpose."

I was seething. How could these women turn against me like this? First, Airmed, my mother, stripped me of what was mine by birthright. Now, my queen dares to stand here and lecture me on right from wrong? I was wronged! All I did was reclaim the power stolen from me. I was cursed by my mother never to contain the power of the necromancer light ever again.

"You still think you were the one wronged. You wanted to use me as your puppet, take my gift, and use it for your selfish conquest. Allow me to show you the damage you've done and have yet to do if all your plans come to fruition."

I stared Tara down. "Do your worst! I do not fear what you wish to show me."

"Very well, Izzy. You can still ask me to go ahead and kill you instead. I'm only doing this as a courtesy to Airmed. She understands that if I cannot convince you, your death will become a loss she must bear. She is the only one who will grieve your passing."

"I highly doubt that." I sneered. Tara nodded. She reached up with the golden claw, and I held her big brown eyes with mine. Her eyes, the last vision of beauty I would behold before my death.

Tara touched the blade to my head, and I felt the sharp sting as it broke my skin. The warmth of the light entered me, and I gritted my teeth as my whole body locked up and began to seize uncontrollably.

A magnitude of visions and emotions hit me at once, seizing my heart and invading my soul. I felt a rush of pain so intense I thought I'd vomit my insides out. The cries and screams of thousands ravaged my throat past the point of burning raw. My heart throbbed painfully, and my head seared in anguish as I felt their misery.

Every bone in my body broke repeatedly. I was stabbed, sliced, poked, prodded, and cut by thousands of knives and swords. The feeling of my limbs chopped and torn from my body made me crumple and cry out in agony.

But it didn't stop there.

Sharp pains struck my neck repeatedly as I was beheaded again and again. Splints shoved beneath my bloodied fingernails. Hot pokers pierced, burned, and blinded my eyes. Iron spikes impaled my flesh. Vices gripped, crushed, and broke every bone in my hands and feet. Flesh was severed from my body.

My arms and legs stretched and tore away from my torso as I was quartered and drawn repeatedly. The pain of thousands of experiences of every conceivable form of torture racked my body again and again and again.

The painful hollowing pit in my stomach from starvation, illness, and mental and physical fatigue of every soldier hit me with excruciating agony. Their heavy-laden, weary thoughts weighed down my mind, ready to give up and die, too tired from fighting for so long. The pain in my feet felt like I had marched thousands of miles on thin skin, nerves, and bones. The rot and stench from their bodies and infected wounds permeated my nose, making my stomach roil. Insects bit and feasted on my festering flesh.

The raw grief of every mother, father, brother, and sister's soul rolled through mine as I saw the deaths of their loved ones through their eyes. It consumed me as their loved ones' deaths felt like my own, and I experienced every one of them.

I felt the violation and mental trauma of the thousands who experienced forced sexual acts against their will. Then I heard the echoes of every crying child torn away from their mother's and father's arms.

And finally, I saw a man who stood over a burning kingdom of blood, bone, and ash. He stood alone and purveyed the destruction with a wicked smile and a twinkle in his blue eyes. I realized that man was me, and I cried out to him.

"WHAT HAVE YOU DONE?"

He looked at me and said, "We are not finished yet."

His queen screamed and ran at him with a knife. He slapped it away and yanked her around by her hair like a ragdoll. He struck her face so hard it knocked her to the ground.

"You defy me at every turn, Tara. It is time I teach you a lesson you'll never forget!"

"NO!" She screamed and held up her hands to defend herself.

The monster grabbed her wrists and slapped her again. Her cheeks and eyes began to swell, and she cried. He tore her dress open, revealing a battered canvas of black, blue, purple, and red. She grabbed the sides of her dress to cover her nakedness.

"Please, my king!" she sobbed.

"YOU MADE ME THIS MONSTER! You no longer give yourself to me, and you no longer share your power!"

"Don't you see what we have done? All the people we raised from the dead? The worlds are in misery! People have gone mad because we ripped their souls away from their peace! The wealthy have grown wicked with idle hands, and the poor wander the streets in worn-down flesh. We have not done humanity a favor by extending their lives! The realms are overwhelmed with a mass populace their worlds cannot support. It was never supposed to be like this!"

"I no longer care! They all bow to me! You will give me what I want, or I will take it from you!"

He pushed her down and exposed her body. She threw her fist, screaming and pleading for him to stop. He went to pull his flaccid member from his pants and tried to get it to rise. When he grew frustrated, his hands wrapped around her neck and squeezed. Her arms and legs flailed. Her eyes bulged and became bloodshot, and her lips turned blue.

Then it was like their souls switched bodies, and I became her, looking up at an evil, demonic beast whose face was red with rage. He was hideous and frightening, with his veins popping and muscles straining.

His red-veined eyes spoke volumes of wrath and hatred. His teeth gritted, and drool fell from his mouth, landing on my face. I felt the pain in my neck as his hands squeezed tighter, cutting off my air, and burning my lungs. I felt my death coming, and I welcomed it.

Her thoughts became my own.

I never loved you! You always forced me and took everything. You are a vile, decrepit beast, a plague to all humanity. Go ahead and finish me, you disgusting pig. I'd rather be dead than spend one more second with you.

The visions released me, and my throat strained as I sucked in air and then screamed. "NOOOO! ENOUGH! I don't want to see it anymore! Please! I beg of you!" I broke down and sobbed in heart-wrenching despair.

Tara stood before me. "Isn't that what all those people said to you? When will everything you've done to them be enough? When will they no longer see the torture and deaths of their loved ones? When will they no longer experience the pain and misery delivered by your command? When, Izrazyk?"

"I, I'm sorry!" I sobbed. Guilt and shame consumed me. "I see, and now I know. Please forgive me!"

"Are you truly sorry, my son?"

The crowd gasped and cried out in awe. They dropped to their knees, and I saw my mother, the Goddess Airmed standing beyond them. The crowd parted as Airmed walked toward Tara and me. Her long blue dress glided as she moved like she was floating on air. Her long, dark hair flowed, lifting and waving, caught up in the breeze.

"Thank you, Tara, for sparing my son and bringing him home."

Tara bowed. "You are welcome, Goddess Mother."

The restraints broke away from my wrists, ankles, and midsection, and I fell forward on my hands and knees. I bowed my head and cried.

"Mother! I am sorry!"

"You have much to be sorry for, Izrazyk. This moment is where you make a choice. You can continue on your path, and Tara WILL defeat you, and you will die. Or?"

I rose to my knees and looked at the two women. "Please, go ahead and kill me. I deserve to die."

"You do not get to choose the easy way out of this," Tara said.

I looked at her. "Then what would you have me do?"

My mother aided me to my feet and dried my tears. She took my hands and cupped them together. A shower of golden seeds poured from her hands into mine. "It is time to return what you have stolen, my son. Go forth into the garden and sew these seeds of healing."

Everything faded around the three of us, and we stood in my mother's midnight garden. Airmed walked by my side and Tara on the other. Tara cupped her hands before me, and I poured some seeds into hers. We walked down the moonlit garden path casting the golden seeds across the rich dark soil. The seeds burrowed into the ground, and new life sprouted and bloomed.

A heaviness lifted from me, and I could breathe again. I saw the error in my thoughts and intentions, and my mind renewed. I also realized that people hated me. Tara was ready to kill me but spared me instead. What would happen if I dared to show my face again? I could no more ask for forgiveness than all the people I hurt would willingly give. No, I deserved to die.

I no longer wanted Tara's power because I would never use it responsibly. I knew she didn't love me, and no woman ever would. I didn't feel worthy of love, yet my mother showed it unconditionally.

How did I begin to make things right? I'd done so many horrible things. Greed, envy, and hate blinded me, and the woman who should have ended me opened my eyes.

"What should I do now?"

My mother handed me a sizable bag filled with more golden seeds. "You must return to Hell, stand before your people, plead their forgiveness, and vow to make amends. You will plant these seeds, and your hands and feet will toil, crack and bleed from the pain you've caused. You will help rebuild, restore and replenish all you've taken and destroyed. The seeds you have just sown have started the process."

Airmed selected five plants from the newly formed blooms and gave them to me. "Go back with Tara and present the first to her family. The second, you will present to Willa. The third will go to the Sevifk and the fourth to the Necros."

"And the fifth?" I asked.

"You will plant it in your city and give the citizens a choice. If they choose you to remain their sovereign, your city will become a haven for lost souls, and evil will not exist inside its walls. It will be impenetrable to all dark forces that seek to harm."

"What will happen to my people if they do not choose me?"

"That is up to them. But you will leave the city in peace. Once you have finished your duties, you will have a place in my home if you wish. "

I bowed to my mother. "I will do these things and more. I will make amends and establish peace. I will give up my life should the people I have wronged deem it so."

"Rise, my son, and begin your new journey." Airmed took my face in her hands, and tears brimmed her eyes. "I have waited centuries for this day. I hoped you would come to see this on your own much sooner. Pride, envy, greed, and malice overtook your heart and ate away the purity of your soul. I chose well when I blessed Tara. She had the foresight to delay the punishment you deserved. She would have defeated you and your armies, but it would have taken so much more from each side and caused insurmountable damage. I had to show you. You had to see what would have resulted had you continued on the wrong path."

I placed my hand over my mother's and nodded. She brought me down and placed a kiss on my forehead.

"I love you, Izrazyk."

"I love you too, Mother!" My voice choked with the emotion I hadn't felt for far too long. Love!

"Are you ready?" Tara asked.

"I am." We returned to Tara's family, and I dropped to my knees and held the first bloom before Tara's father. I waited for him to strike me, stab me, shoot me, kill me. He just looked at me like he felt sorry for me. I swallowed thickly.

He reached forward with something in his hand, and I recoiled. He handed me a small shovel and pointed. "You can plant it over there in front of that cabin."

I nodded and got up. Tara followed me, and I dropped to my knees again. I broke the soil and dug a hole. I pressed the roots down in the ground, returned the loose dirt, and patted it down. Tara went to fill a watering can and brought it back to me. I stood and poured the water till the can was empty.

"You're on your own from here," Tara said.

I nodded. "Tara. I'm so sorry. I don't deserve your forgiveness."

"No. You don't. But, if I hold on to the pain and anger, I will never move on. So, do me a favor, Izzy. Accept when I say I forgive you. I hope going forward you will see that bearing a grudge turns a person into a potato."

"A potato?"

"A potato can't sit around in a dark place forever. It begins to rot, and all those black spots grow inward, making it no good to anyone. People toss bad potatoes. They don't want to keep them around."

"I was a very rotten potato."

"Before you go. There's someone else you should apologize to."

"I'm ready." I followed Tara down a path, and people stopped in their work, staring as we passed. I felt so small under their scrutinous gazes. Any moment someone was bound to come at me and kill me on the spot. But no one moved. They looked away and returned to their work.

Tara knocked on the door of a small dwelling, and a young woman I recognized answered. She smiled at Tara, and then she looked at me and frowned. A man stepped up behind her and put his hand on her shoulder.

Shame hit me, followed by the memory of the pain I'd caused for the four souls I saw within these two bodies. I'd forced Gina to shoot herself. I recognized Alma's violet eyes as they flashed before me, and I saw Esaw's soul with Asher's. I didn't know how this came to be, other than Tara's power must have made this happen.

"Gina, Asher, Alma, Esaw. Izzy has something he would like to say to you," Tara said.

I bowed my head. "Gina, I'm sorry for what I made you do and how it affected you and Asher. Alma and Esaw, I apologize and vow upon my return to free Willa and all the Sevifk. I will release them from their demon forms and send them back home to their families."

Gina crossed her arms, but it was Alma who spoke. "Gina and Asher will never see their families again because they believe them dead. But at least they have us! My husband and I will be waiting for Willa's return." Alma closed the door in my face.

I turned to Tara and sighed. "This is not going to be easy."

"Eating humble pie never is," Tara said.

"I suppose I'll get more than my fill in the years to come."

"Most definitely. That is, if someone doesn't kill you first." Tara smiled.

"I deserve that."

"You'll see in time, Izzy, people will forgive, they will not forget, but as long as you keep doing what's right, your burden will grow lighter."

"You are a fascinating and wise young woman. Tara, I wish you much joy and peace. Farewell!" I bowed. Tara slid the golden gauntlet claw on her hand, and I swallowed nervously.

"Farewell, Izzy!" Tara held the sharp blade over my heart. "May a humble heart's plea for forgiveness be heard and seen by all—May the once mighty ruler bow and fall. May the seeds of forgiveness be sewn and rise. May a renewed and fair man change the breaking tides. I wish him a safe journey as he goes forth on his way, and may each new tomorrow bring him peace each new day."

Her words caused goosebumps to rise from my flesh. I felt the slight sting of the cut from the blade, and I looked one last time at Tara's beautiful face. Then I shed a tear as she faded away.

Chapter 22
ZANE

Blood & Branches

Something felt different in the air. When we left the tavern the other day, my heart thumped like the galloping of Perseus's hooves across the terrain, and an image of Bren holding my beating heart in her hands flashed through my mind.

Willa, her ladies, and I traveled across the dry unforgiving terrain toward a prison colony near the Druid Mountains. We stopped to rest our horses and eat what we could find. It was difficult for me as I tried to maintain my distance from Adria and Saharah. I didn't want to take too much blood from them, so I managed to find some sizeable lizards to quench my thirst. It was the most disgusting blood I'd tasted by far, and I'd be happy to have venison juice right now.

These few weeks in Hell seemed like an eternity since I separated from my brother, and my blood lust sometimes felt overwhelming. I no longer had my safety net and adapting to self-reliance sucked more than a swap full of leeches on my ass.

The drained dead lizards cooked on a spit above the fire, and the smell was unappealing. Adria and Saharah sat and watched and took turns flipping them over. Willa sat cross-legged on a blanket with her eyes closed. No one disturbed her as she reached out to her mother for news back home.

The way things ended in her last connection had me worried. I tried to stay strong and be the voice of reassurance, but my thoughts went to Bren. I hoped she was safe. She had to be. Otherwise, my heart wouldn't beat with such surety.

Willa opened her eyes, and she was smiling. Adrian and Saharah abandoned the lizards and came closer to Willa and Domonique. A breath of relief left her, and Domonique placed her hand on Willa's. "What word does your mother send?"

"It is over. Tara has won," Willa replied.

The women cried with joy and wrapped their arms around one another. I laughed at their happiness as they got to their feet, jumping and dancing. Domonique ran to her horse and returned with a wineskin.

"I was saving this for when we received good news. Tonight, we celebrate!" She took a drink and passed it around. I was thrilled to wash the taste of lizard blood out of my mouth.

"Now, all we have to do is spread the good news that Izrazyk is dead, his army is vanquished, and every Sevifk will go free." Saharah lifted her arms in the air and spun in circles till she got dizzy and fell over. Domonique and Adria laughed.

"Izrazyk is not dead," Willa said. The women and I froze.

"What?" I asked.

Saharah looked confused. "But I thought that you said Tara won?"

"She did. But she spared Izrazyk."

"Huh? Why?" Adria asked.

"Because he is Airmed's son, and she asked Tara to do so."

"You're going to need to explain," Saharah said.

A gust of wind blew, dirt and sand kicked up in the air, and we ducked under our cloaks to shield ourselves. A light appeared, and I squinted and lowered my cape. A vertical line widened into a rectangular doorway, and a beautiful woman stepped through, followed by a man wearing a cloak. There was something familiar about him. Something that made my fangs drop into defensive mode.

Willa and I stood up, and I stayed by her side as we approached the woman and man. The man immediately went to his knees and bowed his head. Willa nodded at the woman, who smiled back at her.

"I bring you a gift, Willa Flores. A gift sent by her majesty, Tara Raybrook of the living realm. Queen of Airmed's children."

"Thank you, portal key master. We were on our way to free the Sevifk and Necros from the Druid Mountain prison, but now with this gift in our possession, it will make our good news irrefutable."

"Indeed, it shall. Do you wish to unveil your gift?" the woman asked.

"Indeed, I do." Willa yanked the hood back from the man's head, and her ladies shrieked in disbelief. My eyes could not believe what I was seeing. Down on his knees, his head bowed, and a strange plant in his hands held up in offering was Izrazyk.

"HELL YES!" I shouted. Izrazyk flinched, and I laughed.

"If it pleases you to kill me, do so now. Otherwise, I will spend the rest of eternity on my knees pleading for forgiveness from all I've done an injustice," Izrazyk said.

"You may plant your offering where you kneel. It will grow here as a testament to your humility, bring healing and feed all who pass through these desolate lands," Willa said.

"Yes, Willa!" Izrazyk picked up a nearby rock and began digging into the soil. He planted the bloom and filled in the dirt.

"Is there any water I can give this bloom?"

"Your blood will suffice," Willa said.

Izrazyk nodded. He took the sharp edge of the rock and cut his hand. He squeezed his palm, and his blood dripped to the ground. The plant grew, and it kept growing, making Izrazyk back away.

In a matter of seconds, a tree stood before us. Leaves sprouted and grew. Golden flowers bloomed and formed into golden pears, apples, peaches, nectarines, plums, and figs.

"Is it safe to eat?" Adria asked.

"It is from Airmed's garden," Izrazyk replied.

"But his blood watered it." Saharah's lips curled in disgust.

"Then he will try the first bite," Willa said.

She plucked an apple and handed it to Izrazyk. He bowed his head and bit into the apple, and chewed. When he didn't keel over, Willa plucked a pear and bit into it. Her eyes lit up, and she smiled. The women came and selected some of the different fruits and took a bite.

"Oh! This is good!" Adria mumbled.

"It's so refreshing and thirst-quenching. Eating this, my soul feels elated," Domonique said.

Izrazyk lifted his head and looked at Willa. "May I speak to your ladies?"

"You may."

Izrazyk cleared his throat. "Domonique. I am sorry for what I did to you in Ardromezor. And I apologize for how I treated you. Adria and Saharah, I apologize for mistreating you. I was cruel to all of you, and you never deserved any of it.

I wish to gift all three of you my castle to do with as you wish. I will no longer live there. I have much traveling to do. But I hope that one day when you see a broken shell of a man at your doorstep, you will take pity on him and allow him a night's refuge."

All of our jaws dropped. What had Tara done to Izrazyk? I had to know! It must have been pretty badass to send the Hedrix demon back to Hell groveling on his knees.

The women didn't say anything, and Izrazyk nodded in acceptance. He must have known that his apologies and repentance would not elicit a positive response. Nobody moved to harm him, and I wondered if Tara or Airmed had something to do with it. I looked at Izrazyk and felt nothing but pity for him. He wouldn't gain friendships or win the humanitarian of the year award.

The woman Willa had called the portal key master, which piqued my interest more than Izrazyk's pitiful display, addressed Willa.

"I have agreed to offer my services for such a time that should free the Sevifk and Necros from the Druid Mountain prison. From there, I will bring your group back to Syadestese City, and the Sevifk and Necros can make their way from there to find their families."

Willa bowed her head. "Thank you, portal key master."

"You may call me Beatrix," she replied.

"You are most gracious, Beatrix." Willa bowed.

"Uhm! Excuse me! Beatrix? May I call you by your name?" I asked.

"Yes, Zane Perrish. You may," Beatrix replied.

"Beatrix. I'm happy to help Willa and her ladies with their mission, but I was hoping maybe if there was a chance?"

"You wish to return to your love in the living realm," Beatrix stated.

I smiled. "Yes, I really do."

"But you will need a body," Beatrix said.

"I know. But I know quite a few necromancers willing to help me out."

"Queen Tara and your brother Dean, being two of them."

"How do you know all of this?" I asked.

"I have my connections. But I have been told not to send you forth on what you request."

"But! Why?"

"Other arrangements have been made for you, Zane."

"By who?"

"I am not at liberty to say. I assure you, you have not been overlooked. Those with greater power than mine have made these plans for you. Have faith, vampire. Your deeds will not go without reward."

So, I had to remain in Hell for an unforeseen amount of time. It sucked hairy balls, but I would make the best use of my time here by continuing to help Willa.

We rode our horses through the portal and arrived at the Druid Mountains prison. The guards opened the gate immediately after seeing the portal open, and Beatrix walked ahead of us. We rode into the courtyard, and Beatrix stood with authority.

"By order of Queen Tara, The Goddess Airmed's blessed and sovereign of her people, I bring an announcement of great importance."

The warden and his top guards approached and bowed. "What news do you bring, Portal Key Master?"

"Izrazyk, the Hedrix master, and his army have been defeated. You are to release all Sevifk and Necros prisoners at once."

The man and his guards looked skeptical. "What proof do you bring to validate these claims?"

Beatrix waved her hand, and Izrazyk stepped forward, concealed beneath the hood of his robe. He lifted his hands and drew the hood back, and the warden and guards gasped.

"It is true. I have lost, and I have rescinded my thrown." Izrazyk reached into his bag and pulled out a handful of golden seeds. He scattered them on the ground, and new blooms sprung up from the ground.

"A gift from my mother, Airmed." Izrazyk cut his hand with the stone and spilled his blood upon the blooms. Trees shot up, and fruit grew. The men's eyes widened in shock.

"Release the prisoners!" the warden shouted.

The order echoed around the courtyard, and hundreds of Sevifk and Necros stepped out into the light. They saw the fruit on the trees and ran, plucking the variety of golden sweetness from branches and eating it. They laughed and cried tears of joy. The courtyard was now an orchard, and as hands plucked apples, pears, peaches, plums, nectarines, and figs, more grew in its place. Once they had their fill, they looked around and marveled at all its beauty.

A man spotted Izrazyk and cried, "The Hedrix Master!"

The Sevifk and Necros screamed out battle cries and ran at Izrazyk, and he fell prostrate to the ground and covered his head. Willa and Beatrix stood before him, and the demons halted. They looked at the women in confusion, but Willa spoke. "He is not a threat to you anymore. You are free! I know you want his death."

"HE SHOULD DIE A MILLION DEATHS!" one man shouted. Everyone cried in agreement.

"And he is willing to surrender his life. But it will do you no good and accomplish nothing! Queen Tara and the Goddess Airmed sent him back here to face all he has harmed. They sent him with the seeds he planted to grow this orchard and feed you in hopes that you would see and grant forgiveness so we can all heal."

Izrazyk mumbled something with his face to the ground.

"What does he have to say?" a Sevifk woman asked.

"Stand up, Izrazyk," Willa said. The demons gasped at Willa using his name to address him. Izrazyk rose to his feet and hung his head.

"I want to apologize to everyone. I was blinded by greed, anger, and vengeance against my mother for stripping me of my power. I came here and stole from your people. I committed horrible crimes for which I deserve no mercy. I implore you to hear me when I say I am truly sorry for everything I have done. I do not deserve your forgiveness, and if you see fit to kill me, I will accept my fate. But, before you do so, I wish to release the Sevifk of their demonic bindings and return what I have stolen from Airmed's children and the Necros people."

At Izrazyk's words, the Sevifk transformed, and the Necros filled with power. They all gaped with wide eyes and hanging jaws as they looked around at one another. They looked back at Izrazyk, and he bowed before them. "I was your master, but now I am your servant. Ask of me what you will."

The woman who'd spoken before said, "We wish to return to our families, and we want to return home."

"We want you to rebuild our villages and supply us with food," a Necros man said.

"I will do all of these things if you allow me," Izrazyk said.

The people discussed this amongst one another. Heads nodded, and smiles broke out on their faces.

"What of our dead? Those who cannot be returned to us?"

Izrazyk hung his head in shame. "I cannot bring back the dead, but I can promise no harm will come to your future generations. My army is defeated, and I will not repeat my mistakes. Once I fulfill all your requests, I will leave you in peace. If you wish to kill me still, I will lay my head beneath the sword."

"What do we call you now?" another woman asked.

"Izzy. Asshole. Idiot. Moron. Whatever you wish to call me," Izrazyk said. Everyone laughed, and Izrazyk looked surprised. Beatrix smiled and opened the portal.

"Come forth all who wish to return to Syadestese City. You will receive provisions for your journey to find your loved ones. Many of you already have family waiting for you there."

I could see the city walls through the portal. The people cheered and gathered to pass. Izrazyk put his hood up and walked behind them, and Willa, her ladies, and I were the last to go through on our horses.

Izrazyk walked through the city with his hood covering his face. Willa and I followed him to the city's center, where a fountain flowed with a statue of the Hedrix master standing at its center. He climbed into the fountain, walked through the water, and began rocking the statue back and forth. Guards came running and shouting, and people gathered around to see who this lunatic was, trying to tear down the monument of their king.

"Halt!" a guard shouted. "You are under arrest by the authority of our sovereign, the Hedrix master!" Izrazyk ignored the guard and kept rocking the statue. The guards lept into the water and held up their spears. "Halt! Or face the penalty of death for defacing our Master's monument!"

With one last shove, the statue toppled to the ground and broke into hundreds of pieces. Izrazyk clapped the dust off his hands while the guards closed in, surrounding him. Izrazyk removed his hood, and the guards lowered their spears and gawked at him.

"Master!" they cried and dropped to their knees.

"I am no one's master. This kingdom is no longer mine. You may arrest me if you wish, but there is something I must do first."

The guards looked at each other confused. The people surrounding the fountain spoke frantically. Willa and I smirked as we looked at one another, then watched as Izrazyk lifted a bloom from his bag and planted it where his statue had been. He scooped water from the fountain into his hands and watered the bloom. It grew, and the rest you already know.

Izrazyk addressed the people of Syadestese City. He explained what had happened and left the people to decide whether or not they wanted him to remain their king upon his return. He told them it would not be for many years, but he made one last decree. That peace should stay within the city walls, and it would be a refuge for lost souls, which included the end of the slave trade, the pardon of vampires, and the expulsion of all evil.

Willa, her ladies, and I took our rest in the castle. The harem was disbanded, but they were permitted to stay if they wished. Izrazyk left all of his wealth to Willa, Domonique, Adria, and Saharah, and he asked that they distribute it to those in need in the city and aid in rebuilding the Necros villages.

He left the city with some of the Necros people to start his mission and sow the seeds Airmed gave him. He began by planting some around the city walls as a way to welcome those who sought refuge.

The night went on with a celebration in the streets. Willa watched from a balcony on the high tower as everyone else enjoyed the festivities. I had just had my fill of blood from a few of the humans who remained in the castle.

"I heard quite a few citizens weren't happy about some of the changes and got the boot," I said.

Willa smiled. "They were weak oppositionists with too much wealth and no heart. The city is better off without them."

"Do you think they'll come back and start something?"

"There's a chance, but the majority won't stand for it, and they haven't the nerve to go against Izrazyk or me. They are a bunch of entitled blowhards. I say good riddance!"

"Does this mean you'll still be staying for a while?" I asked.

"It is my responsibility to ensure everyone is found and returned home before leaving. I made a vow, and I will uphold it."

Most of the Sevifk have been found and freed from their bonds. When Izrazyk spoke the words, it not only transformed the demons before him but all the Sevifk, as we found out when we returned to the city.

"They can't all go at once; it would overwhelm the Raybrooks."

"That's why they are moving to the city for now. They will be safe here till further arrangements are made to send them home."

Willa and I sat in silence for a while. My mind drifted home, and I wondered what was happening with Tara and my brother. Mostly, I thought about Bren.

I didn't know what Beatrix meant when she told me other accommodations were in the works for me. I could still feel my heartbeat growing stronger like it was outside myself but kept getting closer. And I still felt Bren's warmth like she was holding onto me for dear life. What would it be like to have her in my arms again? Given I'd have arms or a body in which to live. I would kiss her like there was no tomorrow because, despite being a vampire, tomorrow was not guaranteed. Immortal or not, nothing was guaranteed. I learned that lesson the hard way.

I looked up to the deep crimson sky and wished there was a star to wish upon, but it was just a gloom of haze.

I miss you, Bren. Keep waiting for me. I'll be there as soon as I can, love.

Chapter 23
TARA

The Hillbillies Ride Again

Eight motorcycles stretched down the highway and headed south. It felt like a freedom ride as my entire family decided to take a road trip together for the first time in over ten years. We headed to the Florida Keys for some sun and sand, and I couldn't be more excited.

We'd left Alma and Esaw in charge at The Hillbilly Roost, which had reopened to the public a few weeks ago. Martina had put on a final one-week performance, and The Roost had a line waiting outside the door. Thankfully we had plenty of new help; otherwise, Bren, Stella, Billie, and I wouldn't have lasted those last few nights.

There were a lot of changes happening all at once. Many of my brothers and sisters left The Roost to begin their search for their families. Some had stayed behind to help the new arrivals transition into the modern world.

I felt sad that Bren didn't come along, but she insisted on staying. She didn't feel right leaving Zane's heart in anyone else's hands, and carrying around a glass jar with a live beating heart wasn't something any human should witness.

Alma had given us one last update before we left. No one had killed Izrazyk, and he was fulfilling his promises. He'd planted the tree in the city center and went on his journey, traveling with the Necros, sowing seeds and helping to rebuild. No one had heard anything about what happened to Malichi, but he didn't make anyone's concern list.

Willa was watching over the city with Zane and her friends. Zane sent his love, which gave Bren, Dean, and me renewed hope. He was safe and well, and that's all that mattered for now.

The portal key master, Beatrix, agreed to live in the castle until the last of Airmed's people made it home. For reasons unbeknownst to us, Zane had to remain in Hell for the time being. Not just because he'd need a body to return, but it was decreed from somewhere higher up. As long as his heart was beating in the blue mason jar, Bren waited.

From the girl I hated in high school to the woman she became; I'd never known anyone could be so loyal and dedicated to another. It made me become her greatest admirer.

I wrapped my arms around Dean as we rode on his black Heritage behind Martina's sparkling purple Triglide, leading the way. Danny and Billie rode his Harley with the cute little sidecar and a baby mobile of little motorcycles swaying in the wind. Billie's baby bump was starting to show, and she wanted to go on this trip before she was too big to ride seated behind Danny.

Dad and Mom, Cannon and Stella, Woody and Rudy followed, and Martina turned into a roadside diner parking lot outside Atlanta. Dean was laughing as we dismounted the bike, and I smiled.

"What's so funny?"

"This is where I met Martina." Dean chuckled.

"Martina always knows how to make an impression, even with the people she already knows."

As we headed toward the door, another group of riders rumbled into the parking lot. They dismounted their bikes, and I read Butcher Bounty Brotherhood on the backs of their leather jackets.

Martina squealed, ran toward one of the riders, and jumped into his arms. He smiled with a mouthful of shining white teeth as he lifted Martina in the air and spun her around.

"Bobby! Just look at you! You look fabulous, darling!" Martina cried.

Bobby laughed as he set her down and his friends greeted Martina with hugs. Bobby was clean-shaven and sported and classic haircut. He looked like he worked out with his biceps flexing in his tight-fitted shirt.

"It's great to see you again, Marti," Bobby greeted.

Martina waved us over. "Dean, you remember Bobby and his brothers? They were here the day we met."

Dean's eyes bugged out. "Bobby? You look different!"

"Yeah, man, Martina hooked me up with her orthodontist friend, and I got these new chompers. I decided why stop there, and I got that weight loss surgery and started working out. Marti has been cheering me on these past few months, and I'm not the crabby asshole you met before. I'm feeling great!"

"I didn't know you two kept in touch! You look great, man!" Dean clapped his hand into Bobby's.

"Yeah, Marti told me about you and your old lady. It's nice to meet you, by the way," Bobby greeted.

"Nice to meet you too," I said. "So, you and Marti?"

"Yeah, Martina and I have become good friends. My brothers and I wanted to visit The Hillbilly Roost but found out it was closed due to illness and some structural issues that needed fixing. We were kind of bummed. I'm happy Marti told us to meet her here today. You all are headed to the Keys?"

"Yeah, baby. Long overdue family vacation. We've all had a tough past few months," Martina said.

"And everyone is okay now?" Bobby asked.

"Right as rain, baby! Come along, sweetheart. I want to buy you lunch and introduce you to Woody The Rooster Raybrook and the rest of our gang." Martina wrapped her arm around Bobby's waist, and he put his arm around her shoulder as they walked to the door. I laughed at Dean as he made a cheesy grin and chuckled.

It seemed a lot outside our little bubble had changed as well, but it felt good to be back out in the world again. And I was looking forward to seeing it all with Dean and Charlie. The little yellow rubber duckie wore his custom helmet, where he sat strapped down on the back of Dean's motorcycle.

The Florida Keys were beautiful. We rented a boat, went island hopping in Key West, and found a fantastic beachfront rental with a private beach and a pool. It was the perfect place to announce our engagement to my family. Well, we might as well say our family. They already accepted Dean as a member long ago.

Dean and I walked the beach hand in hand. We sat and watched the sunset, then built a bonfire. Later that night, Dean and I danced to Kokomo on the soft sand under the stars. We made love and then sat wrapped up together in a blanket, watching the moonlight sparkling on the rippling tide.

"Do you still dream of managing a resort on a beach someday?" Dean asked.

"I do, but I'm in no hurry. I got a letter from the school saying they dropped me because I'd let my courses lapse. I'll have to re-enroll for the next semester and start all over."

"Don't they understand you were saving the world from a demonic tyrannical dictator? I mean, come on! They should cut you some slack, even give bonus credits and hand over your diploma already."

I laughed. "I don't think they'd buy that, Dean. But thanks for being on my side. Besides, if I do some research while traveling the world with you first, I'd understand better than any textbook could teach."

"Now, that is an excellent thought! What do you think of our accommodations so far?" Dean kissed my neck, and I smiled.

"I definitely want to do this again." I turned and kissed Dean's lips.

"Does that mean you're ready for round two?" Dean waggled his brows and grinned wickedly.

I reached down and stroked him. "What do you think?"

"I think I like taking priority over little Charlie," Dean growled.

I paused. "Oh no! We left Charlie on the bike! We should go get him so he can take a swim in the ocean!"

I moved to get up, and Dean grabbed my hips and pulled me back. He began laughing. "Are you planning on streaking through the property with all your family awake?"

I gave Dean a challenging glare. "Only if you come and do it with me."

"Game on!" Dean stood up, and the warm night breeze tussled his blond hair. I gave his sexy body an appreciative once over, then turned to run.

"Tara! Get back here!" he shouted.

I squealed and laughed as he chased me. We ran in our birthday suits toward the house, and the first person I saw was Uncle Woody stepping out onto the veranda. His eyes widened in shock, but he saw Dean chasing me and started laughing. I screamed and covered my boobs with my arm and pelvis with my other hand but kept running past him through the open door.

"STREAKERS!" Woody yelled. All the men saw me coming and slapped their hands over their eyes.

"Gross, Sis! Put some clothes on!" Rudy yelled. Everyone started laughing as I passed the bar in the open kitchen. Stella, Billie, Martina, and my mom saw Dean and started whistling.

"Get her, Dean!" Stella yelled.

"Spank her ass!" Billie called.

I opened the front door and heard my mom yell. "Tara, get your ass back in here, young lady, or I will spank your butt myself!"

"Ooh, child! Your mama's gonna light that tail on fire!" Martina hollered.

"You have to catch me first!" I yelled. I opened the front door and began cracking up as I darted toward Dean's bike and snatched little Charlie free from beneath the mesh tie-down holding him in place. I circled Dean's bike and saw him coming at me with his man package freewheeling in the wind.

I laughed and started squeezing Charlie, making him squeak with villainous laughter. Dean was laughing, and I raised Charlie in the air and cried. "FREE CHARLIE AND ALL THE RUBBER DUCKIES OF THE WORLD!"

Dean captured me in a beach towel and wrapped it tightly around my body. He lifted me over his shoulder and smacked my ass.

"OW!" I squealed. I held Charlie in the air and repeatedly squeezed his squeaker in protest. Charlie pecked Dean's bare ass with each comical strike producing an angry squeak. I continued my vicious assault on Dean's scrumptious muscular buns as he laughed and carried me back through the house. My family was cracking up, and the women were snapping pictures as Dean walked by, swinging freely without shame.

I held Charlie up in the air, and he squeaked out in triumph.

"HE'S FREE!" I cried.

"Mmm, mmm, mmm! He certainly is, baby!" Martina remarked. She held up her glass in a toast and took a picture of Dean's retreating backside with me draped over his shoulder, holding the yellow rubber duck in the air with a victorious grin.

Dean marched me into our room and kicked the door closed. He dumped me on the bed and began tickling me. I laughed and cried out for mercy and dropped poor little Charlie on the floor with a deflated squeak.

"Save Charlie!" I cried between giggles.

Dean laughed and gave me a moment to catch my breath as he bent over to retrieve our pet rubber duck, and I smacked his butt again.

"Oh, yeah? You like smacking the goods, do you?" Dean asked in a challenge.

"Uh-Huh!" I nodded with enthusiasm and bit my bottom lip.

Dean crept toward me on his hands and knees with a devilish sneer. He growled at me and snapped his teeth, and I giggled and backed away. He grabbed my legs, pulled me toward him, and I squealed.

Dean flipped me over on my stomach, pulled the towel away, and ping-ponged Charlie back and forth across my butt cheeks. The rubber duck made puffed squeaks with each bounce.

"Dirty duck, dirty duck!" I cried with laughter.

"I'll give you dirty!" Dean grabbed my hips, lifted me from the bed, so I was on my hands and knees, and gave my right cheek a love bite.

"Ahh! Dean! Stop!" I tried to scramble away from him, but he held my hips tight. He laughed, and I groaned. He entered me, and I moaned.

He started moving, and I cried, "Oh, Dean, don't stop!"

Dean paused. "Did you say stop?"

"Asshole! I said, AHH!" Dean thrust into me.

"What was that?" he asked.

"DON'T ST-AHH!" I cried out as he thrust again.

"I'm not understanding what you want, Tara. Do you want me to stop or?" He pushed into me again.

"AHH! Dammit, Dean! Quit screwing around!" I yelled.

"Alright." He pulled out.

"Seriously, Dean?" I huffed. He sat back on his knees with his erection standing at a high salute laughing his ass off, and I growled.

I pushed him over, mounted him like a cowgirl riding a trick pony, and began to ride at full gallop. I owned this saddle and had this naughty bronc whipped in no time. Winning the golden buckle at this rodeo, I claimed my prize. Dean bucked beneath me, driving me wild. It felt like the first time I claimed him after he stampeded into my heart with his words of proclaimed love and breakfast coffee.

He still turned me on whenever he brought me a cup when we'd wake up, and now I woke from sweet dreams, and being in his arms was pure bliss.

We didn't know what our future would hold, but we'd ride into the sunset together. I knew it would be some time before we could officially travel and see the world with little Charlie tagging along.

Many of my brothers and sisters would come through the portal and need our help acclimating to the world we live in today. But at some point, I knew I could let the people I trusted most take the reins.

As far as Bren and Zane? Time would tell. His heart had grown fully inside the blue mason jar. It may not have a body, but it beat for Bren, and Zane loved her. We knew he'd come back someday. It was only a matter of how and when. I could sense a change coming, and I hoped Bren was ready for it.

Chapter 24
BREN

A Heart In Shatters

I unwrapped the blue mason jar and set it on the table before the window where the moonlight's glow gazed upon Zane's steady beating heart. It was to be a blood moon tonight, so I thought it appropriate for Zane's vampire heart to partake in the occurrence.

I sat at the table and watched as the eclipse began. The shade of red began slipping over the full moon like an ominous crimson haze creeping out of Hell's sky, reminding me of how Jeremiah described its atmosphere. There was no break in the gloom it cast over the dry arid land that stretched on with breaks of woodlands filled with trees that looked like they'd all burned to charcoal with twisted craggy branches.

A knock sounded at my door, and I saw Jeremiah. I opened it, and he stepped inside. Jeremiah smiled. "Hello, Bren."

"Evening, Jeremiah. What do you think of the eclipse?"

"I can't say I care for it very much. It reminds me too much of Hell. I didn't enjoy my stay there."

"I can imagine you did not. Would you like something to drink?"
I went to the refrigerator, pulled out a water bottle, and looked at Jeremiah.

"I'll take one."

I passed a bottle to him, and he nodded thanks before cracking it open and taking a sip. Jeremiah joined me at the small kitchenette table, where he looked at Zane's heart beating inside the jar.

"Man, I still can't get over that. It's the wildest thing I've ever seen, and I've seen a lot."

"I've seen more these past months than most people in their lives. Hell, no one would believe me if I told them everything I saw."

"I can attest to that. I was in denial for the longest time when the Hedrix master dragged me to Hell. The things I saw there made the war here look like child's play."

"Yikes! That makes me worry for Zane."

"He's going to be okay. He's a vampire, and even though vampires are low ranking in Hell, I've heard that his services in defeating the Hedrix army didn't go unnoticed. His people are receiving a second chance thanks to word spreading about Zane's valiant contributions."

I smiled at Zane's heart. "I know. Alma has told me. I think it's awe-inspiring what he's done. I'm very proud of him."

"I see the love in your eyes for him. Which is why I came here tonight to talk to you." Jeremiah cleared his throat and took another drink. He seemed nervous about what he wanted to say, but Jeremiah was my friend, and he could tell me anything.

"Go ahead. I'm listening."

"Well, it seems that Adria learned about what happened with me here, and she will be coming back soon with the next group of new arrivals. Willa has agreed to help her find a suitable body, and I thought that once she arrived." Jeremiah's look was beseeching.

I took his hand and smiled. "Jeremiah, I'll always be your friend, and I look forward to meeting Adria. I hope she and you pick up where you left off all those years ago. I'm happy for you."

Jeremiah squeezed my hand gently, lifted it to his lips, placed a tender kiss, and let go. "And I'm happy for you too, Bren. Do you have any idea when Zane will return home?"

"No. All I know is Zane must wait for the green light from whoever has dictated his fate. He cannot come by way of the portal, and I don't understand why. But who am I to question the supernatural when I am a mere mortal!"

"Bren, you are so much more. There's something special about you, and I noticed it the first time I saw you, and I could see why Zane fell for you."

I blushed and lowered my gaze. "That's sweet of you to say, Jeremiah. And Adria would be a fool to turn you away a second time. You are the kindest, bravest, and most caring man I've met. Well, besides all the men in Tara's family and Dean and Zane." I grinned.

Jeremiah laughed. He was a handsome man. When Tara told me he and Zane could pass for twins with their short dark hair and even darker eyes, I thought of the possibilities. Could I have loved Jeremiah and Zane in a shared body, or would it complicate everything? I suppose it was a moot point now.

Zane couldn't come to inhabit a body, let alone Jeremiah's, and now, Adria was returning. My heart kept time with Zane's, and no two hearts were more destined to be together than ours. I found myself staring longingly at the vampire heart in the blue jar.

"Are you okay?" Jeremiah asked.

"Yeah." I nodded. "I think I'm going to turn in for the night. Thanks for coming by to check on me." I stood to see Jeremiah out. He hugged me like he was saying goodbye. But I knew it was more him letting go of the prospect of being with me as more than friends. I couldn't see him as more than my friend, and I think he had accepted it.

"Good night, Bren."

"Good night, Jeremiah. I'll see you in the morning." I opened the door, and he stepped through. He looked back once more, waved as I smiled, and slowly closed the door. I went back to the table and watched as Jeremiah walked away. The blood moon was in total eclipse and cast its crimson radiance through the window, and I saw particles dancing in the air around the jar like a snow globe only inside out. It was spellbinding.

The jar started to shake, rattling loudly on the tabletop. I panicked and reached forward the grab it, but it fell over and rolled to the floor, shattering to pieces. I screamed, raising my hands to shield my face from the flying shards. My hands and arms were bleeding, and Zane's heart lay exposed on the floor amongst the broken glass.

"Oh no!" I cried. There were fragments embedded in Zane's heart and splinters in my flesh. I began to cry, not knowing what to do. I wanted to save Zane's heart, but my hands hurt with the glass shrapnel stuck in my skin. I quickly washed my hands and arms at the kitchen sink and grabbed a towel to wrap around them.

I searched for a container and found a plastic strainer beneath the sink. Thankfully I had hard-soled slippers to protect my feet as I stepped over the broken pieces. I carefully scooped up Zane's heart and lay it gently in the colander.

I picked out the shards and slivers and debated washing it, but I thought it might help free any tiny fragments, so I took the sprayer on low setting and rinsed the thumping muscle.

There was something I hadn't noticed before. A root hung from the heart's posterior, and the soil must have hidden it. It was so odd! I grabbed another bowl and ladling spoon and scooped up as much dirt as possible. I let my instincts guide me and found my feet leading me out the door. I ran toward the lake with Zane's heart which I'd placed back in the other bowl with the dirt. The red glow from the blood moon illuminated a spot on the ground. And that's where I dropped to my knees and began clawing at the soil with my fingernails.

I gritted my teeth through the pain as the sharp pieces of glass bit at my tender flesh with each movement. I dug deep and with desperation as tears spilled from my eyes.

"Please be okay, Zane," I pleaded.

Once satisfied with the hole's depth, I lifted Zane's heart from the bowl, shook the loose soil inside, and gently lay the beating organ down. I covered it and filled the hole in, wincing as I patted the dirt flat.

I had bled through the kitchen towels and began to drip on the ground. The light from the blood moon grew intense and concentrated on the spot. I sat there on my knees and let more of my essence drip into the soil. I poured all my love into every drop that left my body and hit the earth, willing it with all my soul to bring forth new life.

"Come back to me, my love!" The wind picked up and carried my whispered plea. The soil began to move with a thump, thump, thump, thump motion. I wasn't a necromancer, but I felt something stirring within me, and I remembered when I accidentally stuck myself with Tara's brooch, and her power had entered me.

"Oh no!" I cried. Had Tara's power remained within me, aiding me now? It had allowed me to see and touch Zane in his vapor form, but it had been a month since he died. Would her power hurt Zane? Was it her blood or the power within that harmed him? Dean's power controlled Zane's appetite, but Tara's had knocked him out for a time.

I waited and prayed that I'd done the right thing. Then I remembered Zane had drunk my blood which I offered in small amounts when we were intimate, which didn't harm him. This confusion caused my uncertainty.

"I did the right thing!" I repeated this in my head like a mantra. Everything I did felt right until this moment. With my intuition taking the lead, something or someone of vast significance guided me.

"Please don't go wrong!" I begged.

The ground beneath me began to rumble and crack. I squealed and fell back on my bum, catching myself on my hands and crying in pain. The cracks in the ground radiated with an ominous red glow, and I thought Hell might rise to the surface before me. With panicked breaths, I scrambled backward on my hands and feet in an awkward crablike motion.

The earth exploded, and I screamed as I held my arm over my eyes and felt clumps of dirt shower down on me. I shook my head and brushed the loose soil from my face; in the process, I smeared my cheeks with my blood.

I lowered my arm, and what I saw made my breath hitch and my body lock up in fright. A naked man, no, a vampire, turned his head and hissed at me. His eyes were pitch black, and his fangs were long and sharp. He had no hair on his head or anywhere on his pale body. The eclipse passed, and his flesh took on the white moonlit glow.

"Zane?" My voice trembled. He hissed again, dropped to his hands and knees, creeping toward me in a frightful predator movement, then tilted his head with a curious expression.

"Zane! It's me, Bren! Don't hurt me!" My voice shook, fearful that he might have lost control of the bloodlust in his new body.

Zane froze a few inches before my face. He sniffed me, and his tongue darted out. He licked the blood from my cheek in a long sensual drag that was both terrifying and exciting. I whimpered, and my breaths were erratic. He was like a feral beast, and I was alone with him in the middle of the night.

"Mmm!" He moaned, which sounded all too erotic. He licked my cheek clean, then turned my head and licked my other. Zane grabbed my hands, still wrapped in the blood-soaked towels, and I yelped in pain. His lashless lids blinked, and he cooed.

"Zane? I. AHH!" I screamed as he lifted me in his arms and ran into the woods. The wind whistled as we whipped past trees at full speed. I tucked my head into his shoulder and held on tight. Zane ascended a rocky slope where he stopped and sat me down on a low boulder.

I could see everything from here. The forest and the lake took on a romantic ambiance. At this elevation, I began to shiver from the cold night air. Zane stood over me like a curious wild creature. He didn't speak, only observed me like he couldn't decide whether I was his dinner or something else. What else, it was hard to tell from his perplexed expression. He dropped to his knees so suddenly that it made me jump and yelp.

"Zane? Do you remember me?" He blinked with black eyes that looked alien and disturbing. He retook my hands and unwound the dish towels, revealing my bleeding wounds. He turned them over and back, then began picking the bits of glass from my palms and forearms. I sucked air between my clenched teeth as each pluck bit and stung. Blood oozed from the cuts, and Zane pressed his lips to my hands and began sucking and humming.

Seeing him like this was strange, but I had to admit it turned me on. "Mmm, Zane!" I moaned breathily.

He froze in his ministrations and looked at me. His eyes flared like red rubies, and he licked his lips. My eyes became hooded with desire, and my body responded.

"Zane, I!" He halted me with his thumb dragging across my lips, and I tasted blood as I wetted them with my tongue.

The sound emitted from Zane's throat was between a sexual growl and a ferocious purr. I became aroused, and Zane closed his eyes and took a long, drawing sniff in the air. When he reopened his eyes, they flashed to silver and glowed. I held his stare, and my chest began to heave. He lifted my arms and licked them long and slow, stopping to suck at the small gashes.

The feel of his lips was lush and succulent, and I wanted to feel them on mine. But I also didn't want to make any sudden movements that might trigger him. It was a provocative sensation feeling the smooth flesh and solid muscle of his hands, tongue, and lips move sensually along my arms. Zane cleaned away all the blood, and my wounds were entirely healed by his wet, arousing kisses.

"Zane," I whispered.

He blinked again, and this time when he opened his eyes, they flashed with recognition. "Bren?"

I smiled and nodded. Tears broke free, and I cried. Zane pulled me into his arms and held me tight. He began to weep. "Oh, God, Bren!"

We held each other with our bodies pressed tight. I ran my hands down smooth, unmarred skin with gorgeous sculpted muscles. Zane was that of a beautiful predator made to lure his prey. I ran my hands over his bald head, and he laughed. It was him. My Zane came back to me!

He felt his bald head. "I must look ridiculous!"

"You're beautiful!" I sniffed.

"Pfft, Ha!" Zane looked down at his body and laughed. "Look at me! I'm naked and hairless like one of those blind little mole rats burrowing underground and probably just as fugly!"

I barked a laugh. "You don't look that bad!"

"You still want to be with me looking like this?"

"Oh no, you don't! I haven't been lugging your heart around in a jar for over a month just so you can back out on me now! I've waited too long to be with you like this, and I...." Zane caught my lips with a kiss.

I moaned and opened my mouth, allowing his tongue to swirl around mine. He began pulling my clothes off my body, and I shivered with anticipation of feeling his new flesh against mine for the first time. He pulled me flush to his smooth skin, and I thought I'd die at how heavenly he felt.

"You are so beautiful! I've been dying for this moment, and now it's ours. We can have each other fully." Zane took my hand and pressed it to his chest, where I felt his heart pounding with wild abandon.

"You have a body now. Brand new and completely yours."

"No, Bren! It's completely yours. I belong to you." He kissed me, and I felt his smooth erection pressed against my stomach. Zane was perfect, and he was mine!

He laid me down, and I opened myself to him. Zane lay between my legs, his smooth pale skin pressed to mine. His beautiful silver eyes held me captive, and my breath hitched as he entered me. He groaned in pleasure, then began to move.

"Oh, yesss!" He filled me and then some. Our bodies heated and melded together, and I cried and moaned as we took flight into the heavens.

I was his comet, and Zane was my fiery trail chasing me as we sailed together across the sky. We burned with a feverish fury, and I was moments away from exploding into stardust. What Zane and I had was designed by the maker of cosmic flames that stretched across the expanse of time and space. I have never been loved like this. The convergence of our bodies was magical and divine. I wanted him like this forever.

"I-I love you, Zane!" I panted.

"I love. You too, Bren." Zane panted between words.

Zane's fiery kisses blazed down my neck. Moving around the curves of my breast, he cupped me with firm skillful hands and flickered the tight buds of my ample mounds with a smooth expert tongue.

Zane took me into his mouth, and the titillating pulse of his wet tip against my peaks made me cry out as I came undone. My back arched, pushing my puckered areolas further into his mouth. His fangs pricked my tender flesh, and I sucked a sharp breath between my teeth.

The small moment of pain passed, followed by euphoria, but then he began drawing deeper, and I cried as the next wave crashed, and I tumbled in a wave of ecstasy. My body tingled from head to toe in epic rolling swells of bliss. Zane groaned and shuddered with his release, throbbing in synchronicity with my pulsing channel.

We continued to kiss and touch each other. I couldn't get enough of the feel of my beautiful vampire. This time together was better than anything I had imagined. I'd waited so long, thinking it would never happen. After he died, I was sure it never would. Shame on me for doubting the fates. What they had in store for the two of us outshined the best of my imagination.

But what did this mean for us? Zane was a newly risen vampire. I didn't know how the vampire world worked, but Woody had told me that a sire would expect a newborn to join their coven. It never happened with Zane, and Dean had speculated that it was because they shared his body. Dean's necromancer was dominant over Zane's vampire, which shielded his presence.

Zane took me back to the camper, where we made love again, took a shower, and relaxed. He held me in his arms, and I drifted to sleep feeling complete at last.

I woke the next morning to breakfast in bed. Zane had cleaned up the broken glass and blood and now sat beside me, smiling at me adoringly. A tiny fuzz of blond hair had sprouted on his head and the beginning of lashes, eyebrows, and facial hair.

"How do you feel?" I asked.

"I feel fantastic. How about you?" Zane asked.

"Same. What about the blood lust?"

"It was getting a bit hard to handle in Hell, but I ate some of the fruit from Airmed's trees, which helped calm my cravings."

"There's a tree growing in front of Tara and Dean's cabin."

"How are they?"

"They are enjoying a well-deserved vacation in the Florida Keys with the rest of Tara's family. They'll be back in a week."

I looked into Zane's eyes. "Zane, we all grieved for you, and it was the most painful experience of my life. We missed you. I missed you so much."

Zane took my hands and kissed them. "I missed you too, Bren. I thought I'd never see you again. It felt like I died a second death being away from you, and I thought of you the whole time. And time drags on and on in Hell. It felt like a decade for a day back home."

"We didn't know what happened to you. Tara and Dean were searching, and I carried around the blue jar with your heart growing inside everywhere."

"I felt it like you had my heart in your hands. I felt your warmth, and I heard your voice. You kept me grounded and connected. Thank you."

"I would have done so for the rest of my life. You are all I ever wanted, and no one could ever replace you."

"I feel the same way, my love." Zane kissed me.

"What happened to you in Hell? I heard you were in a battle and helped defeat the Hedrix army."

"I found Izrazyk's city, and Willa found me. She purchased me from a slave auction and snuck me into the castle. She was brilliant in her deception against Izrazyk. All her years of planning brought down the Hedrix, and I was just there to help. It was an adventure that I never wish to experience again. I'm happy to be home."

"That bad? Jeremiah told me how harrowing it was for him."

"Jeremiah? Jeremiah Vansbrie? Willa gave me that name and makeover to hide my identity. He was the one who Tara told Willa was my double?"

"Yes. Jeremiah was a Sevifk that Tara saved from the first group when you, you know." I swallowed down the emotional grief from the thought of Zane's death.

Zane stroked my arm and took my hand. "I'm here now. But I know what you're saying. So is Jeremiah still here?"

"Yes. He is a good friend. His fiancé, Adria, is supposed to return once Willa finds a suitable body and sends her through."

"I know Adria. She's Willa's friend. She is a good person and a fierce warrior."

"A warrior? Wow. Jeremiah told me Izrazyk murdered her and took her to Hell. She turned away from him when she saw him in his Sevifk form."

"It's different in Hell. It changes people, and they have to learn to fight to survive."

"You can die in Hell?"

"Oh, yes. Once you die there, you cease to exist. But, enough about that nightmare. Bren, you'll never have to see it. I want to talk about our future together. Willa told me I'd be on the vampire's radar once I returned."

"I know. What do you think will happen once your kind finds you?"

"I don't know. I suppose I might have to join a coven. I don't even know who my sire is. He turned me and left. It was over eighty years ago."

"I'm worried we may have to live in two separate worlds, Zane. You must be different from other vampires, and I don't imagine having a human girlfriend will go well."

"We will not become separated, Bren. I may have to go out on my own from time to time, but I will always come back to you. Think of it as business travel. But I'm not going out to find them. If they want me, they will have to come here. I don't believe we'll have any issues with a whole camp of necromancers. And until I know how you will fit into the vampire world; you will stay here where you are safe."

"Will we ever have the chance to see the world together?"

"We will. I know Tara and Dean would enjoy coming with us. They can be our backup to keep us safe."

"I have been learning how to fight, but I never got the chance to put it into practice in a real-life situation. When Izrazyk and his demons showed up here, Danny took me, Billie, and Lydia to a safe house."

Zane's eyes lit up, and he bounced up to his knees. "I have to know what Tara did to Izrazyk! He returned to Hell, whipped with his tail tucked between his legs. I was astonished! And elated!"

I laughed. "Tara took Izzy home to his mother, Airmed."

Zane guffawed. "Bringing a man home to his mama will bring him to his knees. But there had to be something else! He left Hell as a cruel, ruthless, take no prisoners prickhead and returned as a saintly kumbaya Johnny Appleseed."

I laughed. "Tara did a number on him. That's for sure! She had the demon convinced everyone was dead, spiked his and his buddies' drinks with that fairie knock-out juice, and took him on a nightmare vision quest. When he came out of it, he was groveling on his knees and begging to die."

"Wow! I wonder what he experienced during that vision?"

"Tara said it was Airmed who not only showed him but also made him feel everything he did to all the people he'd hurt, tortured, and murdered. She showed him his future if he continued on his path. It was one of those scared straight situations only for power-hungry, asshole supernaturals."

Zane laughed. "That's awesome! I wish I could have been here to see that. But now I understand why he changed. He hurt and murdered thousands of people. If he felt everything, I imagine he was experiencing a fate worse than death and Hell combined."

"I know I'll never cross Tara again! So, now that you're back, do you want to call Dean and Tara and let them know?"

"Nah! We'll wait till they return from their trip and surprise them. We'll throw a welcome home party, which they think is for them, but it will actually be for me." Zane put on a cheesy grin.

"Like a coming out of the jar party?" I laughed.

"And celebrating you popping my vampire boy cherry!" Zane said with enthusiasm.

I slapped my hands over my mouth. "Oh my god! You were a virgin, weren't you?"

"Technically! New virgin flesh. I was a one-hundred and six-year-old virgin! So, thank you for deflowering me, Bren Taylor." Zane laughed.

I laughed. "I was your first! How was it?"

"Better than anything I have ever experienced before. You were perfect, love. And, you will be mine always and forever. No one will have this body but you." Zane kissed me.

I wanted this to be true, but like all humans, I would grow old and one day die. I did not expect Zane to go on alone in this world once I was gone. It wouldn't be long before I was Zane's cougar, then things might get weird beyond that. But I had seen those shows about couples with considerable age gaps, and they made it work. I knew Zane loved me enough to make our time together beautiful and memorable.

We had now, and I wouldn't take our time together for granted. I hoped that Zane wouldn't have to fight for our relationship once the vampires tracked him down, and I would stand by his side through it all. And make no mistake, I, too, would fight for us if it came down to it. Like Tara and Dean were a team, so were Zane and I.

A week later, Tara, Dean, and her family arrived home. Gina, Asher, Jeremiah, and I decorated the bar with balloons and a welcome home banner. Zane went to hide in the forest and watched for their arrival. His hair grew a few inches, and his lashes and brows filled in.

He looked more like Dean, except for Zane's piercing silver eyes, which shot straight to my heart every time he looked into mine. The two things he was missing were the scar Dean carried on his chest from Zane's death and the tattoo of the black and white figures representing the brothers. Everything else was the same. Well, I wasn't sure if 'everything' was the same. I never got to experience Zane in his brother's body. And in a way, I was glad.

I knew Tara's heart was going out to me when she said those words about allowing Zane and me to be together. I still think it would have been awkward for all of us. It turned out that fate had another path, and everything worked out how it was supposed to. I now had my vampire and Tara, her necromancer.

The motorcycles rumbled up to The Hillbilly Roost, and Gina went out to tell them to come inside. Asher, Jeremiah, me, and a group of friends cheered when Tara, Dean, and her family walked in.

"WELCOME HOME!"

Hugs, handshakes, and hilarious stories about their trip went on for half an hour. Music played, and we sat around and enjoyed the food and drinks. Tara was beaming, talking, and laughing about their fun time when the door opened, and Zane walked in. He lifted his arms and shouted,

"YOU ASSHOLES STARTED THIS PARTY WITHOUT ME?"

"ZANE!" Tara shouted. Dean's eyes bugged out, and Tara jumped out of her seat, ran, and bowled into Zane's arms. She clung to him like a rabid monkey and kissed his face while he laughed.

Dean approached his brother, and Zane held open an arm to include him in their embrace. I was smiling and crying as I watched them cry, and I went to join them. Tara released Zane to welcome me. I was surprised when Gina and Asher piled in around us, followed by the rest of Tara's family. It became a massive group hug, and Zane was grinning from ear to ear.

"I knew this party was for me! Awe, thanks, guys!" Everyone laughed.

"When did you get back? And look at you? This is not some borrowed body, is it?" Tara asked.

"A week ago. And, nope! This body is all mine! Homegrown and farm-fresh!" Zane patted his chest over his heart.

Dean's eyes widened. "Your body grew from your heart? How?"

"Bren can answer that. I just woke up, saw my woman before me, and it was the happiest moment of my newborn existence," Zane said.

Dean and Tara looked at me, and I explained. "The jar broke during the blood moon. Zane's heart had a root, and I took it with some leftover dirt from the jar and buried his heart by the lake. The moon's ray marked the spot, and my blood must have acted as a catalyst because suddenly, a fully grown vampire was standing before me. He just popped up out of the ground."

"And I was bare and naked as a mole rat." Zane laughed.

"He didn't recognize me at first. Not till he had a little more blood, then his eyes changed, and the rest was, well, it was a beautiful reunion." I smiled.

"You didn't recognize her?" Tara looked confused.

"I don't remember anything before that. I guess it took Bren's blood to wake me up," Zane said.

"And the two of you have been secretly together all week?" Tara smiled knowingly.

"She popped my newborn vampire cherry. It was superb." Zane kissed his fingertips and released them into the air. Dean and Tara laughed while I blushed with embarrassment and shook my head.

"Congratulations!" Dean clapped Zane's shoulder, and they chuckled.

We spent the next few hours catching everyone up and enjoying the party. There was a lightness in the air, and everything felt complete.

Tara and Dean announced their engagement, and Zane grumbled jokingly, saying they had to go and one-up him.

Over the next few days, more new arrivals and Jeremiah's fiancé Adria showed up. She explained to him that she'd never rejected him. She thought the Hedrix was playing a cruel joke when she saw Jeremiah in his Sevifk form, and she cried that night from the heartache it caused. The couple had the chance to talk and reconnect, and their love was still as strong as the day they last saw one another on Earth. Though they both had different bodies now, their souls knew. They were soul mates, given not one but two opportunities to find each other.

Wedding plans and training the new people took up our afternoons and keeping The Hillbilly Roost running took up our nights. And between a diet of my blood and Airmed's fruit, Zane only needed an occasional sip from the bar patrons now and then.

Woody put out the radar for any vampires that might come our way. He said it was only a matter of time, and Zane's existence should be well known. He'd have picked up on Zane's signature like a supernatural beacon if his sire were still alive. All we could do was wait and prepare.

Zane would seem distant at times. He'd gaze off to nowhere like he was watching for someone. I wondered if he was feeling some sort of connection. I'd ask him about it, but he'd just snap out of it and smile at me with adoration in his silver eyes. Zane would give me words of reassurance and tell me he loved me. My mind kept rolling with all the possibilities of what may come. The best and the worst-case scenarios made me anxious. Both meant a significant change, and I didn't feel ready for it. Zane and I just got back together. We fought for each other. Zane had been to Hell and back. No. Nothing, man, demon, or vampire, would break our bond.

Epilogue
ARIES SILVERTON

A Sire's Discovery

I was certain he was dead—the man I sired over eighty years ago, by the name of Perrish. Private Dean Perrish was the name he'd given me when we met in the bar that night. I could sense something different about him above all the other new soldiers.

I knew he'd make an excellent addition to my family. He had the appeal I was looking for with his lady killer looks and strong character. Dean was a man who'd talked like he'd seen life through two men's eyes. And I was about to give him a gift that would give him an advantage over most young men going into war who surely would die.

The transition would be challenging, but Dean looked like a fighter and would rise as my second. I would teach him everything he needed to know, and this war would provide an opportunity to tame his bloodlust in the battles he'd face.

This war was the humans, but I, too, would partake in the blood bath that would both quench my thirst and add to my reputation as the leader of my coven.

I'd brought Vivienne along to seal the deal. Her power of persuasion was her temptress, and she'd hooked Dean without resorting to compulsion. I followed them as she led Dean back to her hotel room, where I waited outside the door and listened while she did her little tease and restrained him.

Vivienne gave the signal, and I walked into the room, slowly closing the door behind me. Dean looked up in surprise. "What fucking twisted game is this?" he shouted.

I sat beside him on the bed, and he struggled against the ties on his wrists and ankles. My eyes took hold of Dean's, and he froze beneath my coercion. Vivienne smiled as she sat in a chair and lit up a cigarette. She crossed her shapely legs, took a drag, and blew smoke rings through her red-painted lips.

"This is no game, Dean. I am here to recruit you. You've been through the wringer with training, and now you face a monster. I mean Hitler, of course! He must be wiped from the face of the Earth, and you will get your chance to participate in winning this war. His army doesn't stand a chance with my soldiers in this fight.

I am here to add you to my ranks, Private Perrish. Vivienne spotted you and drew me in your direction. She has a good eye for new talent, and I sense you've got what it takes to make the cut. You may speak, but do so calmly, soldier."

"You're no army lieutenant! Who are you really?" Dean asked.

"Like you, I am a soldier in this war, but I'm not a man like you either. I can give you a gift, Dean. I don't make this offer to just any man or woman." I winked at Vivienne, and she rolled her eyes. She's heard this spiel several times in our two hundred years together.

"No one is a man like me," Dean said.

"No. I imagine not. Vivienne tells me she can see two auras that blend like you're a man with two souls. It intrigues me to come across someone so rare. Do you know what it means?"

Dean shook his head and glared at me.

"Well, I find you fascinating. I have seen a lot in my long life, but I have never come across someone like you before. I want to share something with you that will make you invincible in this war and open your eyes to a new world. There is good and bad in both of our worlds. But with your experience, you will have an advantage over those before you. I will make you my second in command."

Dean's brows creased. "Second in command of what? What is this? Some kind of spy recruitment? This is a fucked up way to induct someone. I don't want to be your spy. I joined the army to fight for my country."

"As did I. I fight to maintain the freedoms this country provides for the people. Humankind deserves the right to live free and in peace. My people depend on them to thrive so we too can live."

"Your people? What do you mean by that?"

"Allow me to show you." My fangs grew into long sharp points, and Dean's eyes widened in fright. He tugged at his bindings, and I compelled him to hold still. He tried to scream, but his mouth would not open as I had forbidden it. He really had no choice. I was not going to let go of someone so rare.

Vivienne licked her lips and leaned in as I opened my mouth wide and took hold of Dean's hair, pulling his head aside and exposing the fast-hammering artery. My prize was but a heartbeat and a bite away. I leaned in and whispered in Dean's ear. "This will hurt for a time, my friend, but you will pull through."

My fangs sunk into Dean's neck, and he groaned in pain. This pain was not the worst of what he would feel, but it would pass in a few minutes. Though to him, it may feel more like hours. Dean Perrish would perish from this life and rise a new creature. He would become a force above humankind, an immortal with the strength of one hundred men, a speed that surpasses a bullet, and reflexes so fast that they will escape the human eye. He will be able to jump and climb to and from tremendous heights and pounce upon his enemies and prey without them knowing what hit them.

The first taste of his blood solidified my choice. There was a power waiting to be unleashed in Dean's veins. I released my venom and pulled back. Dean began panting and sweating as it began to enter his system.

Before the screaming began, I nodded to Vivienne to go to work. She would get dressed and go from door to door, compelling people so they would ignore Dean's screams.

I headed for the door and looked back at my new fledgling. I smiled and said, "You'll make a fine addition to our ranks, soldier. I'm looking forward to us working together."

I walked through the door, which was the last time I saw Dean Perrish. He was an enigma to this day. I didn't feel my connection or bond with all I had sired before him. I went back a few days later, and he was gone. I should have stuck around and kept a closer eye on him, but pressing business took me elsewhere.

Vivienne had checked on him, but she said he was taking longer to rise than most. She left to feed and came back later to an empty bed. We searched for Dean, but he'd disappeared. I panicked because I couldn't get a read on him no matter what I tried. What had happened to him was the biggest mystery and scandal to travel through all vampire sects.

Decades later, there was one account of a female who encountered a man of Dean's description, but she didn't get a feel of him being our kind. Necromancer is what she had said, and it was baffling, to say the least.

And then there was nothing. Nothing until two weeks ago when I woke with an intense sensation like a beacon had been flipped on, and I knew. It was him! The connection surged to my heart like two frayed wires coming together and completing a circuit.

Nearly two months prior, I had felt a sharp pain in my chest which brought me to my knees. It felt like a loss I couldn't explain, but something felt utterly severed. I spoke with Felix about it, and he said it sounded like what happens when a fledgling dies. The sire experiences the pain of that loss.

Did Dean die and come back? A vampire dies by one of two methods, stake through the heart or beheading. They do not return. Unless?

I thought back to the account of the female and the necromancer. There must be a connection. I should have pressed for more information, but I hadn't seen any coincidence other than a resemblance.

The female didn't report this account to me, and I never knew to which coven she belonged. She must have been a rogue. The message reached me through the grapevine, which a story can become misconstrued the further goes its reach.

There were reports of a stirring of a nest of supernaturals. One of my people overheard a discussion by two travelers with the gifts of the goddess Airmed about a necromancer who defeated a demon.

I was interested in this demon's name because there was one I sought who'd murdered our queen and defamed our race. Vampires were superior to man in this realm, but those in Hell became servants to the select races of demons.

Queen Cleopatra, the same from human history, could travel between realms and bring news back and forth to our people. Humans believed the story that the Egyptian queen died from a snake bite. Well, that wasn't entirely true. She died from a bite, but it was a different kind of venom. And her mummified remains were that of a servant girl close to her description.

She ruled over the vampire race for nearly two thousand years. Her sire, King Syadestese, perished nine hundred years ago. He'd established a kingdom in Hell, seized by the same demon I sought. Cleopatra and her king no longer exist in either realm, but our race still honors their memory.

I prepared to travel from my newly acquired home on an island off the coast of Brazil. I bought the run-down resort for a steal. A family had gone missing nearly two years before and was never found to this day. Reports claimed they disappeared after a strange light phenomenon occurred from the cave down on the beach.

I sent Felix and Vivienne ahead to the states to begin the search. I could feel Dean was somewhere in the southeastern part of the United States. I received a call from Vivienne in Miami, and a bartender mentioned seeing someone who matched his description a few months ago. He was wearing a black leather jacket and riding a motorcycle. He worked his way around the ladies and took a different one home every few days. That sounded like the predatory moves of a vampire or a gigolo. Vampires tend to be the same as thirst, and sex goes hand in hand.

Dean was no longer in Florida. This I knew. No. He was further north. Felix called me a few days later from a roadside diner north of Atlanta where a gang of bikers was talking about a club called The Hillbilly Roost.

Felix approached the men and asked if they knew a man named Dean Perrish. The leader, Bobby, asked what business it was to him, but then Bobby began talking once Felix stared into his eyes and loosened his lips.

In the Smoky Mountains of Tennessee was a densely wooden one-hundred-acre plot of land near Tremont belonging to a Woody Raybrook. He owned and ran The Hillbilly Roost, and up until three weeks ago, the establishment was closed for a few months due to illness and building repair.

But there was something else entirely different going on, according to my sources. And it went back to the discussion of the two supernatural travelers and the demon defeated by a necromancer.

I arrived in Knoxville, Tennessee, in time for the local college's spring break. A group of young men who looked like jocks sat at a table in the restaurant. I listened from my seat at the counter. One of the men started the conversation, which piqued my interest.

"Rudy will be back next season. His leg healed, but he had a funeral to attend followed by a family emergency."

"Is everything alright?" a second member of the group asked.

"Yeah. It's all good now. Rudy invited us to come to his uncle's bar tonight. It's only an hour south. You guy's up for it?"

"Hell, yeah!" the other three responded.

"Man, I saw a few of Rudy's uncles when he was in the hospital. One was huge and scary, and his uncle Woody was intimidating too."

"Oh, dude! I remember seeing him. I tried to talk with that guy, and he looked at me like he knew I was talking shit. I had to excuse myself before I did shit my pants. The guy was intense. Are you sure you want to go there?"

"It's fine, Derrick. Rudy's family is cool. We'll check it out and hang with Rudy for a night before heading south."

Bingo! I found my next meal and a ride to where I needed to go. I waited until the four men got up to leave and followed them to their vehicle. "Excuse me, gentlemen!"

All four turned to look at me. "Can we help you?" the most talkative of the groups asked.

I held his eyes, and he froze. Then I went down the line and had all four hooked with a droning gaze. "You all don't mind if I tag along. I am thirsty and could use a drink." I smiled.

The ring leader blinked. "Oh, sure, man. Come abroad! The more, the merrier, right guys?"

The men nodded their heads, and another said, "Yeah! There's room for a fifth!"

I sat between two men in the back seat, and they began talking about their trip and all the 'cool shit' and 'hot women' they'd get with while I sat patiently, entertaining their youthful hijinks with an occasional smile or slight comment.

An hour later, the crew leader pulled into a gas station and went to fill up the tank. The shotgun rider went inside the store to get junk to eat, and I took the opportunity to have a snack.

I drank my fill between the two in the back and exited the vehicle, leaving the men slightly light-headed, but they'd live. I went into the forest behind the store and found a place to wait for Felix's call.

My phone rang. "Tell me what you found!"

"I've found him." Felix's responded. "He is at the Raybrook establishment, but there is a minor complication."

"Which is?"

"He lives amongst a coven of necromancers."

"How many?"

"So far, I've seen around twenty, but there may be more."

"Why would he?" I stopped. It occurred to me why I hadn't found him till now. Someone was shielding him. It was a necromancer and had to be someone extremely close to him.

It was why vampires were forbidden from associating with necromancers. For one, they could control the undead. Second, necromancers have aided rogue vampires in the past, shielding them while they ran from their covens.

Eventually, they were found and punished, but how had Dean remained hidden for so long? This issue was still beyond my comprehension. Maybe it had to do with the stir between the necromancer and the demon.

I would maintain a distance for now and send spies. I ran back out to the vehicle, where I caught the young man named Derrick before he got back in the SUV with a mound of junk food in his arms.

"I need your number. You and your friends will gather intel on what you learn about a man named Dean Perrish." I put my number in his phone and called mine so we could contact one another. He nodded with the others, and before I let them go, I gave them a few instructions.

"You will not mention me, and you will find Dean and talk casually, asking him general questions about his life. You will call me tomorrow, and when you hear my voice, you will follow my commands."

They nodded again, and I released them. I could not simply go up and knock on doors in a nest of necromancers. I was strong enough to abstain from the influence of one or two, but a whole group was beyond my skill set.

I found my way to a distant ridge where I could view Woody Raybrook's land well. I could smell that Dean had been here with a human female, and he drank her blood. It was weeks ago, but the faint scent was still there, and whoever she was, she smelled divine.

The rumbling of motorcycle engines roared in the distance, and music played. I observed the densely wooded acreage and a lake with three wooden crosses erected in the water.

This land had a supernatural and all-powerful presence. If I were to make myself known too soon, the scenario might not play out in my favor. I needed to make a plan.

TILL WE MEET AGAIN
Blood is thicker than water, they claim
Which one will rule and which one will sway
The influence of man or compulsion of beasts
The heart will tell to say the least
Loyalty of familial flesh
Command by razor-sharp tooth
Perhaps combine all
And reveal the truth

Here goes a big old southern fried THANK YOU to my beautiful readers. I hope you enjoyed the Dark Trespass Necromancer series, and I look forward to the future as my supernatural family moves ahead.

The Hillbilly Roost shall remain, and all are welcome to stop for a drink. Just don't go snooping beyond the trees. It might cost more than you think.

Someone may come along and save your ass. But that's for The Rooster to decide. You shouldn't go where you're not supposed to in the first place because there's really no place to hide.

And as you know, Woody doesn't like blood getting all over his property unless necessary.